*chasing
the
blue
boat*

PRAISE FOR
CHASING THE BLUE BOAT

I loved this book so much that I read it within a small window of time. The descriptions blew me away by bringing every detail to life. The author, gifted in storytelling, has created a tale with characters who will keep you wiping tears in one chapter and cheering their courage in another.

LINDA METCALF
PhD, TEDx Speaker, Texas Wesleyan University Professor, and author of ten books on solution focused therapy

Connie Kallback put her compassion and skills to work in writing *Chasing the Blue Boat* to tap into emotions ranging from grief to love. A faith-centered novel, it is a rich nugget of literary enjoyment with authentic characters, symbolism, and foreshadowing well worth your time.

GEORGE WATSON
Author of three Prentice Hall books for teachers, author with his wife Kathy of *Positive and Courageous: 100 Daily Pillars for a Man's Soul* and *Authentic and Courageous: 100 Daily Boosts for a Woman's Soul*, and Share a Prayer, a weekly devotional blog

Chasing the Blue Boat wastes no time in pulling you into the story's vortex using people, places, and events that stir your emotions. In this way, Connie's novel grabs you early, makes you care, then leads you down a path you can't wait to take. From tragedy to triumph, this story told through the eyes of a young girl, is a classic in the making.

JERRY VALLOTTON
Author of *The Toss: A New Offensive Attack for High-Scoring Football*, serves in Little Country Church, Redding, California, as elder, youth leader, and on-loan speaker/preacher

CONNIE KALLBACK

A NOVEL OF LONGING

chasing the blue boat

Ambassador International
Greenville, South Carolina & Belfast, Northern Ireland

www.ambassador-international.com

CHASING THE BLUE BOAT: A NOVEL OF LONGING
©2024 by Connie Kallback
All rights reserved

ISBN: 978-1-64960-604-4
eISBN: 978-1-64960-655-6

Cover Design by Hannah Linder Designs
Interior Typesetting by Dentelle Design
Edited by Kate Marlett

Scripture quotations are from the King James Version of the Bible. Public Domain.

No part of this publication may be reproduced, distributed, or transmitted in any form or by any means, including photocopying, recording, or other electronic or mechanical methods, or for the purpose of training artificial intelligence technologies or systems, without the prior written permission of the publisher, except in the case of brief quotations embodied in critical reviews and certain other noncommercial uses permitted by copyright law. For permission requests, contact the publisher using the information below.

This is a work of fiction. Names, characters, and incidents are all products of the author's imagination or are used for fictional purposes. Any resemblance to actual events or persons, living or dead, is entirely coincidental. Any mentioned brand names, places, and trademarks remain the property of their respective owners, bear no association with the author or the publisher, and are used for fictional purposes only.

AMBASSADOR INTERNATIONAL	AMBASSADOR BOOKS
Emerald House	The Mount
411 University Ridge, Suite B14	2 Woodstock Link
Greenville, SC 29601	Belfast, BT6 8DD
United States	Northern Ireland, United Kingdom
www.ambassador-international.com	www.ambassadormedia.co.uk

The colophon is a trademark of Ambassador, a Christian publishing company.

To Gary

AUTHOR'S NOTE

When I sat down to write *Chasing the Blue Boat*, I had no outline. I knew only that it would begin with an episode from my young life that could have ended in permanent injury or death for my brother and me. It scares me still if I think about it. I have no idea why we did it, except that kids do crazy things.

Then, a strange thing happened while I wrote about the main character Dana watching her brother Luke beg their mom to let him go on a boat ride at the lake. Inexplicably, a terrible accident that friends told me about years ago popped into my mind. During a boat outing, a wave tossed their son's friend overboard. I knew instantly what would happen to Luke, but I didn't want that for him. I fought it and cried while my fingers flew across the keyboard.

This is to say that certain plot points may be difficult to read about. As in everyday life, the characters deal with harsh realities; but not all rely on God. You may find yourself wanting to remind them that faith in God can comfort them and pull them through. All they need to do is call on Him.

Others in the story do understand that faith brings the hope to go on, and joy comes in spite of grief. Those charismatic characters—who are strong believers—help Dana and her parents reach a positive ending. For those who cry through the sad times, I hope uplifting humor throughout will bring many a chuckle.

Although I borrowed a few scenes from real life, the characters are fiction. Commiserate with them in their loss and disappointment and laugh with them as they draw closer to God and find redeeming grace in forgiveness.

CHAPTER 1

FENTON, NEW YORK

1971

For as long as Dana could remember, Luke turned every day into a challenge, especially in the summer when they had more time to roam free—swinging from a piece of hemp rope suspended from a branch, scaling picket fences, climbing the stone wall around a sinister house for a glimpse of a bandit hideout. He teased her to chase him, swooping through the backyard to raid Mom's garden where they ripped carrots from the earth, wiped the dirt off on their pants, and ate them whole. Then they'd lie on their backs on the grass, imagining their futures in the clouds. She wished her mind spiraled the way his did.

School ended, yielding to another round of adventures. Her anticipation grew when Luke hinted at something big that had to be kept secret from Mom. She listened while he explained every detail of the plan.

"Got it?" He barked orders as though he were commanding a whole platoon instead of one nine-year-old girl.

She nodded, narrowing her eyes.

"When we get there, I'll go first."

Nothing new about that. Being two years older gave him the right to set the rules.

He laid out the next step. "You tell Mom instead of me. She always believes you."

Like a soldier assigned to scouting duty, she hopped from the front porch, pushed through the lilac bushes, and squinted through slats of the fence at their mother hanging laundry. "We're off to the library." The words sailed through her cupped hands.

Mom turned to the fence, took a clothespin from her mouth, and swept her chestnut hair aside. "Why? School's out now."

Dana faltered, a sign to her brother to take over.

"Getting a jump on summer reading." He grinned.

Mom gave a thumbs-up, the "be safe" sign in their family, and bent to her basket. The clothes hung limp on the line until a breeze released invisible beings inside to dance.

Dana and Luke sprinted three blocks to the Carnegie Library, the centerpiece of Fenton. She paused at the base of the grand stairway and lifted her face upward, hoping to conquer it and the ledge beyond by judging the distance from the ground. To build some courage, she dallied a few steps away by the cornerstone. The year 1895, chiseled deep into the stone, prompted her to trace the incised numbers with a finger. She wanted the action to transport her away to any time before today. Maybe staying there long enough would help her relive last summer's big library celebration.

The whole family—Dana, Luke, and their parents, Jesse and Rachael Foster—had reveled in a festival attracting a good part of the town's population to the expansive grounds. A banner proclaimed in huge red letters, "75 Years of Reading: 1895-1970." From makeshift booths dotting the grass, people bought hot dogs and sodas while a three-legged race, an egg toss, and other contests offered trinkets to the winners. Dana pulled a number from a goldfish bowl and won a tiny aluminum horseshoe with the imprint "Good Luck" wrapped around a penny. Even though Mom disapproved of wishing on objects, Dana didn't see any harm in keeping it. She took it with her everywhere, including this risky trip to the library. Reaching into her pocket, she gave it an extra rub.

The wide stairway led to an open-air foyer, where two massive columns announced the entrance. She and Luke took the stairs at the nonchalant pace of visitors checking out books.

Instead of heading for one of the heavy doors at the top, Luke sneaked behind a column and peered from behind it, smirking like Peter Pan. Waist-high sidewalls, wide as picnic benches, flanked the foyer. He straddled the one beside him. Bending his chest toward the surface, hands gripping both sides, he jockeyed his hips sideways and dropped his feet to the outside edge. In another move that took mere seconds, he stretched cat-like across the diagonal space to the building's adjoining ledge. It rimmed the outside of the library to form a shelf, projecting outward enough for child-sized shoes to fit with plenty of room.

Heart thumping, Dana followed his every move. The ground lay twenty feet below. If she slipped, the grass would cushion her fall, even though it wasn't as soft as her mattress at home. She didn't dare look down again. The first glance had made her stomach want to bring up her lunch.

Luke sidestepped several yards in front of her, pressing his belly against the wall and straining his eyes toward the corner. He hesitated only once to swing his head back to her. "Let's go all the way around!"

She froze. The world around her stopped. No dog barked. No horn honked. Not one bird left a pattern on the horizon. To ensure a firm foothold before her first step, she leaned into the wall. Hugging its hard comfort gave courage to her outspread arms. She focused on the corner ahead and caught Luke's profile against the sky, his close-clipped hair colorless in the sun. His shadow on the stone would leave a permanent image in her mind.

Feeling the way with his feet, he negotiated the corner. On the other side, a series of towering windows framed a spacious office inside. He passed by the first set as Dana approached them.

Inside, a woman behind a desk raised her eyes to a pair of skinny knees. Jumping from her chair, she nearly tripped as she ran to the door.

"She saw me!" Dana's intended whisper became a hiss.

"Go back! Quick!" Luke reversed his steps. "Move!"

Forgetting their earlier caution, they flew around the dangerous corner to the sidewall and the top step in what seemed a second. Skimming the whole flight of stairs, they raced for home, feet barely touching the pavement.

Safe at their own block in the oldest neighborhood in the center of town, they slowed to catch their breath. Branching maples created a quilt of shade on the sidewalk, giving relief to their all-out dash. Up ahead, their cottage-like home looked out of place, squeezed on the corner mansion's side lot. Defying its small size, their house drew attention to its columned veranda with a knee-high wall spanning the entire front and wrapping around one side like a vigilant serpent. The porch covered more square feet than the three bedrooms inside.

"What a bummer! We just got started." Luke jammed his hands into his pockets. "But wasn't it great?"

She bobbed her head. "We saw the whole town up there!" A large dose of enthusiasm ensured her role in his next wild idea.

"You know you'll need a disguise to go to the library from now on, don't you?" He stopped to rip a sucker sprouting from a grooved tree trunk.

"Won't Mom think we're crazy masquerading when we want to check out a book?"

"No problem for me. I've been going by myself for years."

His not-so-subtle reminder of being older stung; but at least, he didn't call her a baby this time.

A bird feather on the ground helped her resolve the disguise problem. "I know! I can wear my Sacagawea costume from the school play. I'll wear the black braided wig and headband. With feathers." A triumphant pirouette flung her hair in long honey waves across her eyes.

"Don't be stupid."

Fist on her hip, she countered him. "What if there's a special program, and Mom wants you there?"

"I'll figure it out." He snatched another twig from a tree between the walkway and curb and snapped it in two.

His action took little effort, like everything else he did. She'd practice it in secret by herself.

Their daring spirits flagged for a few days but without school to keep them busy, they had time to test their limits. Luke hinted about the library again.

"What about costumes?" To give him time to think, Dana refastened a loose sandal strap.

"Aw, everyone's forgotten by now." His nose wrinkled, showing his teeth. He confessed to asking his best friend Teddy Olson, who lived a quick bike ride up the road, to join them. "His mom won't let him. Crumb. Bet he didn't even ask her. I think he's scared." He plucked a stone and kicked it ahead of him on the sidewalk. "He doesn't recognize fun when he's tripping over it. He's chicken, isn't he?"

"Uh-huh. Not brave like us." She marched beside him, straight-shouldered.

"Nothing scares us. And we're more careful than he'll ever be." He seized the rock and flung it across the empty space between two houses. It flew into a distant tuft of weeds. "There's no way we'll ever get hurt."

"We'd only fall on the grass." Her sandals didn't have rubber soles like her sneakers to grab the edge.

His eyes fixed on a far-away spot.

What was he thinking? Did he want Teddy there in her place? Some thanks after her show of courage and pretending to enjoy it. She swept her eyes toward him without turning her head. "Do you think Mom knows?"

"Nah. She doesn't need to." He pointed at her, almost touching her nose. "And don't you tell her."

In the block before the library, they passed a small city park and its long rectangular pond, the pride of the grounds, stocked with goldfish. Luke cut across the manicured lawn. "Let's go find that fat one. Remember its splotchy white marks and the streak by its mouth?"

"The freaky one?" She followed where his footsteps flattened the grass. He was doing it again—launching their next venture—but by the time she talked herself into it, he'd change his mind. Her ideas, when she suggested them, thinned in the air before reaching his ears.

Slabs of thick slate framed the pond, a foot and a half above the surrounding pavement. She crouched on the edge and leaned over the water to see moss speckling the bottom and sides. Fish ventured from beneath lily pads. The curious ones kissed the water as they waited for crumbs. "Too bad we didn't save some crust from our sandwiches."

Luke plunged his hand in and wiggled his fingers to taunt the fish. Tiring of it, he arched his back to ease an imaginary kink. "Too hot out here today." Pretending to lose his footing, he fell against her, knocking them both into the pond. Legs and arms flailing, they splashed hard and came up sputtering. Dana gasped. In hip deep water, they soaked every hair on their heads.

Her knees scraped the edge while climbing out. She wrung out the wadded hem of her shirt, making a small stream on the pavement. "The water felt so good. I wish we could stay and swim."

"Not a good idea." He sat on the side to untie his shoelaces. "The groundskeeper threatened to report Teddy and me to the police if he catches us here again this summer."

"And you didn't tell me?"

"Didn't need to. Nobody's here now." He tied the laces together to throw the sneakers over his shoulder. "Helps them dry quicker."

"I'm leaving my sandals on." Again, she refastened the strap, thankful it didn't loosen in the pond.

"Wow! The cement is burning!" He bounced to the grass in his bare feet. "What's wrong with kids living a little?"

They turned for home, dripping.

"What will we tell Mom?" A rivulet ran down her neck while she waited for him to choose an answer from his surplus of excuses.

"We can stay outside while our clothes dry. She'll never know the difference."

Mom's pottery craft and household chores liberated them to dawdle by the street. He counted on it. Making a quick change in gait, he flopped on a patch of grass in a comfortable sprawl.

Dana had a choice—follow his lead or go home drenched. She stretched out on her belly to accommodate his stalling tactic but wished for a towel.

He tossed his shoes to bake in the sun while he acted on his sudden need to relax. On finding a small stick, he held it between two fingers and waggled it like a pencil.

"You remind me of Dad when you do that."

"I know. It helps us think better."

She thought about his attempts to imitate Dad. Poking out her jaw, she blew a puff of breath upward to shoo a bug near her face. It persisted until she swatted it away. "But you're not like Dad in other ways."

"Such as?"

"He doesn't have fun like you do."

"Aw, he's a grown-up. They don't know how to enjoy life." He threw his make-believe pencil to the curb. "I'll be different. I'm going to have fun till I die. You watch me." He shot from the ground like a tightly wound spring.

She didn't have his easy agility. He coached her to turn cartwheels the way he did, making her practice the moves; but nothing worked. She couldn't keep her legs as straight as clock arms.

Their clothes had dried by the time they reached home but not the sneakers.

Mom met them on the front porch. "Airing out your shoes, Luke?"

"Yep. Wanted to go barefoot. It's summer, after all."

"Luke Foster, it's one thing to disobey me and another to lie to me. I have you on both counts."

He opened his mouth; but for once, nothing came out.

"The town forbids swimming in the pond." She stepped close to feel the wet canvas. "Leave these on the stoop to finish drying. You're confined to your room for the rest of the day. Except for supper." She turned to Dana. "You, too. I'm sure you weren't the ringleader, but you don't need to follow everything he does." A slight pat directed her toward her bedroom. "I'll call you to set the table."

Dana hung around by the entrance to the hall, smarting at being punished for something Luke had started.

Luke skulked through the kitchen to the back door as Mom's voice followed him. "You're supposed to be your sister's protector, not the one who helps her get into trouble."

He slowed but didn't turn around. "She doesn't need protection."

"But she might at some point. What if someone picked on her?"

He pivoted. "No one bullies my sister. They're afraid of what I'd do."

Dana smiled to herself. Her confinement might not be so bad after all.

CHAPTER 2

The need for a friend hit Dana hard a few days after the dip in the pond. A call came from Teddy's family for Luke to join them on a boat ride.

"Can I go, Ma? Please?" He shifted his weight from one foot to the other, his knees bobbing like a dancing crane.

Mom took a break from working on a long-necked vase. "You told Dad you'd mow the lawn today."

"I know; I know. I'll do it first thing tomorrow. I promise." His whole body begged. "It might be weeks before they go again."

"I guess another day won't make a difference. Just this once." She readied her brush. "Don't forget."

"I won't, Ma. Thanks."

Dana followed him outside as he hopped on his bike, stood on the pedals, and rode from sight, his long legs pumping to a blur. She stared down the empty street, expecting to find a visible trail he'd left from taking the ride so often.

She wandered back into the house to Mom's worktable. "I wish they'd asked me to go, too."

"Maybe when you're older."

It wasn't what she wanted to hear. The front door offered an outlet. Grass bent under her sandals as she shuffled to the sidewalk heading toward Teddy's, opposite of the way to the library and goldfish pond. Teddy's family might drive by, see her walking alone, and ask her to join them.

Dragging herself past the church next door, she crossed the street to a vacant lot on the next block and stopped by a field of ragged foliage. Luke and Teddy had let her tag along on the day they ripped out clods of wild grass growing in that empty lot.

Swinging them around with soil and roots still attached, they adopted the role of David confronting Goliath, their name for the house beyond the field. Hurled clumps thudded onto the roof. No window opened in the empty house.

"Want to try it, Dana?" Teddy passed her a tuft of grass as long as her arm. "Swing it like this." His hand hung down, wheeled forward to high above his head and back around in a smooth, underhand throw. "Let it go when your hand comes in front of you about eye level."

Her best effort landed in the weeds a few yards away.

Luke took over. "You have to release it when it's high enough to sail in the air." He demonstrated the move and made her practice before giving her another one.

Boys were born knowing how to do everything.

Before the Olson family moved nearby, Dana and Luke had battled boredom together. They roamed from neighborhood yards to the overgrown woods behind the church, where they crouched on hands and knees among tree roots to see people in the basement meeting room. Once, Luke had sneaked around to the mail flap in the main front door, lifted it, and yelled, "Shave and a haircut!" She'd had to scurry away with him to avoid getting caught.

While he baited a fishhook with live worms, grasshoppers, or crawdads, she hung around to watch. Bait too small to fit on the hook squished to nothing. He chased her with them, but she learned how to pretend she wasn't afraid by tuning him out. No fun teasing a girl who didn't scream and run away.

The arrangement had remained—Luke as the actor with her as the observer until this year when she had joined him to keep Teddy from replacing her altogether. In some ways, she liked it better as the watcher.

One morning over a breakfast of oatmeal, his words got to her. "Crawdad guts." He jabbed a finger at her bowl. "See? You can tell by the creamy white color."

Cooked cereal, never her favorite, plunged to the bottom of her list. Mom would never make them eat crawdad guts, but the stuff in front of her was as lumpy and icky as the real thing. A ball of mush clogged her throat and refused to go down. She filled her spoon again; but as it poised in the air, she gagged.

Finishing his own bowl, Luke did a tantalizing jig of freedom in the doorway.

She dabbled in her bowl to make the mess appear half-eaten. Her hand crept into her shorts pocket for the lucky penny.

Sudsy water foamed high in the sink where Mom was finishing the dishes. "Eat up, Dana. I want to put these away."

"Luke said the oatmeal has crawdads in it."

"Don't be silly. You know he's teasing." Mom scrubbed smudges from the trim beside the pantry. She pulled the plug in the sink to let the water burp down the drain, then lifted the laundry basket to her hip and headed for the basement where the wash machine waited. A final message wafted over her shoulder. "Your penny won't help you."

Since when did Mom have x-ray vision?

The untasted bowl of cereal sat on the table. Twenty minutes passed before Mom's basket dropped to the floor, announcing her return. "Still here?"

"I can't do it." Dana clutched the edges of the seat.

"Go, then." Mom shooed her away.

Dana slid from the seat, hiding her smile. The penny warmed in her hand.

In many times like that, Luke lured her into trouble while she was minding her own business. Another incident, though—a blameless one from two years ago—crept most often into her mind.

Uncle Barn—short for Barnabus—arrived for a visit between air force assignments. He brought gifts: turn-of-the-century paper dolls for her and an intricately crafted blue sailboat for Luke that they barely noticed. They spent most of the day riding on Uncle Barn's shoulders or commanding him as their sled dog while he towed them on a tarp across the lawn.

Mom cried when her brother left the next morning. His new assignment to a base out west might keep him away for months or years. In sympathy with her mood, rain fell through the morning, creating temporary creeks beside the curb on the way to storm drains at most corners. To Dana, it meant a chance to get acquainted with the paper dolls.

In the afternoon, Luke found her on the bedroom floor, surrounded by paper scraps and cut-out shapes arranged in a semicircle, lying in flat outlines against the rug. He held the boat high in one hand like a prized trophy. "Hey, the storm's over. Want to witness the maiden voyage?"

She followed him outside. The orphaned dolls didn't win a backward glance.

They skipped down the steps, across the lawn past the knotted oak in front, and stopped by the sidewalk. Leaves overhead released their last sporadic drops into the fresh, moist air of a world cleaned by a hard rain. The smell tickling Dana's nose would link itself forever to the blue boat.

Runoff from the downpour flowed in deep, rippled patterns at the curb. Luke dropped to his knees to launch the boat into the current. It took off—upright on its first try—bearing the image of a full-scale vessel, its prow straight and proud, skimming uncharted waters.

Captured by its unerring balance and agility, they became sailors aboard a craft on a fast-moving river. They raced with the speed of Spartans to keep up. Paying no attention to their surroundings or the water's increased momentum, they flew to the end of the block.

Before they reached the corner, the boat plunged into a storm drain. It was gone. Swallowed whole. The swiftness of it froze them in place.

Water continued to flush the opening, empty except for a messy wad of debris deep inside. It tipped in a magnificent arc in the curve of the waterfall, bearing its regal mast firm and upright until it vanished.

Recovering from stunned silence, Luke stood still while his eyes searched for a sign of the gift it stole from them. "I guess we have to say, 'Goodbye, little blue boat.'"

Her first encounter with sudden loss left Dana sucking air in great gulps. And though they never spoke of the boat again, a festering sadness lingered. She couldn't forget the unswerving, sleek figure, sails pointing skyward all the way. Then it was gone. Its abrupt disappearance wouldn't leave her.

Luke wasn't home when Dana helped Mom set the table for dinner. Dad arrived home from work as foreman at the Yardley Textile Mill. "To the lake again?" His eyebrows pinched together at Mom's news.

"You know how they enjoy the boat. It's not every day." Mom poured iced tea into frosted plastic glasses. "They have so few chances to go during the week when it's not crowded. Teddy's dad can't always take the day off." Her voice rose to disperse the dark cloud near the ceiling.

Dad hung his golf jacket in the closet and shoved the door shut. "I told him the lawn needed mowing. Wanted him to be aware and do it on his own. Show some initiative." Fishing receipts from his pocket, he filed them in a slim drawer under the kitchen counter. "I keep thinking he'll grow up and surprise me."

Mom caught his glare. "At eleven, Jesse? You know the choice you'd have made at his age."

He rested his wrists on the table as he waited for dinner. "Had no option out in the fields working for my old man. No time for boat rides." His eyes slid to the door and back to his watch. "But I never missed a meal. Where is he?"

"I'm sure Barbara will be calling to ask if he can stay for supper or to say they stopped somewhere." Hands in potholders, she lifted a steaming casserole from the oven.

After Dad gave the blessing, they ate; but no message came.

Mom used idle talk to quell her concern. "We turned over the leaf pile this afternoon where we're going to plant more garden." We turned over the leaf pile this afternoon where we're going to plant more garden. Rich black soil. It should give us some nice vegetables."

Dana cooperated in the distraction. "Found worms, too. They're good for the garden, aren't they, Dad?"

"So they say." His face relaxed when he looked her way. He rolled his glass, tipped it, and took a sip.

Mom stirred a teaspoon of sugar into her tea. "How's work?"

"Everything's running fine *there*." He spit out the final word for emphasis. Lifting his fork, he eyes it like a foreign object. "You let him go when you knew he had work to do." He began eating his salad, scowling at the bowl.

Little remained of the man who had bounded into the hospital room after Luke was born. Dana had heard the story more than once. Fearful at first to say he wanted a boy, he held out a tiny outfit with "Slugger" imprinted on the front and the tiniest baseball cap Mom had ever seen. Although Dana knew he may have dreamed then of Luke becoming a baseball star, she listened these days to his life-isn't-a-game message conveyed far too often. Worse than that, a series of changes causing turmoil at the mill followed him home. She wished for the days when he came home hiding a surprise chocolate in his pocket.

When the phone rang, Dad leaped up; but Mom already had it.

"The boat?" Her hand flew to her cheek. "Is he . . . " A frantic nod. "We'll be right there."

His chair scraped the floor, but the receiver already rested in its cradle.

"Accident at the lake. Have to get to the hospital."

He grabbed his keys. "What about Luke?"

"Michael said to hurry."

The oyster casserole, Luke's favorite, sat abandoned on the table.

CHAPTER 3

The glass doors of the emergency entrance at Fenton Memorial Hospital parted automatically, sensing urgency, admitting Dana and her parents to the beige-walled reception area bustling with people. They hurried to the desk, passing Michael and Barbara Olson where they waited for the Fosters. Beside them, Teddy wiped unstoppable tears. Michael, in the shorts and T-shirt he wore while steering the boat, scrambled to keep in step.

While Mom and Dad spoke to the desk attendant, Dana pressed against her mother. They turned around together, her parents standing strong as a double statue for the moment.

Michael placed his hands on their shoulders. A wag of his head took the place of a greeting. Droplets beaded on his face. "Teddy and Luke were sitting in the back, on the side. We've always warned them against it." His voice broke, but he continued. "The boat slammed the water. Bucked Luke off." He choked to a whisper. "Propeller blade caught him in the shoulder. Nicked his neck, too." His hand flew near his collarbone to demonstrate. "I jumped in. Pulled him to shore. Not far. She drove the boat in." His hand opened toward his wife. "A doctor, fishing with his family . . . helped us." A moan escaped before he covered his mouth.

A woman in a white uniform placed herself in front of them. "Are you Mr. and Mrs. Foster, Luke's parents?"

They nodded.

"He's sedated and as stable as possible." She held out a clipboard. "We need your signature for surgery."

"For what?" Dad faltered instead of sounding in control.

"Damage to the neck and shoulder."

Hand shaking, he signed the paper.

Mom did her best to keep from collapsing. "Please, can we see him?"

"Quickly. Follow me." She led them down a hall and pulled aside white drapes to a small space, more like a compartment than a room. A boy on a high, narrow, mobile-framed bed lay among tubes connected to bags hanging from metal poles. A sheet and a beige hospital blanket draped from his chest to his feet. An apparatus over his mouth and nose and white dressings swathing his neck and shoulder left a small part of his face for them to see. He looked nothing like Luke. Closed eyes replaced blue ones, sunken in and partly concealed. Any visible skin—patches of forehead, cheeks, and around his eyes—wore a pasty white pallor, emphasized by an earlobe turning blue.

Mom, crying, kissed his head. "We love you, Luke."

A man and woman in white whisked him down the hall in the portable bed.

The three of them returned to the emergency waiting room. Mr. and Mrs. Olson entwined their arms around Teddy, broken down with sobs.

Dad's gaze burned into Michael. "You didn't see them sitting on the edge?"

"It happened too fast." Michael pressed his fist to his lips to hide the quiver of his chin. "I'm sorry." He repeated it and beckoned them to join their family circle. "Come, pray with us."

When all joined hands, Michael prayed for guidance for the doctors in the operating room and for Luke during surgery. After an amen in unison, they sat down on chrome and black Naugahyde couches to wait.

In Mom's tight embrace, Dana's arms and ribs felt like Dad's hands clamped together with knuckles whitened. Mr. Olson's prayer coursed through her mind again. She prayed silently. *Please, God, don't let Luke die.* But what about the still form the nurse had led them to? Had she taken them to the wrong person? It couldn't have been Luke in the makeshift room with a curtain for a door. The smell of rubbing alcohol and other chemicals bristled through the air. Impulsively, she had reached to brush his cheek but drew back. It didn't seem like him at all. She tried to picture Luke before his bike ride to Teddy's, but everything about him remained a blur.

The emergency entrance admitted a boy older than Luke, treading across the entry mat on his own but holding upright one hand dressed in gauze. The bandage, wrapped multiple times around, leaked spots of red. Although she felt sorry for him, she wished Luke had his injury instead of the one from the boat accident. Not being able to use his hand for a while had to be better than lying immobile in a hospital bed like someone she didn't know.

The long wait they prepared for lasted less than an hour. An assistant, a woman in a white jacket, called Mom and Dad in to speak to the doctor. They left Dana with the Olsons. "I want to go, too." She reached for Mom too late. From across the room, an open palm waved her to stay there. Mom hurried to catch up to Dad.

Dana wouldn't hear the detailed story until her mother spoke of it years later.

The woman showed them to a small, private, pale blue room with more fake leather chairs, end tables, and a box of tissues. A pastoral watercolor scene hung on the wall.

The surgeon's experience in delivering bad news didn't make his meeting any easier. "You must know a doctor at the lake with his family called an ambulance for your son from the beach house there. Because of them, we thought we might be able to save him."

A tall man, the surgeon lowered his head to ensure they grasped the underlying meaning. Sometimes, people in shock weren't able to accept what he had to tell them, forcing him to be even more specific.

Jesse's arm, in a firm embrace around Rachael, fell away like a limb hacked from its trunk.

The surgeon continued. "He lost a considerable amount of blood before arriving here." A too-long pause became uncomfortable. "Before a significant repair became viable, he was gone." He folded and refolded his hands in a series of gestures; but instead of reaching out to them, he stooped over in his white coat and held the pose without moving. His voice came out in a lower tone. "I'm sorry. There was nothing more anyone could do—not the other doctor or the ambulance crew or anyone."

Jesse stared at the wall, while Rachael stared at the doctor's mouth shaping each syllable of the dreaded message. She withdrew her hand, wet from her cheek, but made no sound. What the doctor said couldn't be true. She must have misunderstood.

The truth became clear when an assistant directed them to another room. More papers to sign. Arrangements to decide upon. While Jesse did the talking, Rachael remained silent, trying to breathe. How could she face tomorrow or any other day without Luke?

After the final decision, the assistant escorted them to the door. For Rachael, despite the endless path down the gleaming white hallway to the waiting room, walking forever without ceasing would have been better than giving in to reality. She reached for support, but Jesse's tight fist hardened his arm. Her hand hung loose.

The walls wavered. The floor slanted. If she looked up, objects began to spin. Making it back without falling became her new goal.

In the waiting room, Dana ran to her mother. "How is he?"

"He's gone." A barely audible whisper breathed the words.

"Gone? Gone where?"

"To Heaven." Mom swayed with her earlier unsteadiness, bowed her head, and closed her eyes.

Dana's stomach hurt the way it did when she fell from the oak tree in the front yard. Air burst from her lungs. She ran to the hallway where they'd rolled Luke away. She'd find him and prove everyone wrong.

Dad caught her before she darted more than a few feet. "Your brother's not here anymore." His face crumpled into a shapeless mass resembling Neenah, a cloth doll from Dana's preschool years. His head dropped to meet his shoulders.

"Stay here." Mom led her to the other family once again.

Mrs. Olson's free arm enclosed her. The other held Teddy.

No one spoke, but the renewed sound of weeping from one of them broke the quiet and spawned more tears from someone else.

Dana willed herself far away. Mrs. Olson patting her arm, the way a mother helps her baby go to sleep, entered her awareness. She wanted to go home and burrow under the sheets to get rid of this bad dream and awake to see Luke in his bed in the morning.

She almost fell asleep by the time Mom and Dad returned.

"Let's go." Dad didn't speak to the other family or even look at them.

Mom pulled on his arm. "I want to wait until they take him."

"You won't see them. They'll do it out back." He plodded toward the exit to the parking lot, the others following behind him, the Olsons at the end, trailing in silence except for Teddy's muffled sobs.

Dana said goodbye to Teddy because it seemed right somehow. Then, she took Mom's hand and didn't look back.

To Dana's disappointment, Grandpa and Grandma Norwood stayed with Aunt Elaine, Mom's younger sister, on their arrival from their New York Finger Lakes farm. They spent their days, though, at the house, comforting and setting out food for meals from friends or freezing it to keep Mom from having to cook for a while.

On the day of the funeral, they crept through the back door early to prepare breakfast. A repeated tug on a gas engine growling to life drew them to the living room closer to the sound. Mom had drawn back the curtain and leaned into the front window while Dad mowed the lawn, the same one Luke promised to mow days earlier.

They left the doorway and set about their work in the kitchen, asking Dana to find elusive bowls and utensils.

Coffee, perked with energy to defy the gloom, waited for Dad to rush into the kitchen after parking the mower in the garage. "It was too tall." He gave his explanation to the question no one asked. "Couldn't wait any longer. People will be here." He scrubbed his hands in the kitchen sink and took his cup of coffee to the bedroom to get ready and change into his dark suit.

Like Dad, most people at the funeral wore black; but Mom and Grandma seemed uncomfortable in black dresses that suggested anything other than their usual joy. Even so, they maintained a respectable image. Mom's hair draped around her shoulders. Grandma's silver strands, mixed with darker ones, swooped from her temples to highlight a ribbon tied behind her head.

Dressed in his Sunday suit, Luke appeared to some to be peacefully sleeping. They must have known the phrase, "sleep, my child," in the organ's background music and wanted to make Mom feel better.

From a side door in the choir loft, a woman wearing a choir robe glided toward the center near the altar but stopped beside the huge wooden cross, centered on the wall. She sang *The Lord's Prayer*.

Pastor Connor prayed and talked about Luke. "In his few years, he lived a full life and leaves us a legacy of enduring memories. He gave a great gift to his family and friends: the gift of tomorrow. In the memory of him rests the beauty of each day. The sun will beam brighter in its shining. The presence of rain or ordinary actions like bouncing a ball will bring an appreciation deeper than any who knew him have ever before realized.

"We do not know when our time will come; but when it does, we, like Luke, will meet our Savior as He takes us into His arms. There will be no hurt or pain as there is for the ones left behind, missing him. But one day, we will join one another again without mourning or weeping, only rejoicing.

"I ask you to accept the grace of our Lord in our sorrow and in tomorrow's joy."

Everyone filed from the church and into cars for the trip to the cemetery. Baskets of flowers guarded the gravesite. Each family member held a dark red rose. When the pastor finished the final prayer, Dana stepped beside Mom and Dad as they placed their roses on the casket. She wished she had brought different parting gifts as mementos of Luke's life on earth—one of his prized rocks shot through with shiny flakes of muscovite, last fall's dried yellow oak leaf bigger than her hand, or the root beer-colored arrowhead from Dad. She didn't know how to make that happen.

Finally at home, Grandma ushered Mom aside before talking to visitors. "Let Dana stay with us for a few weeks. You and Jesse need some time alone."

"I don't think I can exist without her beside me. I need her now more than ever."

Listening to her mother, Dana grew older in one swift minute but had no time for reflection. She practiced her best manners on neighbors and families from church. Without being obvious, she marveled from afar at the food people brought—a whole ham, casseroles, salads, and desserts. It reminded her more of a birthday party instead of the saddest day she'd ever known.

Mom fought for composure amid the embrace of friends. "We didn't get to say goodbye." Grief smothered the last word, causing her to return to an earlier message. "We didn't tell him how much we loved him." When it brought tears, she bowed her head. Finally, she settled on, "He's in Heaven, where we don't have to worry about him."

Dana hoped that phrase might lift a small part of her heartache and carry it away.

Dad shook people's hands, speaking as little as possible. To some, he uttered, "It was inevitable."

Visitors whispered to each other. What a peculiar thing to say. Most attributed it to stress or anxiety pills he might have taken to make it through the day.

To others, he confided, "He had a chore to do, but she let him go," or "He shouldn't have been there."

Those who heard him seemed to conceal their astonishment without alluding to his comment. What response could they make? They offered their sympathy and walked away. No good ever came from getting involved in a family conflict.

Dana couldn't ask Mom to explain it while so many people hovered around her.

CHAPTER 4

Dad's return to work after the funeral gave Dana relief from the gray atmosphere in the house. Free-flowing conversation no longer accompanied dinnertime. Regular routines, meals, and bedtime remained as usual; but other than those things, little in her life stayed the same.

The typical time for going to the Fenton Market changed after Dana and her mother ran into Pastor Connor's wife, who asked about the family, then talked about Luke's abundant energy and how everyone missed him.

"Yes, he was precious to us." Mom's usual cheerfulness failed her; and before she retrieved a tissue from her purse, the tears started.

Dana left the two women consoling each other by the produce section and stole over to the bakery area to see the automatic doughnut-making machine, where fresh dough sizzled in hot oil. Through the glass, she saw a round shape of fat white dough with a hole in its center plop out of a pipe and ride the circle of steaming oil, following those already floating like kids on inner tubes in the river. At the halfway mark, a spatula flipped it over to display its deep-fried bottom before it finished its trip and skidded down a ramp to a holding bin. As the pile accumulated, a bakery worker rolled them in powdered or granulated sugar mixed with cinnamon before packing them into white paper bags, not included in today's shopping trip. Doughnuts belonged to special occasions.

Luke had always viewed the whole process with her. She didn't mention it to Mom on the way home. Keeping his memory alive by talking about him—maybe not every day, but often—had been Dana's expectation. When it didn't happen at the dinner table, she approached Mom alone. "I thought about Luke last night and—"

"Not now, Sweetie. A woman is coming to order a teapot she wants me to make to match her kitchen." She continued sweeping the side of the dining room that claimed the only bay window in the house, useful for storing pottery creations in various stages of completion.

Dana began again when the lady left.

"Let's not talk about it." Mom busied herself in her work.

"Why can't we?" She caressed the hidden penny.

"I think it's too distressing for your father."

But Dad was at work. Dana ached from the restraint of holding her memories inside. She wandered down the hall, struggling to convince herself that the accident had never happened.

A visit into Luke's bedroom revealed it was just the way he had left it, except for the neatly made bed. She climbed under the blanket, hoping he had left some warmth there; but the cold sheets smelled of detergent and fresh air. It must have been hard for Mom to wash away the last sleepy smell of Luke in his bed.

Thinking about it later, she initiated a bedtime ritual of puffing up the sheets and blankets in her own bed, where she would sit in a billowy mound. "God, please give me a chance to see Luke again. Tell him I need him here." She tried to imagine being in Heaven. "Luke?

Are you okay up there? Do you look the same? Do you have long hair down your back like Jesus?"

Now home from work, Dad heard her and creaked the bedroom door ajar. "Who are you talking to?"

"Thinking out loud is all." She pressed the blankets flat. "Bed's kind of lumped up."

"Get some sleep." He blew a kiss from the doorway.

She kept her prayers silent after that but continued to mound the bedding. All she wanted was to have Luke home again. She didn't care anymore if he took the trip to Teddy's every day, as long as he came home every night.

While private memories kept her going, she didn't share them. She waited for Mom to talk about Luke, but her desire didn't extend to anyone outside the family. A closed core deep inside guarded her around others. It relaxed at night or whenever she strayed back to being with him.

Dana sat on Luke's bed during a trip to his room and rested her eyes on his dresser. Had anyone checked the drawers since he last dug through them? An excursion through the top one brought folded piles of underwear and socks. The next drawer stored shirts and, behind them, handkerchiefs. Probably gifts he'd never used. Under summer shorts in the third one hid two fuzzy tennis balls, a yo-yo, and a box of arrowheads and rocks. A stack of framed and unframed pictures of Luke filled one side. Mom must have buried them there, school pictures and all, except for the double frame in the dining room featuring Luke at age four and Dana at age two.

A photo for her room might help her feel he was still there; but if she took it, she'd have to confess to snooping around.

Digging farther back into an apparent heap of rags, she found a strange shape—the hull of a toy boat. Some streaks of blue paint survived amid scratches and scrapes. On the top, a broken shaft protruded behind the prow, near center, where the main mast had been. How was it here after it had tipped into the darkness of the storm drain? She rubbed the nicks and larger indentations, trying to heal them. "Oh, Luke, I wish you'd told me. We could have been sad together."

She carried the damaged boat hull to Mom in the dining room. "I know I shouldn't have, but I grubbed around in Luke's drawers and found this." She held out the remains. "Know what it is?"

Mom's eyes grew misty. "The boat from Uncle Barn."

"It ran so fast in the gutter and zipped down the drain. I saw it happen in less than a second. No way to catch it."

"I know. Luke told me. He retrieved it with the skinny garden rake. He showed me this when he returned." She took it from Dana and held it for a moment. "A nest or bundle of twigs down inside the hole caught the sails and mast and held it there. Pulling it out nearly destroyed what was left of it. It was already in bad shape." She handed it back to Dana. "He begged me not to tell anyone. Especially Uncle Barn."

"He loved this boat. So did I." Dana stroked the side, thinking. "Can I keep it?"

"Of course. He'd want you to have it, I think."

She ran to find a new hiding place before Mom's permission changed. Searching for a corner in her own dresser, she thought about Luke and dashed out the front door. Clutching the boat, she scaled the oak, the one she and Luke had adopted as a magnificent tree house of multiple rooms and decks. It had become a command center for him to direct the army below or a tank to shoot grenade-like dirt clods. Without him, it endured as a refuge where she hid undisturbed or a waiting room outside of Heaven for visitors to request a meeting with someone. Luke needed to know the blue boat was safe with her before it hid in her room.

The Olsons quietly moved away. Rumors of their departure spread through the neighborhood.

Mom told Dad, who responded, "Good riddance."

Dana made sure he had left for work before asking, "Why did he say that, Mom?"

"I'm sure he didn't mean it."

"I don't understand. He didn't sound happy." She stood beside her mother at the stove.

"It's a way of talking about items people don't want anymore—things they're glad to get rid of."

"Not Mr. and Mrs. Olson and Teddy. They're nice."

"He's sad about Luke. He thinks he'd still be with us if they never lived here." A pie crust rested in her hands. "What kind of filling shall we make for this?"

"The fancy one Dad likes. Thick and creamy with cherries." She searched in the refrigerator for cream cheese. "But do you think Luke would be alive if the Olsons didn't live up the street?"

"If I hadn't let him go." Her mother's voice drifted away.

Dana spoke past the cool air flowing outward. "What if you didn't give permission but he went anyway?"

"He wouldn't do that." Mom shook her head.

"He did lots of things you never knew about." Dana honored her promise to Luke not to disclose certain incidents, but dipping into her memory storehouse brought plenty with no vow attached. "What about the time he rode off on his bike and went fishing without telling you? And you found out because a fishhook caught his ear and left it bloody?"

A pink hue crawled up Mom's neck as she bent to a bottom cupboard shelf to find the mixing bowl.

"Don't you remember?" Holding the cold package, Dana spieled on. "If he took the boat ride without asking, it wouldn't be your fault."

"We can't say it's anybody's fault. Sometimes, things just happen."

More examples came to mind, but Dana stopped. Quiet reigned in the kitchen.

Drowning—that's how Mom looked before she sank into a chair.

Dana melted beside her; and for the first time since Luke's accident, the two of them cried together.

CHAPTER 5

When friends' visits waned after a few weeks, Rachael found Jesse in his easy chair one night after dinner. "It's time for us to get away—a place to take Dana where we won't see anyone we know."

"Can't I read the paper in peace anymore?"

"Give me one minute, and I'll leave you alone." Her request sounded crisp even though that wasn't her intention. "What about the shore? A cabin at Cape Cod. We've never been there." Waiting for his reaction on the sofa's wide arm, she added, "Elaine's friends have to cancel. We could take their reservation."

The newspaper rustled in answer.

"A change from camping in the Adirondacks. Not reminiscent of past years."

"I'll think about it."

"School starts in little more than a month. We have to decide soon."

The accident hung in their minds like yesterday. She pushed aside the sheer curtain at the bay window. The sun on its downward slide deceived her with the radiance of a joyful day. High in the oak tree's leafy shadows, Dana scrunched her back against the trunk as she sat on a branch, legs dangling on either side in a pose that made her legs less knock-kneed than next to each other.

Moving closer to the window, Rachael checked a smudge to assure it wasn't permanent. Beyond the smear, she saw Dana more clearly, small against the wide trunk that emphasized her aloneness.

"We need to go. It's not fair to her if we don't." She let the curtain go slack. "We all need to get away."

<hr>

Dana sat alone in the back seat of the Dodge, where she always rode beside Luke. Pretending he was there making goofy faces, she ignored him by surveying the sky. A single cloud attracted her to its loneliness. What if Luke was watching them from up there? She reached out to entice it to the car. "Come with us." Did she say it aloud? Holding her breath, she waited, but no one moved in the front seat. When she gazed out again, it had floated away.

She closed her eyes then to picture the ocean in the brochures, showing nothing but sand spreading out to the horizon. She imagined the beach sand between her toes. Without a single shade tree, the sun's fiery heat would surely drive her into the ocean to cool down. The sensation she'd heard about—the tugging of the waves—would be hers to experience.

The rental cabin came in sight, third in a line of four-room cottages, all clones of the first. It provided a kitchen, living room, and two bedrooms just a short walk from the beach.

While Mom took inventory of pots and pans, Dad brought in the food box and waited in the doorway for instructions. She said without a glance, "Leave it on the table. I need to make sure everything's clean." A soapy rag swabbed the counter. "You two go ahead and explore. I need to unpack for supper."

The one-block trek along a footpath became endless. When the ocean finally came in view, Dana broke away and sprinted toward the sand.

Dad caught up and swept his hand in the air across the panorama. "See that? It's low tide."

Not understanding, she frowned.

"Ocean's going out from the land, leaving more and more beach. Makes it easier to find shells exposed by the water on its way out."

Before long, shells littered the sand. Many of them she'd seen in books, but the shapes of others belonged to exotic places. One broken piece resembled a petrified honeycomb with a dozen tiny hollow columns connected together.

"Part of a bigger shell once, but it's been eroded by wave action." It flew into the air as he tossed it, caught it, and squinted inside, using one eye as a scope. "Might have dwarf sea fossils still in it." Though it rattled when he shook it, nothing fell out.

He inched along the beach until a sharp object nicked his toe. Digging into the sand, he brought up a familiar but miniature shell. "A tiny conch." He handed it to Dana, top first, to show off its whorled design.

"Like a whirlwind!" She held it up against the sky and turned it over. It gaped open in a polished white mouth with the rumpled, turned-up edge of a swollen lip.

"Sailors called them whelks or conches. They used large ones as horns. Had to cut a hole at the end to make them work." He pursed his lips and blew, but no sound came out. "This one's too tiny and broken." Several chips showed at the edge.

"What happened to it?"

"Been knocked around. Like some people." He set off to patrol the sand before he had to explain himself.

She tagged behind him, holding the shell. "Can I take it home?"

"Sure. A keeper from the beach." He tucked it into his pocket but brought it out again. "They say you can hear the ocean's roar in it."

She pressed the tiny opening to her ear but took it away, disappointed.

He held it against his own. "Try it again. It's captured the sound of the waves."

Listening, she pictured herself there during a storm. "I hear it! I hear it! I can't wait for Mom to hear it, too!"

"It's like taking a piece of the ocean home with you."

"I want some for a collection. An assortment." She craned her neck toward him but reined in her enthusiasm. "Not enough to be greedy."

He offered her his baseball cap upside down. "Fill this. But you'll have to leave the rest for another gatherer or sea animal wanting to use them again."

"They do that?"

"I'm not sure, but they might." He shaded his face against the horizon. Faded blue eyes peered out under blond-white brows like those of a sun-bleached old salt inspecting the sea.

Her eyes, in contrast, darted in every direction.

"If crustaceans are living inside, they'll die and stink something fierce."

It sounded like one of Luke's outlandish sayings. She wrinkled her nose. "I'll be careful."

"You're finding these on the beach because the sea creatures are gone. Once in a while, you'll find a live one where water's been trapped, but I don't see any pools here."

She skipped beside him like a fawn. "I love shells! Is that why you and Mom decided on this place?"

He left her question unanswered and scraped a concave line in the damp sand with the toe of his sandal, mounding it to a peak at the end. "You're lucky to be in the right place today."

A full hour passed as she collected one shell after another and scampered back to him. Toes buried deep in the sand, she listened while he pronounced a name for each one. She admired the thin shells of mollusks, long and dark, and the fluted striations of thicker, multicolored, round oysters.

Dad carried the filled hat, brim forward, wedged between his arm and ribs. His free hand reached for hers as they ambled to the cabin.

She hadn't felt such a warm hand in a long time.

The family spent their daylight hours on the beach. Dad relaxed only there or in the water. Barricading himself behind a newspaper or magazine became a more disturbing habit in the cabin's smaller space than at home.

Every morning, they drove to town. While Dana and Mom bought fresh groceries and rambled through a quaint shop or two, Dad called the mill to check in. On the fifth day, he left the phone booth in a hurry. "An emergency. The big brass is on their way. I have to get back."

Dana almost dropped her packages on the sidewalk.

"If it were earlier in the week, you could stay here. I'd come back for you on the weekend, but tomorrow's the last full day left." A slump replaced his usual stance. "Sorry. Have to go if I want a future with Yardley."

They packed and left on a quiet return that lacked reflection or any kind of joy. Dana watched the scenery pass by like her life where people came and went. Uncle Barn and Grandma and Grandpa arrived for occasional visits; and a new teacher had greeted her every year, along with kids in different classes. She never expected the changes to include her brother dying and leaving forever. In every sliver of silence, her mind moved there.

Dad talking, actually having a conversation with Mom, directed her attention to the front seat.

"Roger's Car Sales has a '69 Chrysler 300 sedan with twenty thousand miles. Cream colored. It's a good buy." That got Mom's attention.

"Does the Dodge have a problem, Jesse? It's been fine when I've taken it out."

"Leaking oil. The big sheet of cardboard I left under the car has multiple stains on it. You'll see it in the garage. Already asked about a trade-in, but I'd get little back. I'm thinking of keeping it for you."

"Do we need two cars?"

"Might be invaluable if the rumors at work are true. They want me to oversee a project in a North Carolina mill for a week or so at a time. Having two cars saves you from two round trips of driving me to the Millingford Airport to go south and again when I come home. An hour each way."

She breathed out long and slow. "Do what you have to do."

The steady hum of the engine propelled them down the highway, interspersed with varied sounds of wind as they drove by trees, unbroken spaces, or structures on the way to the next town.

Mom turned for a better view of Dana in the back seat. "When we get home, we'll go shopping for your school things. Are you counting the days to meet your new teacher? Luke had her in fourth grade, too. I think he liked her most of all."

An instant void filled the car like the lull following a thunderclap. The Dodge accelerated. A sound like asthmatic wheezing broke the silence, but none of them was afflicted with anything like that.

Dana rubbed Mom's back, hunched in the front seat, to try to stop the shaking.

CHAPTER 6

Rachael sensed a transforming of their lives, subtle at first but inevitable as maple leaves turning crimson. The change overtaking them became ominous—a nameless feeling that lurked beyond the doorways, behind the couch, and under the carpeting; but she couldn't catch it to give it a good shaking and demand what it wanted. More than once, she tried bringing it up to Jesse; but he wasn't in a talking mood these days. Their easy conversations springing from his evening arrival at home seemed years ago. And now, as he traveled, opportunities dwindled even more.

Dinner during his weeks home marked the single daily event when the three of them inhabited the same room. Months ago, when Luke had completed the family at the table, Jesse gave grace while others took occasional turns. Since the accident, though, he refused.

One rare night when he was in the kitchen before dinner, Rachael spoke to him. "Will you return thanks for us tonight?"

"I told you I'm done. I want no part of it." He threw an imaginary wad toward the garbage can. "God has cast me aside."

"How can you say that? You're the one who's turned away. He's always there."

"Not when Luke was dying."

His words burned, but she went on. "He brought us through our darkest time. Don't you see that?" She let it sink in before continuing. "My comfort still comes from Him. Strength, too. How do you think I keep going?"

"It doesn't work for me." He looked away.

"He can help you."

"You've forgotten. I lost my son." His jaw hardened. "Needlessly."

"Please, Jesse. Not again."

"Do you want me to stay or should I go elsewhere for supper?"

Her hands flattened against her cheeks to stop the dizziness. "Sit. Please sit down." With resolve, she willed her body to guide her from the room and returned, Dana following behind her.

Rachael gave grace for them that night and every night thereafter.

In every action and thought of every day, she fought to keep the darkness at bay, knowing her declining liveliness did nothing to help. Prolonged staring through the bay window often got in the way of finishing a piece of pottery. She and Jesse, and Dana as well, needed a whole new day to dawn; but regardless of what she said to Jesse, it was impossible without Luke.

After vacation, Rachael began driving home right away after church to avoid talking to anyone. Within a few weeks, though, she rejoined the coffee hour after Sunday services to give Dana a chance to play with friends on the church's expansive lawn. At first, they stayed together as a way of protection; but they didn't have to worry. Wary church members approached without mentioning Luke—or Jesse, if he wasn't there—and spoke of recent events only.

Attorney Taylor Hamlin, a head taller than anyone else in the crowd, became the exception the first Sunday in November. He stood in the coffee line in front of Rachael. The big man set his cup on the table, poured one for her, and moved aside while she stirred in a little cream. To counter his hair receding early, Taylor shaved his well-shaped head, revealing more of his natural tan skin tone. A few premature gray hairs mingled in his dark beard, clipped neat and short.

After the usual how-are-you greeting, he downed a good part of his cup in one quaff. "How's Jesse? Haven't seen him for a while."

"He's spending time at a mill in North Carolina. Installing the new production line he oversaw here." She attempted a smile. "Usually leaves on Sunday morning. Takes the day for his flight, plus to and from airports and checking into a hotel to be ready for Monday." She didn't share that Jesse preferred sleeping in on Sunday during weekends at home rather than attend church.

People who often joined conversations in progress allowed them to talk undisturbed.

"How's everything going in the pottery studio?"

"You know about it?"

"I've seen your work in art shops. Nice." His head bobbed in approval.

"They're in several galleries." She resisted the urge to sweep spilled sugar from the tablecloth while an unexplained comfort level kept her talking. "Unfortunately, they don't bring in much money. If the house had more space, I'd teach classes. My glazing area is the dining room's extension. A sun room, actually. Too small." Why would she tell him that?

He stepped back in surprise. "Would you consider working outside your home?"

"I may have to start thinking about it." For some time, she had daydreamed of a way to turn her pottery into a career; but a real job meant a new direction and security, too, in light of Jesse's recent behavior. She'd have to manage her pottery in less than a full-time pursuit.

"My office assistant is retiring first of the year. I'll need someone to take her place."

"I have experience. Not recent, but I worked until Luke was born." His name sneaked out before she could rephrase.

He wasn't shaken like other people who fumbled for words on seeing her distress. "Give it some thought. Why don't you drop by the office? It might be a fit for you. Call to set a time in the next few weeks, and I'll show you around." He reached inside his suit coat to an inner pocket and produced his card. "I hope I'll hear from you. Who knows? The Lord may have directed me to this place in the coffee line for a reason."

Rachael floated across the lawn to find Dana. She hadn't felt this carefree since Luke was with them.

After school on one of the first days after Thanksgiving break, Dana couldn't hang her jacket up fast enough when she saw Mom place fresh bakery doughnuts on the table.

"Hold on." Mom's palm glistened from holding a cold decanter. "I have an announcement. I'm going to work in Mr. Hamlin's law office at the beginning of the year." She poured a full glass of apple juice. "Remember him from church?"

Dana frowned. "Do you have to?"

"We can use the money." She kissed the top of Dana's head. "I don't have to be home while you're in school." In a change from her usual pre-dinner bustle in the kitchen, she sat down. "My hours will be the same as yours at school. I told Mr. Hamlin it was my main condition in returning to work." The plate of doughnuts traveled to a spot in front of Dana. "He sent these as a gift to you."

Sorry about not being more polite at the mention of Mr. Hamlin's name, Dana wanted to thank him; but he wasn't there. She sniffed at her glass before taking a sip. "What if I get sick at school?"

"The school nurse will call me at work so I can bring you home."

At the first bite of maple glazing, Dana grinned with her mouth full. Only one person knew about her top pick in flavors to tip off Mr. Hamlin. She switched off the fleeting impulse to tell Mom to relay a thank you to him, and asked instead, "How will you know what to do at the office?"

"Not much has changed since my working days before your dad and I married." She smoothed her hair, as though she were suddenly self-conscious of the way she looked. "Before his assistant retires, she'll show me their routines. I'll take you to see where it is after Christmas, before school starts again." She cut a doughnut in half for a small taste. "Something for us to do when Grandma and Grandpa leave."

Dana gave herself a second helping.

The kids at school had no idea how it felt to dread the coming of Christmas. The joy in their voices buzzed in electric current through hallways and classrooms.

At home in the year's happiest season, Dana and her parents endured what used to be the best part: getting ready. She helped decorate the tree and display the manger scene but left Luke's most treasured ornaments hidden in the box. Together, they hung wreaths and garlands around the rest of the house but missed the ambiance surrounding Christmas. Even the thought of dressing gifts in shiny paper and ribbons lost its magic.

On Thursday afternoon, Dana and Mom, in the midst of making cut-out cookies, greeted Grandma and Grandpa Norwood, true to their plan to be there in time for Christmas Eve on Friday. Everyone exchanged hugs and kisses, hoping to repeat the scene of previous years.

Dana left splotches of flour on Grandma's dignified face. Brushing away the white dust, she took care not to smear Grandma's reading glasses hanging from a chain around her neck. "I didn't have school today, and it doesn't start again until after New Year's."

A cheer came from Grandpa. "How about your dad?"

"Only off until Monday."

Grandpa turned to Mom. "How's he doing?"

"Don't see as much of him as we'd like." To his raised eyebrows, she added, "He's at the southern mill half the time. When he's here, system breakdowns keep him working long hours. I've had to leave supper for him to eat later in the evening. Sometimes, he gets fast food near work." Her left thumb rubbed the underneath side of her wedding ring. "It's good he's busy, though, I think."

Footsteps at the back stoop preceded Dad stomping the snow off his shoes. He wrestled the door shut and shook his father-in-law's hand the same as a business associate. "Good to see you, Dan. How was the trip?"

"All clear except here. You have all the snow." He cleared his throat, trying to keep his gusto, but failing.

Dana hugged Dad around the waist with an orphan's intensity while Mom fluttered her apron and said, "Dinner's in half an hour."

The men found their way to the living room.

Pretending to rearrange the gifts under the tree in the dining room, Dana hid near the sunroom wall to listen unseen.

Dad dropped into his overstuffed chair. "How's the Air Force treating Barn?"

Grandpa chose the couch, keeping Dad in view. "He's TDY in Texas."

"TDY? What's that?"

"Temporary Duty—short-term assignment. He'll return to Warren Air Force Base in Cheyenne soon."

"You must be proud of him."

"Likes what he's doing."

"A missile base, is it? With operational missiles?"

"Minuteman. The silos spread from Wyoming into Colorado and Nebraska." Grandpa smoothed the arm of the couch as he talked.

"Haven't seen him since his last visit when he brought the kids a blue sailboat as smooth as any made by a skilled craftsman." Dad's hands came together in front of his chest, holding the imaginary boat. "Don't know if they ever played with it, though. Funny, I never saw it again. Luke probably took it to the lake and lost it."

Dana resisted the impulse to jump out and tell him the truth.

Seeming to be shocked, Grandpa pressed deeper into the cushions but continued their chat. "I hear the mill's keeping you hostage."

"Pioneering some new lines. Keeps the technicians troubleshooting double time." He plucked a cigarette from his pocket. "Similar problems down south as we've had here."

"You've taken up smoking?"

"New bad habit. Eases the stress." At the flick of his lighter, an orange flame erupted.

"God can help with that, you know."

"Rachael reminds me." Dad inhaled with the gasp of a diver emerging from the sea. "Sorry." He coughed. "I try to keep it outside. She doesn't like the smell."

"It permeates anything porous—drapes, upholstery, clothes." Grandpa placed both hands on his knees and leaned forward. "Other than the mill, how're you coping, Jesse?"

"Been better."

"If you need to talk, I can listen."

"Thanks." Dad swept the built-up ash into a tray beside his chair and parked the cigarette. The smoke rose unattended. Unraveling yesterday's newspaper, he feigned interest on page two.

Grandpa reread the outside headline for several seconds. "Let me see if there's enough coffee to sneak a cup before dinner. Want some?"

"No, thanks. I'm good."

Dana held her breath to keep from crying. She had lost Luke but not the blue boat. If given the chance, she'd have lost it all over again to save him.

Neighbors without nearby families gathered at the Fosters' house for Christmas dinner. Last year during preparation time, Dana and Luke had made a contest of who could set the most places at the dining room table, extended full length by two extra leaves. She couldn't remember who won, but she could still see Luke frisking from the kitchen and placing a stack of plates beyond her reach in the center. Even so, he triggered fun in a way no one else could.

As hostesses, Mom and Grandma roasted the turkey. Everyone else brought the trimmings. The drumsticks, usually reserved for Luke and Dana as the only children, evoked Luke's presence last year. One stayed reverentially alone on the platter.

Little laughter joined constrained talk around the table. But near the end of the meal, a man asked Dad about the weather in North Carolina.

"Better than here!" He smiled like someone telling a joke. "No snow to speak of. The mill's in the western part of the state. Sometimes gets a dusting, but overall, the climate's mild. In dead winter, black ice can be bad, morning or night. It's the least of my headaches, though. I hail a cab or shuttle from the airport and stay at a place in walking distance from work."

"And why is it you're going there?"

"Getting a new system up and running. Same as we did here. Not without its problems." He shrugged.

"Make the trip often?" The question came from curiosity rather than nosiness.

"I'm gone anywhere from several days to a couple weeks at a shot. It'll settle out." The finality in his tone halted any further questions.

Mom and Grandma began clearing the table. Other women took their cue to help serve pumpkin and pecan pies while Mom carried the half-eaten turkey to the kitchen. She tucked the leftover drumstick into a far corner of the refrigerator.

Wishing she hadn't seen that, Dana returned to the dining room, not to the table but to the pottery area cleared of tools and half-finished work. She blended in there like an inanimate clay object to listen without drawing attention. Coffee and dessert could run on indefinitely.

"I hear the church next door is expanding." Everyone turned to the woman who was first to reap local news. "They're planning to build a fellowship hall on the parking lot's space."

Dana and Luke had adopted that lot as their skating rink. During rain, car tires sank into the unpaved dirt, dredging muddy tracks that froze in winter. They would scoot across the alley to put their skates on by the largest patch of ice. Skating a few feet at a time didn't stop them from seeing themselves as future Olympic champions. They chose nicknames for themselves and created posters to publicize their fame.

She hadn't skated alone, even though deep plunges in temperature had frozen the lot twice.

Another neighbor joined the conversation. "I hear they're going to demolish two old houses on the other side to create a new parking lot. The grounds are a mess right now. Trees and bushes have grown wild as a jungle. Haven't been pruned in years."

The jungle, one of Dana's hideaways, once hosted a forbidden picnic with Luke. They carted her dolls' frying pans with cut-up chunks of bologna to the overgrown thicket of shrubs beside the windows of the church's basement meeting room. The scheme was simple—make a small fire, fry the bologna, and eat it there in the bushes. Two heaping handfuls of weeds and grass spurned the flame of their matches. Success came after several tries, but the tendrils of smoke alerted people in the room below. No one waved. When a man gave a furious rap on the window, Luke stomped out the thin flame. They scooped up their planned picnic and scuttled through the bushes.

"The church will own a good part of the block." The first neighbor rejoiced at finding a neutral topic. "It's definitely growing."

Dana wanted to run over to the church and beg the person in charge not to alter any of it. If everything kept changing, the world she knew with Luke might go away altogether.

CHAPTER 7

1972

One evening in January, Dad came home in time for dinner—a rare occurrence. At the serving of hamburger patties, scalloped potatoes, and asparagus, Dana enjoyed the comfortable familiarity of a family meal—except for the empty chair. Both Mom and Dad asked about happenings at school as if they'd rehearsed but forgotten to coordinate. Their unusual politeness became a red flag. An unknown force beyond Luke's absence strained the exchange. Dana couldn't figure it out.

Mom finished ahead of them. She left the kitchen but reappeared in different clothes. "I have a women's meeting at church. I'll say goodnight now because you'll be asleep when I get home." She kissed Dana and held her longer than usual. "See you in the morning." Clutching her purse and keys, she closed the back door slowly to keep it from banging on the way out.

In the living room, Dad browsed through book titles in the bookcase—not a typical action for him after dinner, his hour for reading the paper. When the sound of the car tires crunching the gravel ceased, the house maintained its stillness. He turned to Dana. "I need to talk to you." He sat in his usual chair.

Standing in front of him, she thought about the strangeness at dinner warning that everything was off in some way.

He took both her hands in his and locked her in his gaze. "I have a new job in North Carolina. Yardley has offered me the manager position at the mill down there. I have to report soon. Early next month."

"You mean, we're moving away?"

"I'm the only one going."

"What about Mom and me?" Heat rose to her head.

"You'll stay here like you always have."

"And you'll live by yourself?" Her hands in his became fists.

He dropped his chin, fixing his eyes on hers.

She wrenched her hands away. "We'll be here alone?"

"Not alone. You'll be together, you and Mom. You won't have to change schools or anything." He pulled her to him, but she drew back, unbending.

It was becoming clear to her. "How can we live without you?"

"You'll do fine. The two of you."

"No! You're supposed to live here!" The room grew murky and ominous as a cave with no exit. "You're my father. You belong here with us."

"I'll still be your father. I'll always be your dad. Forever." Words intending to convince turned to begging. "You can visit me whenever you want."

"I don't want to visit you. You belong with us." Her hands swiped sideways at tears coming from a plentiful source inside. "Don't go." She thought she'd crack in two. "Please, Dad, don't go."

"I have to."

Again, he tried to embrace her. But she ran, screaming, "No!" through a hurricane of blackness to her room to bury herself in bed.

Curled up there, she replayed everything he had said; but she didn't understand. Was it clear enough? If he accepted another job, she and Mom would move with him like the Olsons did. He must not have thought it through.

But the following days showed he was doing exactly that—moving away alone.

Dana tossed about in bed, searching for a way to make Dad stay. A plan slowly formed in her mind. She slept and somehow awoke early enough to catch him before he left for work.

"Wait." Not knowing what else to say, she brought her hands from behind her back, holding final proof of the blue boat's existence.

"What do you have there?"

"Luke fished it from the storm drain. Didn't even know it got stuck. Thought we'd never see it again." Her hand swooped to show the boat's final move. "He dug it out where it caught in some stuff at the side, way underneath. I guess that's what happened. He hid this beat-up piece in his drawer. Mom said I could have it."

She held the boat out to him.

Puzzled, he hesitated, then cushioned it in his palm. "The boat Uncle Barn gave Luke." He turned it over. "Always wondered what happened to it."

She took it as an invitation to retell the entire story. Reliving it in detail, she chased the boat along the curb in her mind.

Dad's misted eyes turned away to a supposed noise.

"It's all we have of him." She peered up, begging. "Can you fix it?"

His usual composure returned. "It'll take work."

"But can you?"

"I'll try." He rubbed his temple, staring at the remains. "A definite challenge. You must know that."

"Do it for Luke. Okay?"

He stooped to kiss her. "Gotta run." At the door, he paused. "I love you."

Then, it came to her. "I'll be on the lookout for what it needs. Material for sails. String for ropes. Paint." Her spirit soared. "We can work on it together." If she couldn't have her brother, the next best thing was Dad beside her restoring Luke's treasure.

Hand on the doorknob, he turned back. "Don't plan on it, honey. Can't do it at the moment. Place keeps me too busy." He saw her smile die and added, "Someday soon." He held the boat aloft in a less-than-convincing sign of hope.

The back door closed, blocking Dad from sight, along with her final glimpse of the battered hull. Alone in the kitchen, she thought about it. Maybe he was too tired to think about Luke anymore. Or her.

As the days passed, she searched for his work on it, but where? Not in his work area in the basement or puttering at the kitchen table. He was never there.

In a desperate move, she stopped talking to him altogether. When he came home before bedtime, which wasn't often, she pretended he wasn't there. When he spoke to her, she turned away—abruptly, so he'd notice.

Anger perched on her shoulder and coached her to reject him, but nothing she did brought change or happiness to either of them.

Dana's only relief came from a new student, Mary Jo Dwyer, who entered fourth grade in late autumn. In that short time, they had become close friends. Whenever the girls raced to Mary Jo's after school, Dana never forgot to call home, the most important rule in her diminishing family.

The girl's parents had divorced a few years earlier; but last summer, her mother had remarried. The stepfather had brought his preschool-aged daughter, Paula, to join the family, and they had moved to Fenton together. Dana couldn't imagine all those changes. She'd already survived so many of her own.

On the Saturday after Dad's news, a sunny winter day, Dana headed for Mary Jo's, five blocks away on the other side of Parkview Elementary. Her feet smacked the earth, slowing a few times for a walloping, satisfying stomp. She couldn't do that in snow or rain. By the time she reached the house, her cadence turned to a trot.

She joined Mary Jo and Paula, playing fetch with Max, their Labrador retriever. She imagined the muscles in her arm growing stronger each time she threw the stick. "I wish we had a dog."

"We can share Max with you." Mary Jo waited while he returned not to her, but to Dana. "He likes you."

"How do you know?"

"Watch what his tail does when he sees you."

Before Dana could bask in the dog's acceptance, movement at the front gate distracted them.

Carter, the fifth-grade bully, did his best to control every house in the neighborhood. He stopped and held his hand on the latch. "Are you babysitting your *baby* sister, Mary Jo?" His voice rose to imitate Paula's voice but couldn't get beyond a sarcastic whine.

"Go away." Mary Jo swung around to confront him. "You have no business here."

"But I can help." He burst through the gate, brandishing a water pistol.

The girls retreated to the middle of the yard.

Flat footed and panting, he chased after them. An unexpected halt placed him in front of Paula. "Here, d'you want this?" He held out the plastic weapon. As she reached to take it, he flipped it and aimed streams at her hair.

Shrieking, she put her hands on her head and wailed.

Mary Jo hurried Paula into the house, yelling at Carter to go home.

Grabbing Max's stick, Dana turned on Carter, forcing him deeper into the yard. Although she dodged repeated spurts, her jacket dripped by the time she caught him at the fence. Max barked beside her.

Carter clambered over but, once outside the yard, poked his head up. "Wah, wah. You're like that little baby." His smirk revealed a gap from a missing tooth.

Stored-up anger fueled a spontaneous reaction. She smashed him square on the nose. Blood spewed like a breaking dam. Carter howled as the bright stream coursed to his chest. He ran through adjacent yards, hands tenting his nose.

She waited by the fence until he blended into the trees. The whole scene took a while to process. The sensation that her fist wasn't attached to her arm when she punched him and the stark red blood made the event surreal.

A list of fears came to her. Mary Jo's mother might forbid her from visiting again; or worse, Mary Jo couldn't be her friend anymore. What if the police arrested her, or she had to apologize to Carter's parents? Or if Carter landed in the hospital, Mom might make her visit him. She tried to envision handing a bouquet of flowers to a bully.

Max, the only witness, wagged his rear end, ready to play. Sprayed water made his black coat sleeker than before.

Close to freezing in spite of the sun, Dana waited a few more minutes for Mary Jo's return before leaving for home, closing the gate with a secure click.

Dana's altercation became news to Rachael when she ran into Abby, Mary Jo's mother, at the Fenton Gallery.

Abby rested her hand on Rachael's arm. "Don't be mad at her. Mary Jo told me everything. She thinks Dana's a hero. I don't mean it's good that she bloodied his nose, but the boy is a terrible bully from what I've heard. It's likely he won't torment the girls or anyone else again."

"It's not like Dana." Rachael floundered for an explanation. "She's going through a hard spell. Her father is leaving soon." To explain further, she continued. "We're getting divorced. No one in my family, all the way back to Eve, has been divorced." She'd done it—aired her problems to someone she had spoken to many times but not enough to be a confidante.

"I know what it's like, thinking you're the only one to go through it. Mary Jo's father walked away, and Clay has no idea of Paula's mother's whereabouts; but we're so happy being normal together, we think they did us a favor."

The words, intended as comfort for Rachael, weren't enough.

"Unfortunately, you and I are part of a larger club than you know. My house is open for a cup of tea any time you need a sounding board."

"I may take you up on that." Rachael forced a smile. Her first concern was Dana. "As much as I think I know my own child, I can't fathom what she did." She tried to tell if Abby also thought Dana's behavior unusual.

"You may be expecting too much of a little girl who's been through more than one life-changing ordeal, as you have."

"But I'm an adult. Age and experience help to sort things out. I'd feel better if I knew the wounds of her childhood will heal eventually."

Rachael's future held many cups of tea with Abby, but that day's decision was to postpone the Carter talk to sometime after Dana's birthday.

CHAPTER 8

While Dana was away at a slumber party, Rachael used the opportunity for a private talk with Jesse. She sat on the couch across from him. "Have you noticed a change in Dana here lately?"

Surprised that she was talking to him, he raised his head.

"She's angry, Jesse. I've never seen her like this. Ever. Not the sweet girl we've always known." She moved toward the arm, closer to him. "I'm not sure this whole situation has been handled the best way."

"What situation?"

"Yours. Choosing to leave."

"You mean, *I* didn't handle it the right way."

Her silence accused him.

"What do you want me to do?" He lit a cigarette there in the living room where he'd promised, again, to smoke only outside.

"Ask for a provisional transfer, a temporary change of location to return here eventually and give us another chance." She continued when he said nothing, her voice growing louder. "This is too sudden. Dana lost her brother. It's too much."

"And I lost a son." Jesse's tone rose to match hers. "I didn't ask for him to die."

"Don't you think I'd change that day if I could bring it back? It's a shock for me to lose my son and my husband within a few short months!" Her planned heart-to-heart was dissolving into a shouting match.

"My life is upside-down, too! I don't know how to cope with losing Luke. I can't fix it in any way, and now I'm going to a state where I don't know anyone."

"It's your choice," Rachael retorted.

"What?" His shoulders shot backward.

"The whole town knows. You asked for the transfer."

Stunned, he sank into his chair, then stabbed his cigarette into a tray and stomped out the front door.

Through the glass, she saw him standing on the veranda, a solitary figure with nowhere to go. After a time, he stepped aside to sit on the glider. In the waning light of dusk, the spark of his lighter flared as he lit another cigarette.

If she were able to evaporate like an ephemeral being, she'd do it. In a previous time, his apologies came easily, holding her in his arms and saying he hadn't thought it through. They'd find another way.

The shadows in the corners deepened around her in the living room. She had sought him out about Dana. How did it go wrong? Her feet, at someone else's insistence, propelled her through the living room to the veranda where they stopped in front of him. "Dana turns ten this week."

He exhaled his smoke away from her.

"The party for the girls will be on Saturday, but January 25 is Tuesday. You need to make her day unforgettable." She didn't wait for his reply.

Dana marked her birthday with a silent protest to Dad.

He held open the Chrysler's front passenger door for Mom and the back door for her. "Best car I've ever had. Isn't she a beaut?"

Undaunted by no response from either, he maintained his cheeriest self as he drove downtown. "We're going to the Robin Hood Grill, the new place. I hear the steak sandwiches are great."

Without encouragement, he forged ahead. "It's early enough to take in a movie after dinner. How's that sound to you, Dana?"

A voice muttered from the back. "What's showing?"

"The Rialto is running that one released in December—beds and brooms in the title."

"Yeah, if you think you'd like it."

"You will, too. Not brand new, but it has great visual effects, so I've heard. Has anyone at school seen it?"

"Don't know."

At this, Mom shot an I-told-you-so look toward the driver's seat.

Dad gave exclusive attention to the process of parking in a space by the curb two storefronts from the restaurant.

Outside, Dana staked a spot on the sidewalk in a military stance and slung her purse over her shoulder as she stepped out of the car. "How did you leave work early, Dad?"

"I had an important date." He shut the car door behind her.

She waited for him to turn around to face him squarely. "With me or Mom?"

"Both—but your new double digits make this a special day."

"Yeah, it's special for me when my father is leaving." Her purse strap strained in her grip.

"Dana!" Mom couldn't condone the outburst of daughter against father, even if she had a reason.

But Dana persisted. "Think you'd have a happy birthday if your father was abandoning you?"

Dad's eyes narrowed. "We didn't have much in the way of birthdays. We were working to survive. I was lucky if I had a cake."

Mom gave up and turned away, but the words didn't stop.

"What if your father was moving away alone? How would you feel then?"

He flinched at her accusation. To regain composure, he sought a grounding point and placed the flat of his hand on the car's hood, one of the few things harboring no animosity. "Honey, I'm sorry. I still love you, but things haven't worked out the way we planned. Some day, you'll understand. When you've grown up." He curled his arm around her, and she jerked away. His hands hung like heavy weights at his sides while his wife and daughter cried. "Let's get in the car."

Wiping tears, Dana folded herself back into a corner of the back seat, wishing she could grow small enough to disappear.

Dad slumped in the driver's seat with the ignition key in his hand.

Dana choked back sobs. "Do you have to go?"

"I've already received the transfer."

"Then we can move with you."

His eyes grew dark. "We've gone over this too many times."

Mom turned in the front seat. "You need to finish school in Fenton this year, Dana. It's not good to leave in the middle of a year. See how we do here—the two of us together—until summer. Then, we can revisit it."

A new possibility. Why hadn't they told her earlier?

Dad twisted to see the back seat. "Shall we claim our seats for dinner?"

Mom coaxed Dana. "We want to celebrate you. Let's go."

She finished her last sniffle.

As they straggled into the restaurant, Dana lagged behind.

In a hushed tone, Mom said to Dad, "I told you to hold off."

Inside, he stated his reservation name, appearing relieved by the subdued lighting.

While they ate, Dana did a silent head count—one, two, three. Luke would have been number four but more like four, five, and six because his presence always claimed extra space.

At home, it was down to two of them at supper without Dad. The accident had broken the crucial family link. If she knew how to be strong like Luke—outspoken and sure of herself—Dad might not leave.

Sunday afternoon floated by in an anticlimactic haze after the previous day's birthday party. Six girls brought the gifts Dana hoped for and more.

Mom coaxed her to the pottery studio. "Can we talk for a minute? About what happened in Mary Jo's yard?"

Dana took a chair but found a new fascination on her chain-link belt and the intricate detail of each metallic piece.

"Do you remember?"

She held her breath, waiting for wings or a new invention to carry her away. To where, she didn't care. "Who told you?"

"Saw Mary Jo's mother. By chance."

Excess air pushed into her cheeks like hot air balloons before deflating. "Is she mad at me?" She held her breath waiting for the answer.

"You're still welcome there, but we need to think about a better way of handling a difficult situation."

"He's nothing but a smart aleck."

"That may be. But we have to learn how to coexist with them, too."

"What else could I do? He barged into Mary Jo's yard. Trained his water pistol on Paula, a four-year-old."

"Sometimes, powerful words—or the way you assert yourself when you say them—can have a strong effect and avoid violence."

"Should I have watched him bully someone and get away with it? Like he always does?" Her eyes turned smoky. In a husky voice, she said, "I had to do it. Luke's not here."

When Dad left the first weekend in February, Dana shuttled between relief at not having to ignore him anymore or planning for him to come home again. He called frequently the first weeks without a schedule or regularity, but she answered in monosyllables. That forced him to either ask more questions or drop the conversation. Still, he persevered and continued to call, usually on weekends. It didn't take many of those talks to find it took as much effort to be mean to him on the phone as it did in person.

The phone rang on the first Sunday afternoon in March. Mom's answer revealed it was Dad.

Dana yanked her jacket from a hook and yelled, "I'm riding bikes with Mary Jo," and left before hearing a sound of protest. Inside the garage, she heeled the kickstand upward and wheeled the bicycle through the side door, away from the driveway. A path between the square house on the corner and the next one provided a shortcut for her escape.

The temperature had dropped after church. The rubber on the handlebars threatened to freeze her bare hands. She cheered for the pair of mittens in her jacket pocket. Now, what to do? Mary Jo's family was away, visiting her grandmother for the whole weekend.

To resist the cold, she pumped the pedals fast, whizzing the bike toward the library. Her breath puffed out in visible clouds like a dragon shooting fire at its enemies. The thought of the new fierce image warmed her.

She parked her bike in a stand, thinking it strange hers was the only one. The tall flight of stairs took longer to climb alone, but at the top, the curved metal door handle didn't budge. Under the stone lion's head guarding the entrance, she peeped inside. The empty room jogged her mind. The library was closed on Sundays.

Shivering on her way down the stairs, she tried to think of a close-by place to go, and it came to her—the grocery store with its heat. The bicycle resisted in the cold as she wrestled it from the stand. White specks dotted the air. Snow. Not what she needed.

She rode on the sidewalk, empty because no one else braved the wind and cold. A dull, gray Chevrolet with deep rust on its frame slowed beside her. The teenage driver and another boy leered at her. She sped up. The car's rattling engine kept pace. When she slowed to let it pass, the driver tapped the brakes until the Chevy barely moved. She almost stopped pedaling, but the top of her head thumped with her pulse in the frosty air.

The boy in the passenger seat rolled down the window. "Hi, Beautiful. What ya doin' out in the snow?" The rusted car stopped. He jumped out, grabbed her shoulders, and kissed her full on the lips before he darted back into the front seat, cackling. The car roared off in billowing exhaust.

The bike pointed up the street. Her cheeks burned. Her feet churned to help the wind blow away the image of the boy's dirty mouth. She pictured his face on the ground and spit on it as the sidewalk fell away. Her thoughts whirled as fast as the wheels. The cold caught her, making her regret leaving home. It was Dad's fault. His phone call brought the cold bike ride and the despicable boys. But she had to keep the whole thing to herself.

As pedaling grew harder, her imagination threw a toasty ski outfit around her—a blue one. The need to find somewhere to think and hide for a while brought to mind the church's back wall and tangled bushes, a shelter from the wind, where she and Luke often played.

Cars filled the church parking lot, even though it was mid-afternoon. She propped her bike beside the house and stole across the alley to the area behind the church. Lights beamed from the basement meeting room. By squatting at ground level, she could see through a window. A bride, inside a circle of women wearing Sunday-best clothes, stood still while a woman styled her veil.

Mom and Dad had married in the summer, she was sure, but innocent-enough thoughts about it grew into resentment. If the wedding hadn't happened, she and Mom wouldn't be alone. But then, would she and Luke have been with Mom and some other man or with Dad and some other woman? Carrying it further, she may have had a sister instead of a brother. Sure, a sister who could never take Luke's place.

She left the window like an elusive creature in the shadows and prowled away. Telltale footprints in the snow exposed her momentary presence. Stowing the bike in the garage, she climbed the stairs to the stoop, tiptoed inside, and left her jacket on a hook. All clear in the kitchen. She began to sneak through the dining room.

Mom sat in her workspace, hands idle in her lap. The tiniest sound must have startled her. Leaping up, she folded Dana in her arms. "Where were you? I was afraid you might freeze. I searched for you everywhere."

"To Mary Jo's. No one was home."

Mom's hands shook as she draped a double-knit crocheted shawl around Dana. "You've been gone a long time."

"Rode to the library. Started snowing when I left." Her gaze traced the pattern on the dining room rug before crawling up the far wall toward the church. "Do you know there's a wedding today?"

"I saw the cars."

"I started thinking how it must have been when you and Dad got married. The ceremony and the weather and everything. What was it like?"

"Not snowing. A sunny day in June. Grandma and Grandpa held the reception in their yard behind the house. You've seen the album." Seeing Dana's reticence, Mom guided her into the kitchen and took a milk bottle from the refrigerator. "You must be cold."

"Are you sorry you married him?"

"Of course not." Milk poured from the bottle into a pan. "I wouldn't have known you." No mention of Luke.

Dana pressed her nose to the window for an oblique view of snow-brushed shrubs and small trees.

The pot's contents bubbled around a wooden spoon. "I called Abby's number, but no one answered. Weren't they going away this weekend?"

Dana spoke to the windowpane. "We talked about riding bikes. Guess Mary Jo forgot about not being here."

Ensuring the cocoa was hot, Mom set two steaming mugs on the table.

Every crevice of Dana's brain avoided further quizzing by allowing the steam's dissipating tentacles to capture her.

"I know you don't always want to speak to your dad. I don't, either. But he'll always be your father, and I need to keep in contact with him because of you."

"And Luke."

"Yes. And Luke."

The short silence provided time for each to decide where to go next.

Dana spoke first. "You know how the assistant principal calls me in sometimes to talk about Luke? She said people hide photographs of someone who died—not to forget his life, but to keep from being sad again. It's healthy, she said, to acknowledge him. Acknowledge his life. It must be one of her preferred words." She kneaded her cold fingers.

Mom's palm, warm from holding her mug, rested on Dana's arm. "So we shouldn't shy away from talking about him?"

"Yeah." She sat up taller. "What does Dad think?"

"You'll have to ask him when he feels like talking."

"It will never happen."

"We have to give him time. People handle grief in different ways. Right now, I think he's busy running away."

She didn't know adults did such things, but she had to agree with Mom.

CHAPTER 9

The closing of school neared, marking the end of fourth grade and one year since Dana had wandered with Luke, seeking out new challenges. She measured time as before or after his accident and wondered if she always would. Facing her first full summer without him, she pondered another problem. Mom was working. Where did that leave her? Staying home alone?

It became apparent one Saturday that Mom had been working on a solution when Abby and Mary Jo smiled through the front window.

Abby tapped Rachael's arm as she walked through the doorway. "Paula's at a friend's house. She won't get in the girls' hair while we're busy. Once in a while, things work out right."

They migrated to the dining room table and settled themselves while Rachael produced a tray of sandwiches and crocks of clam chowder soup. Across a corner, the girls chattered like chipmunks. No one would have guessed they were together the day before.

Seeing them preoccupied, the mothers talked over the plan for summer. Rachael summed it up. "Taylor would like me to be in the office three days a week, if possible. I can do some work at home on the other two. How does that sound for you?"

"Perfect." Abby's thumb danced down her glass, creating streaks in the condensation as her eyes rolled toward Dana. "Can you tolerate spending three whole days a week with Mary Jo at our house this summer?"

"I'll find a way." Dana giggled with Mary Jo as they devoured soup like starving waifs in a novel she'd read and then scampered outside.

While Abby stirred honey into hot tea, she admired the mug's design as one of Rachael's originals. "The recreation group is giving swim lessons at the high school pool. A good thing for the girls."

"Dana already knows how to swim."

"So does Mary Jo. But it's an advanced class. Teaches safety, rescue, and survival skills. Plus, something called 'speed techniques,' in case the girls want to go for the gold." She waited for the thought to sink in. "I'll sign them up for Tuesday and Thursday mornings so you can get some work done."

During the two remaining afternoons, the girls joined Mom in her pottery area. Using fat rolls of hemp twine, they worked on macramé projects of wall hangings, key chains, and plant hangers, the last being most successful. But boredom set in after they braided more than one.

"I'm going to weave a collar for Max." Mary Jo spooled out a few feet of thin rope.

"Max won't be happy." Mom held out a strand. "Rub it between your fingers. Not soft or smooth. You'd have to line it with cushioning material."

To convince herself, Mary Jo gave it a squeeze. "Not good for bracelets, then, either."

Dana wished she could be as comfortable around adults as Mary Jo, but the lasting effect of that exchange was the suggestion for bracelets. It took hold of Mom and Dana in the following days and expanded into wider jewelry possibilities. With the eagerness of archaeologists digging for a find, they explored craft shops, excavating assorted beads of plastic, wood, and faux gems in myriad shapes and sizes. Lustrous ones gleamed. Those in a flat finish produced interesting patterns.

The range of textures and colors flooded Dana's imagination. Sifting through a batch in shades of violet, she chose a handful in hues from bright to pastel. "Aunt Elaine's best color. A necklace for her birthday."

"Gifts for friends' birthdays, too." Mom held a cluster of smooth beads as blue as lapis lazuli. "We'll need a bigger supply of wire and fasteners. If we buy in bulk, we'll have plenty to share with Mary Jo."

At home, Dana searched for a hidden box that safeguarded a treasure from an Adirondacks riverbed years ago. A nut-brown triangular rock an inch long distinguished itself by a single white line cutting diagonally across it like a brand. The best part was an eroded hole near one of its three rounded points that would support a chain. She scurried to the kitchen. "How's this for making a neat necklace?"

Just by looking at it, Mom could feel the stone's smoothness. "Polishing will make it shine. Remember the thin silk taupe ribbon we bought? We can braid it and thread it through the hole. It'll be beautiful." She held it to her throat and turned to her reflection in the window glass. "I might need to borrow it for an occasion."

Dana couldn't ask for a better compliment.

Although summer ended too soon, Dana began her best school year ever. Her fifth grade teacher, Miss Richardson, exhibited energy that bounced her dark, loose hanks of hair out of control as she challenged each student to improve. The idea of setting personal goals, regardless of what others were doing, appealed to Dana. She felt as though she'd grown several years older within a few months. Something else helped, too. Most of the Parkview students no longer shied away from her as the girl whose brother died.

Still, Luke's accident wouldn't leave her. One irretrievable second stole her brother forever. During swim lessons, she had visualized being bucked off the boat and practiced swimming fast or diving to avoid the spinning blades. But even with a plan in mind, reacting wasn't easy. The element of surprise was a force in it all. He couldn't have known.

Escape came from immersing herself in the lives of people she read about. Among the best were stories of Annie Oakley. Applauding the skills of the young sharpshooter, Dana steered her eyes more than once over the pages about Frank Butler marrying her a year or so after she beat him in a marksmanship contest. Dana couldn't imagine any man, or boy, taking a liking to someone whose skill surpassed his.

Pictures of Annie wearing long dresses like most women in the quarter century before 1900 surprised Dana. They were nothing like the cowgirl outfit with short skirt and vest fringed in fake leather from Grandma and Grandpa before she had entered school. For Luke, they had brought a cowboy hat and a pair of chaps. She had loved her Western clothes, but she yearned for a hat like his as they rode imaginary horses—Luke's, a black stallion, and hers, a palomino filly—over the wide prairie of their front lawn.

Being alone together freed Dana and Mom from having to anticipate Dad's reactions, but they still missed the days with Dad and Luke before the world turned upside down. Mom responded by bringing Luke's school pictures out and placing them beside Dana's throughout the house. Occasionally, they talked about what he said or did and were able to laugh about the way he cartwheeled across the lawn.

Once, when they exchanged those stories, Dana recalled one that involved Mom. "Remember how Luke and I teased the wringers in the old washing machine back then? We wiggled our fingers where the rollers came together, daring them to catch us." She reenacted the action in front of imaginary rollers.

"And I warned you it wasn't safe."

"We didn't listen, but you were right. It caught mine and pulled my hand all the way through. You had to give it a hard whack to make it stop." She chopped the side of her hand downward.

"I'll never forget." Mom relived the way she hit the release knob to spring the wringers open. "That's when I quit using that machine and bought one of the new automatics." She thought for a moment. "You were three then."

"Even though I was little, I can see it like yesterday how it bruised my arm below the elbow. I went to my bedroom crying, but Luke came by. I asked him to wrap my arm in the end of his T-shirt. Don't know where that idea came from, but here's what's important. He did it, whether it made sense or not."

"I'm hearing this for the first time."

"He stretched the bottom of his shirt. Rolled it like a bandage around my arm so carefully. Wasn't bleeding, but it hurt." She rubbed her arm as if it had just happened. "You know what? The soreness disappeared for a while. It really did. Can you imagine?"

Mom closed her eyes. "An act of kindness from Luke."

"I wish he were here to wrap us both in his shirt. We could use it."

Little did Dana and Mom know how soon they'd need the help of Luke's T-shirt.

A sudden change took them off guard in mid-November. Dana heard it from the dining room while Mom and Elaine finished the after-dinner clean up.

"What's Jesse doing these days?"

Giving a jolt of surprise, Mom lifted her hands from soapy water in the sink and whispered, "Funny you should ask."

Elaine draped her towel over the back of a chair. "Give me the scoop."

Trying to keep her voice even, Mom let three words slip out. "He's married again."

Elaine nearly fell on the floor. Unable to speak, she sputtered.

Dana eased around the corner as Mom blotted a dab of suds from her cheek.

In the midst of shock, Elaine blurted, "That didn't take long. When did you find out?"

"Yesterday. I asked about his progress in finding somewhere permanent to live. Turns out, wife number two owns a house."

"How convenient."

"You'd think I was his new confidante, the way his enthusiasm rose as he listed her attributes."

"Like what?"

"She's a great cook. He even repeated it. Maybe he couldn't find anything else to say. Imagine him telling me that."

A slap on the counter accompanied Elaine's shriek. "Some men will do anything for a home-cooked meal!" Rachael's calmness clearly baffled her. "Did you have any idea he was seeing someone?"

"When he mentioned the woman who works in the personnel department one time too many, I suspected but didn't want to admit it. I thought he was still trying to find himself." What started as a chuckle ended with tight lips.

From the doorway, Dana saw her mother's attempt to stay lighthearted in her delivery of the news. Their eyes connected. All she could say was, "Mom?"

"I didn't want you to hear it like this." Crossing the kitchen, Mom wiped her hands on her apron before the three huddled together.

"Will we see him again? Ever?"

"Of course. I told you; he's still your father. He'll come to see you as he always has. And someday, he'll want you to go down there to see him, too."

Dana wasn't sure about that.

CHAPTER 10

1973

Working in the kitchen with Mom gave Dana a communication advantage; but even with their growing closeness, she found it easier to talk during a physical task that kept her from direct eye contact. It proved true one night in January while setting the table for two. "I've been thinking about my birthday."

"Your eleventh!" Taco seasoning filled the kitchen as hamburger sizzled in a frying pan. "The twenty-fifth is on Thursday this year. Your father will be here to take you for a birthday dinner."

"Why? I haven't seen him for two months."

"Getting resettled hasn't been easy for him, but he does want to see you."

"Sure. Lots of proof of that."

"Try not to be angry. It cheats you of happiness coming your way."

After her last birthday, the disaster before Dad left, her hopes weren't high. "Do I get to choose where to eat?"

"I guess, but it might be smart to have two or three choices." Mom placed vegetables and cheese for the tacos on a lazy Susan. "Give yourself permission for a good time." Going to the stove, she glided her arm over Dana's shoulder. "Meanwhile, we'll plan the party you want with your friends. It'll be here soon."

As it turned out, Dad took her to the top of the list, The Pizza Palace. He led Dana to an isolated booth at the back, away from prying eyes outside. Leaving her for a moment, he leaned on the front counter while he ordered the largest pie with everything on it, including extra cheese.

Back at the table, he poured cream soda into a tall glass. "This is for you."

"I haven't had this since forever." She held the bubbling glass at eye level, pleased he remembered.

"Any plans for your big day?" He settled himself at their booth to listen.

She sipped through the straw as she considered his question. "I'd love a roller-rink party, but Mom thinks they're for older kids." In truth, it cost too much; but she wanted Dad's reaction.

"I expect she's right." He tipped a cola bottle into his glass and stripped the paper from a straw. "So have you decided what you're going to do instead?"

"Grandma and Grandpa came last weekend. Tomorrow night, Mary Jo and my other friends are coming over." She listed them: "Jennifer, Ellie, Deena, and Olivia. With Mary Jo and me, that's six."

"What'll you do—the six of you?" His voice went up when he was interested.

"It's a slumber party. Mom already gave me my first present—long flannel pajamas, white with tiny blue flowers and blue trim on the collar and pocket." Her hand swept across her collarbone. "My best color. Soft, too. Can't wait to wear them."

He rested his glass on the table. "What do you do at slumber parties? Sounds like it doesn't involve too much sleeping."

She giggled. "Mostly, eat. Mom is in charge of food. Cheesy chips and pretzels and pizza again for the main thing. I guess later, we'll have ice cream and cake or cupcakes."

"What about music?"

"Mary Jo offered her tape player, and everyone will bring some of their tapes to give us a bunch to choose from. Before her suggestion, I planned to use our 8-track 'cause it's all we have. Don't have many to play, though."

That was his cue. He reached into a bag on the floor. Out came a twelve-inch-square package professionally wrapped in paper with multicolored flying balloons on a white background. A red bow, as big as the box itself, topped it. "These should help with the festivities."

She removed the bow before ripping the paper. Before her sat the portable cassette player she had dreamed of. Too much to ask from Mom. Tapes of several popular singers tumbled out. "Wow! Even ABBA and the Bee Gees. My friends will flip out!"

He shared her enthusiasm. "I play them in the car."

"Thanks, Dad! This changes everything."

"I predict the cassette will take over the market. It's smaller and more compact. You can store more in a smaller space. It's a feature people prefer."

"I already do."

"And that's not all!" He unhooked a small microphone from a hidden compartment. "You can record."

"They'll love this!" She held it up. "Testing. Testing. We'll have fun with this."

He pulled a package of blank tapes from the bag. "For you and your friends to record on your own."

She leaned over the table to kiss him. "It's the best present." Stuffing everything back into the bag to make room for the arrival of pizza, she perceived something new. His mouth turned up at the corners.

After he served her the largest slice, he settled one on his plate. "Any other gifts you're hoping for?"

"Knee-high socks. I'm crazy about them. Don't have any yet." She bit off the smallest end of her pizza to test if it had cooled. "They make them in stripes and tons of designs. I've been telling everyone how much I like them. Do you think they'll take the hint?"

"You'll find out."

"I don't think they're too expensive. Or a jewelry box—a small one."

"You'll be surprised at whatever they bring."

"Uh huh." She dreamed ahead to the party before she began eating in earnest.

He restarted the conversation unpredictably with an invitation. "I want you to come down this summer to meet Kaye."

She choked but hid it by gulping her soda and coughing to pretend it went down the wrong way. She thumped her chest a couple of times and asked, "When?"

"Don't know yet. We're renovating the house to have a bedroom for you to stay in." He sketched a diagram of the house on a napkin and explained the changes in detail. "We're in the bidding stage for who will do the work."

Her eyes washed over the other tables to see who else was there.

"If it isn't ready, we can stay somewhere else for a few days." He'd get her attention yet. "Want to fly down?"

"You mean . . . in a plane?"

A broad grin captured his face. "That's the preferred way."

Six months after her birthday, Dana boarded a plane for Charlotte, North Carolina, and found an aisle seat matching the number on her boarding pass.

Following a string of other passengers, a woman with a round shape stopped beside her, eyeing the window. Before Dana could stand up, the woman offered her the seat. Against her deepest wish, Dana followed the polite refusal rule.

On hearing it was Dana's first airplane ride, the woman insisted. Stuffing her battered travel bag in the overhead compartment, she deposited her ample girth into the aisle seat. "I fly this trip often." She let out an audible sigh. "What I need is shut-eye. I'd be wasting a good window."

The engines revved. After a bumpy ride down the runway, the wheels left the ground. Houses below and yards with swing sets glided under a wing and out of sight. Within minutes, a shopping mall, a ballpark, and rows of cars in a factory parking lot receded from her lofty view. A lake narrowing into a curving river gave way to cultivated farmland.

Her seatmate had already fallen asleep, but sleep did not court her. When an air pocket threw her stomach up to her throat, it felt like the time she and Luke had challenged themselves to stand in the back of Dad's old panel truck before he had traded it. They had kept their balance without touching the sides as they raced over hilly roads. If they hit a pocket going downhill, they'd shout, "That's a stomach! Do it again, Dad!" She wished Luke had been able to feel that up in the air.

He missed out completely on plane rides. But if he were here, she wouldn't be on her way to see Dad or meet a stepmother, someone she had never foreseen in the complications of living. What did she look like, this woman she never wanted in her life? Was she willowy with smooth hair like Mom? Dad hadn't shown her a photo. Of course, she hadn't asked, either. Did her stepmother want to meet her new stepdaughter? To help time pass, she created conversations between Dad and his new wife, but invented dialogue didn't come easy for a father who wasn't a natural talker.

The captain halted her thoughts by announcing preparation for landing, and soon, they were taxiing to the terminal.

In the sea of faces, a familiar one appeared. Dad, in his signature golf jacket and khakis, rushed toward her. A small woman, not much taller than Dana, trotted beside him.

Auburn curls framed Kaye's rounded, pixie-like cheeks that promised friendliness. Her nose, tiny and slightly turned up, earned her a one-word summation: cute.

"This is Dana!" Kaye squeezed Dad's arm. "A little blue-eyed blondie. She's as gorgeous as you said, Jess."

Dana found it strange for someone to speak about her in third person as though she wasn't there. But . . . gorgeous? Dad must have said as much to his new wife.

Reality hit her. She had a stepmother. It was true. She'd met her, a fashionable woman wearing a pleated plaid skirt above the knees. Mom had nothing so trendsetting. Kaye's outfit, far from ordinary, clearly came from a professional line. Her stylish cream-colored jacket accented the predominant color of the skirt with tan and cocoa woven into the plaid.

The thought of being pretty accompanied her during their side trip to baggage claim. Dad had never said that to her—not once.

Kaye's flair for filling silences with chatter helped their comfort level while they waited at the baggage carousel. She ticked off the changes under construction at the house. "We're having an old TV room converted into two bedrooms. One will be for you when you visit. It's currently messy and torn-up, but the design makes the best sense for us. We can always build an entertainment room in the basement. Your dad's handy that way." She peered at Dana from under a light canopy of well-applied mascara. "But you already know that."

"Are you doing the work, Dad?"

"Too much for me now. Might do a room when I can."

"Sorry we can't take you there. It's not what you'd call livable, even for the two of us." Kaye sighed. "A good thing we're both working all day. We're lucky to eat and sleep there."

Dad switched from the house to a current problem plaguing him. "The oil crisis makes it hard to buy gas. We're better off not traveling far."

"Was it a hassle filling up to come here?" Dana choked it out.

"Waited close to an hour in line." At her worried expression, he added, "You're worth it."

Dana rejoiced over two compliments in ten minutes—a record. When she identified her bag, Dad swept it up and guided them to the exit, his other hand on her shoulder.

In the car, Kaye chatted on. "We have reservations at a hotel here in Charlotte tonight, but we're going to Boone tomorrow. Neat things to do in the mountains, including a bluegrass festival."

Bluegrass—a new term for her. It sounded like food for a horse. Who had a festival for horse feed? Not wanting to sound stupid, she didn't ask.

The hotel room included two double beds with a dividing wall between them, forming an alcove for the second bed, a fine arrangement for reading a book instead of talking or listening to Kaye. Her constant stream of talk rolled on like a never-ending river.

Soon she heard a unison goodnight followed by the click of the light switch, compelling her to shut hers off and contemplate the ceiling in the dark. The thrill of her first flight and seeing Dad again was already waning. She had finally met her stepmother but didn't need a fixed diet of her. What she wanted—having her father back—appeared impossible.

The scenery grew more alpine on the road to Boone as they approached the picturesque town tucked into the valley. The campus of Appalachian State University drew Dana in with its red brick buildings like stairsteps ascending the surrounding mountains.

While they walked from one location to another, Kaye recited facts from a pamphlet about the campus. At midday, they stumbled upon an old-fashioned drugstore with a lunch counter and a well-preserved soda fountain. Its row of round spinning stools, upholstered in shiny cherry material, enticed them to sit down.

"Is this oilcloth?" Kaye ran her hand over the slick surface of the stool near her. "These are practically historic."

"See the spigots?" Dad pointed, not thinking how many times he'd said it wasn't proper. A soda jerk, the person making the fizzy drink or ice cream soda, dispensed the flavored syrup and carbonation by jerking the spigot's handle. "Get a special drink to go with your sandwich. This is a rare opportunity."

During their lunch, she took in the store's wares. Items for sale overflowed the shelves, hung on hooks, and swung from the ceiling. Juice drinks and flavored pop vied for center stage beside magazines, pet supplies, and camping equipment, including camouflage clothing. Bunches of lollipops peeked from glass jars next to jawbreakers in twisted colors. Ads for products or concerts shouted from every supporting column. She wondered how to describe it all to Mom when she got home.

The next day took them to the Tweetsie Railroad, a park so named by the "tweet, tweet" echoing through the mountains from a vintage coal-fired locomotive hauling the train through a three-mile loop. After a lunch of hot dogs and ice cream, Dad hopped on the Tilt-a-Whirl with her, one of the few rides for adults. Kaye, afraid of getting dizzy, stayed outside the gate. Looking back, Dana took note of the delicate makeup enhancing Kaye's eyes and smoothing her skin tone. The process for applying it must have taken years to learn. Her manicured nails sported a pale tone of classic polish. She clearly spent little time in a garden or working outside. Mom kept hers short for gardening, typing, or shaping clay for ceramic pots.

The bluegrass festival began mid-week, highlighting a group of violins—called "fiddles" by the locals—accompanied by bass, banjo, guitar, and, in one band, spoons. A clogging contest stirred their curiosity. The name led Dana to expect the dancers to wear wooden clogs like old-fashioned Dutch shoes, but it was more like a variation on tap dancing.

On their final day, they visited Grandfather Mountain and saw black bears—a mother named Mildred and two cubs—in a new natural habitat. The enclosed acres gave them space to create their own dens or enjoy the limelight where Mildred charmed visitors by catching peanuts in her mouth.

From there, they explored the Mile High Swinging Bridge, the mountain's ultimate test of Dana's courage.

"Want to go across with me?" Dad placed his hand on her arm and confirmed that Kaye chose to stay behind.

Dana stared, against her will, into the eighty-foot chasm between two mountain peaks. It reduced the view from the library ledge to mere inches. Her stomach began its familiar churn.

Sensing her fear, he slipped her hand into his. She didn't complain about being too old. No one saw her—at least, no one she knew. At each step, the huge bridge swayed and bucked.

"Put your other hand on the railing. If it bothers you, don't look down. Zero in on the solid rock at the other side."

If Luke had been there, he would have run ahead of them with his hands free; and she would have had to follow.

When they had made it to the other side, they waved wildly at Kaye, shrunk in size like a figure at the wrong end of a telescope.

Relief flooded through Dana when they made it back across, culminating in the best camaraderie of the entire trip. It had taken all week to feel that way, just as she was going home.

Dana's final surprise came on the way back to the airport when Kaye delivered the news she'd hidden all week. "Next year, the house will be totally fixed up; and you'll have a new baby brother or sister."

"I will?" She hadn't considered the possibility of Dad having a baby with this new wife.

"What do you think it will be? A boy or a girl?"

Reluctant to say, she guessed, "A boy?" Then she said, "A girl is okay, too. Either one." It was worse than being called on in school and not knowing the answer.

Kaye said in a confidential tone, "I think your father wants a boy." She fluttered her eyes at Dad. "I won't be working while the baby's little, so you can stay as long as you want next summer."

The double whammy of news caught her off guard. Her eyes slid past Kaye's perfect hair toward the windshield.

CHAPTER 11

Dana met Mom at the airport gate and began her travelogue about the week. She continued at home where they sat down to an already-prepared meal of fried chicken served cold and a salad of greens. "Are these from the garden?"

"Lettuce has long passed. Doesn't like the heat of midsummer."

As they ate, Dana finished a complete recounting of the trip—the bears, swinging bridge, railroad, music festival, and all. At the end, she told Mom about the coming baby, expecting her to be startled; but she wasn't.

Instead, Mom redirected the conversation with news surpassing Dana's. "I'm going to have my own business—a consignment shop! I can sell my own pottery and other peoples' crafts. Might teach a few classes there. Taylor—that is, Mr. Hamlin—is doing the paperwork. What do you think?"

"Wow! You decided this while I was away?"

"Haven't found a location yet, but it's neat to think about, isn't it?" She didn't give Dana a chance to answer. "Elaine wants another outlet to sell her paintings. And you can help, too, on weekends and in the summer."

"How about the bracelets and macramé? Can I sell those?"

"I don't know why not. It'll be our shop."

The baby-to-be was already forgotten.

"We've discussed it over dinner—Mr. Hamlin and I. He hopes to spend time with both of us and get to know you better." She finished the chicken thigh on her plate and dropped it in the bone bowl, ready for the garbage. "He offered to take us to see the play at the Booth Theater on Friday night." Her voice rose. "Sound like fun?"

Annoyed at Mom for accepting the invitation before asking her approval, she reached into the freezer for more ice. "Is Mr. Hamlin married?"

"Not anymore. He married during law school; but after a few years, they separated. Never had children. His wife wanted to be a mother, but it didn't happen. He thinks she might have blamed him."

"How was that his fault?" Sometimes, the weird thinking of grown-ups baffled her.

"It doesn't mean it was. Some people find it easier to point a finger when they're unhappy."

"Like Dad?"

Mom blinked and waited for an explanation.

"Did Dad leave because he blamed you for Luke's accident?"

"I'm not sure. He wasn't the same person again, was he?" She grew quiet. "Neither are we, but we've carried on. Your father's had more difficulty adjusting."

"Didn't take him long to move away and find someone else."

"Is he happy?" Her mother looked almost hopeful, expecting an answer.

"No one has been happy since Luke died."

When Dana had accompanied her mother a year and a half ago to see the new workplace, she had met Mr. Hamlin at his office. Dad hadn't left home yet, and the thought of another man befriending her mother hadn't existed. Then, Dad remarried, and the world rotated out of kilter again.

As Friday evening approached, her concern mounted, spurred by her vague annoyance at Mom. She rehearsed her sternest expression in the mirror and then a placid, disinterested one; but when the doorbell rang, she forgot which one to wear.

"Good to see you again, Dana." Mr. Hamlin extended his hand. His normally smooth face crinkled.

Apprehension dissipated as he spoke. They were, after all, going to a play—nothing more.

"The Fenton Theatricals are putting on *Wait Until Dark*. If you haven't seen it, you're in for a real show. It's filled with suspense." He gave a playful tap to his temple, checking himself. "What else can we expect from Agatha Christie? Naturally, it's suspenseful." His smile returned. "Ready?"

They migrated out the front entrance.

"I've been waiting for this," Mom said as she locked the door.

Mr. Hamlin stepped aside and waited to escort them down the steps. Mom lifted her purse strap onto her shoulder, and the three headed to his car.

Some of Dana's friends complained about going to a boring play with their parents, but her live theater experience came only from school plays. Her curiosity rose.

During the performance, she subtly kept Mom and Mr. Hamlin in her side vision to see if he held her hand or draped his arm around her; but the play's action drew her attention. She focused on the stage and nothing else. At the height of two scary scenes, she vaulted from her seat.

He teased her about it afterward. "I think jumping beans hid in our row before the show."

Mom took it in stride. "You said it was a thriller, didn't you?"

A short walk from the theater took them to The Backstage Tea Room, where the adults ordered coffee and Dana ordered a flavored tea.

Mr. Hamlin offered his suggestions. "I have two out-of-this-world desserts to recommend here—coconut cake with a high frothy icing or lemon queen dessert. The second is more like a key lime pie than cake; but, of course, it's lemon."

When Dana chose the lemon, he waited for her to take the first bite. "How do you rate it?"

"Yummy. Incredibly yummy."

"I'm partial to lemon dessert for its dual tastes of bitter and sweet. Nothing beats it." He sank his fork into his cake and added, "Like some people, except you don't taste them."

He had tasted lemon, she was certain.

While they ate, he posed a question to Rachael. "Have you told Dana about the consignment shop?" He sat back as the two traded ideas and joined in when they remembered to include him.

When the bill came, the waitress left a parcel the size of a shoebox on the table.

"Since we're on the topic of shops"—Mr. Hamlin reached forward and moved the gift in front of Dana—"from what your mother tells me, you can use this."

Her eyes grew wider than her attraction to the stage.

When she didn't make a move, he encouraged her. "Be brave. Find out what's inside. We want to see, too."

Wispy pink paper with silver-edged patterns yielded at her touch. Matching ribbons fell away. Inside a glossy hot pink toolbox, numerous compartments brimmed with decorative beads, chunky or delicate, as well as crimp beads and small fasteners.

"A jewelry kit! Wow! It has everything!" She sidled around the table to hug the man who was as tall sitting down as she was standing.

Dana wore the latest bracelet of her creation to the dinner table several nights later, which spurred ideas about what to make for the future shop. Talk about jewelry and beading continued through the meal.

As they finished, Mom wadded her napkin in a final gesture. "I have something to show you when the dishes are done."

"What is it?"

"It's a keepsake, actually." The minute the last plate rested in the cupboard, she waved for Dana to follow. On an overhead closet shelf in her bedroom rested a miniature cedar chest, a gift from a furniture store to graduating high school girls in Mom's hometown. It bore a small brass plaque that read, "Congratulations to Rachael Norwood." On opening, it emitted a bold, fresh-cut tree scent, deeper and sharper than pine. "I've been thinking it's time for you to have this." She pulled out a velvet burgundy gift box.

The softness of the box attracted Dana, but she put off the temptation to rub it. Inside, at the end of a fine gold chain, hung a one-inch-long dragonfly. Its head, legs, and upper wings, a little over an inch wide, reflected gold and the lower wings, silver. Ten diamond chips studded its entire body, the largest at the top, tapering to a tiny one at the bottom below its golden legs.

"It was a symbol of your father's love for me. Now, it's for you."

"I remember you wearing this. Haven't seen it for a while." Dana lifted it from the box, unable to believe it was hers. In the mirror, the dragonfly sparkled at her throat.

Dana wore it every day until a time she would wish she'd left it in its box.

***

After Dana said good night, Rachael sat alone, thinking about the necklace. Jesse's behavior following Luke's accident contradicted his polite manner when she had first met him in Tannersberg, Fenton's twin city, where she had landed a job in a large attorney firm upon finishing secretarial school. During a visit to the farm to introduce him to her parents, they hinted about his introversion, fearing it might dampen her easygoing spirit.

Her mother found the words. "We love you, Rachael, but we're not sure he's strong enough to hold you."

"Of course, he is. He's self-made. On his own since high school. You'll see when you know him better."

When they became engaged, Elaine spoke to her, too. "Are you sure, sis?"

"I've never been so sure. He'll be a good provider and a good father. You'll see." She insisted no one knew him as well as she did. That was sixteen years ago.

She wanted to drop her thoughts there but reminisced one more time, reliving the moment when Jesse had presented the necklace to her. They had picnicked at a local lake and stayed through sunset, strolling through a secluded beach he had wanted to share with her.

As the last rays of light altered the sky to glowing red coral, they had shuffled slower in the sand. He had held her hand while the other dug into his pocket to produce the gift box. Inside rested the delicate dragonfly. He had draped it around her and clipped it, careful not to pinch her skin.

"It's a beauty-and-the-beast gift." He had elaborated when she didn't follow the connection. "Not only is it from the beast to the beauty, but it has its own symbolism. Dragonfly combines two nouns. Think of the dragon as the beast and the fly as a butterfly, beautiful but free to fly away if life turns too beastly."

That's when she had fallen in love with him. Before their walk on the beach, she wasn't sure. How could she resist a man who offered a unique gift and described himself as the beast from the most romantic fairytale of all time? How ironic that he would be the one to fly.

She decided to defer telling Dana until she was older—or not at all.

CHAPTER 12

An empty storefront on Main Street held promise as a pottery shop. Dana cringed at the thick cobwebs shrouding the windows. The space, unoccupied for more than a year, needed repair and extensive cleaning.

Taylor, which Dana called him now, helped Mom negotiate a good rate because of it. "Great location." He shifted his inspection upward to the hammered tin ceiling, painted off-white, the single thing that required no renovation.

Mom agreed. "The possibilities are endless. Like a blank slate, you know?"

The exterior walls of the buildings on either side functioned as inside walls for the shop, one darker brick than the other. Two large showcase windows flanked the entrance door where Dana admired the Alice-in-Wonderland brass knob and elongated keyhole like a vertical mouth singing a high note.

Taylor traced the door's mahogany finish and whistled at its smoothness. "The antique surroundings will set off your pottery to advantage." He rubbed his hands together and made a quick decision. "I'm free on Saturday. You ladies don your work clothes, and I'll see you here at eight."

"You're one for helping damsels in distress, aren't you, Sir Galahad?"

He unfolded his arm from his side and made sweeping arcs with an imagined scimitar. "Let the magic begin." He stopped short and grinned. "I was going to say, 'Abracadabra,' but I'd be mixing metaphors. And fables."

Mom's laughter carried Dana through the week, but her own excitement approaching the weekend eclipsed her mother's. She felt like a part owner. After all, Mom said she was.

On Saturday, Taylor clattered inside, carting a bucket, mops, rubber gloves, rags, and a box of industrial products containing everything from glass cleaner to grease and tar remover.

Ready to begin, Dana grabbed the bucket; but before she filled it, he handed her a pump bottle. "Spray this on a two-foot section of floor and let it sit a minute or two before mopping. The stuff has a strong smell, but it's a miracle-worker."

Before many minutes passed, Dana held up the mop. "Hey, look!" Underneath the grime lay bronzed gray stone tile.

"Not bad." He knelt to rub a recently cleaned piece to assure it was stone. "It may need some grouting, but I can polish it off in a weekend."

"My business loan might shrink in size before we're done." Mom breathed a sigh. "It may take us a week or two to do the floor; but we know how to work, don't we, Dana?"

"Sure, even if we have to change the water every section."

Turning to Taylor, Mom asked, "How did you become a jack of all trades?"

"I worked in construction during college." He edged closer to them. "As the extra guy, I had to fill in wherever they needed me. Learned a wide range of skills." His arm encircled Mom's waist with an easy, inconspicuous motion. "I scoped out the future and saw I'd have to help a couple of ladies reconstruct this place into a pottery shop."

Even though Dana questioned whether his subtle action was appropriate, she enjoyed being included in the ladies' category.

He released Mom and began to tackle spots of cement splattered on the brick.

"Leave those for a while. The weathered brick will form a background for the display shelves. Want to hear my solution for disguising the largest splashes?" She had their full attention. "I'll tack burlap fabric over fiberboard as a bulletin board to exhibit items lightweight enough to hang from stickpins. Your necklaces, bracelets, and macramé crafts, Dana. Mary Jo's, too. Every crafter can have a unique bulletin board to fit between shelf units. A personal photo could identify each board if that's what they want."

"Sounds like a definite plan, madam. It'll be easy as this." He began to sing "Heel and a Toe" from a familiar square dance tune as his feet tapped the floor. He caught Dana's hand to twirl her around. "Do you know the do-si-do?"

They dance-stepped forward, passing each other, circling back-to-back, and returning to their original positions.

"You know how to do that?" Dana's question echoed in the bare room.

"Picked it up in school, same as you."

Mom clapped. "I wish I had a movie camera. No one will ever believe me." She joined the other two, crumpling with laughter. "How can we get serious work done after that?"

"If this is work, I'll take it any time." He tapped a few more steps before stopping. "The place is returning to life. See it? Everything here is getting a new start."

A new beginning. That's what they needed.

When Dana entered sixth grade, she spent time after school and Saturdays in September helping Mom get the shop ready. She was cleaning another section of floor one evening while Mom lost herself in the planning list. They raised their heads to see Elaine swoop in and twirl in exaggeration before she took stock.

"I'm here to help. Aside from the art show this weekend, you can count on me until the grand opening, whenever it is."

"First weekend in October. That's our target."

"At the peak of leaf season for tourists and the following holidays. Good seasons for gift buying. I approve."

"You second the plan?"

"I do. Let's see what's left." Elaine eyed each item on the to-do list. "Something's missing. What about a sign above the door?"

Mom raised her hands in surrender. "How did I forget? We don't want to hide our unique name."

"Clark, the high school art teacher, has a signage business. Also does advertising posters. Want me to ask him for an estimate?"

"As soon as you can." She cut to the door, Dana and Elaine following, and turned around outside to reimagine the entrance. "Guess where the name came from."

"Reveal, please."

"Well, Dana had told her friends about the shop by saying, 'My mother is a potter.' It stayed in my mind, and it helped me to envision 'My Mother's Pottery' in large letters and then underneath 'and consignment.'"

Dana's smile grew as wide as the doorway.

On hands and knees, Dana worked in stained coveralls on the second portion of the floor.

Mom, in a paint-spattered T-shirt and frayed sweatpants, bent to a task across the room. She jumped when Taylor bounded through the door, swinging a gallon of paint from each hand. "I didn't think we'd see you tonight."

"Brought paint left over from the house. Thought I'd slap it on the rear wall, the only one not bricked. And freshen the back room."

The wall concealed a room intended for multiple purposes as office, workroom, and lunchroom. An ancient sink and drain board with legs supported itself beside a working refrigerator.

"Don't waste any effort in the back room. I'll make it livable later. The shop has to be ready first."

He rose to full height at attention. Then, relaxing, he scanned the room. "I see progress here already. The chain gang's been busy."

To keep from staining the cleaned tiles, he laid a large tarp on the floor. After painting a small area of the rear wall, he stepped aside. "Passable?"

"More than passable. It's what this place needs. Don't you think so, Dana?"

"Yeah. I mean, sure." Her shyness took over and kept her from adding anything else. She reran it in her mind while she worked.

At six o'clock, he convinced them to take a break and go to dinner at The Garden Patch down the street.

Mom held her arms out wide. "Dressed like this?"

"They won't mind as long as I pay the bill. C'mon. It'll be fun."

Between bites of sirloin-tip salad, he presented an idea about the back room. "I did some legal work for a plumber in town when he started his business. He can put in a modern sink and junk the old one."

"I can use the money for more important things." Mom folded her napkin and left it on the table.

"I'll take care of it. My gift to honor your bold venture."

"But that's an old cast iron sink and more durable than a modern one. It'll be a work horse for my pottery." She pulled a penciled diagram from her purse. "The back room will be a studio where I can work and watch the shop simultaneously. Besides, the sink doesn't have a single chip in it. And it has character."

"Let me know what I can contribute."

"You really are already doing it. Without you, we'd have no display boards, grouted tile, or painted walls. I know the shelves aren't up yet, but they will be. We can't do them alone." Her animation gave way to future thoughts. "Down the line, I might find a small end table to fit under the sink for towels and other supplies. It will be a home away from home, and I won't have to spend time in the basement."

Dana finished a bite of lasagna, glanced at Taylor, and reached into her well of courage. "The taupe color you're painting the rear wall brightens the room."

Mom moved her chair close to Dana's to show their unity in opinion. "You have a good eye, you know."

He threw his head back and slapped his hand over his heart. "Moi?" Exuberance infused the air, and Dana breathed it in.

Amid the buzz of final preparation, Dana stepped back from a shop wall to assess her personal board. One week from today marked opening day.

Aunt Elaine drafted her as helper to hang paintings; but before they began, she called across the room to her sister. "When is the sign going up? Have you heard from Clark?"

"Today! You'll see it done."

A rap at the door alerted them to a smiling man who stepped inside. A scar ran from his tousled brown hair across one eyelid. "Today's the day. We're ready to put up your sign." Before he turned to go outside, he deposited a box on the closest counter. "Your posters."

Dana thought the art teacher's eye in a partial wink gave him the aspect of someone telling a joke.

Mom pulled the lid off and smoothed her hand over the top poster. "Nice work!"

"I try." He glided to the sidewalk, where two men wrestled a sign from the bed of a pick-up truck.

"Don't let those eyes fool you." Aunt Elaine slipped next to her. "They see more with a glance than most people do with a stare." She answered Mom's unspoken thought in three words. "A childhood accident."

Dana detected movement through the front windows. Two ladders rose into the air and leaned in position at each side of the door. "Hey, we don't want to miss this."

They ran outside to witness the process. The men hoisted and fastened the sign to brackets already inserted above the shop door. Block letters spelled out "My Mother's Pottery" in the color of red clay, outlined in a darker shade against a beige background for contrast. In lower case, "and consignment" sat below the main title as an afterthought. A wide swath of color in a mix of browns, rust, beige, and sienna bordered the entire sign.

Mom stepped back to appraise it. "Matchless! Call me anytime for a recommendation." She waited while Clark and the other men reloaded their equipment. "Do you have the bill, or will you send it?"

"Ask Elaine about that." Clark jumped in the truck and took off.

"The truth has to come out." Aunt Elaine grew quiet to add to the suspense but couldn't stay that way for long. "Mom and Dad wanted to be involved, too. They paid for the sign and posters. I promised I'd bring my camera today so they can see it."

The following week, Mom and Dana mailed a picture to her grandparents. Dana imagined the smiles on their faces when they saw the eight-by-ten photograph of her and her mother under the new colorful sign.

When Grandma and Grandpa called, Dana and her mother danced, the two of them alone, in the dining room. The shop was becoming a reality.

The big day, Saturday, October 6, arrived. Dana brushed away the haunting dream of an empty shop without buyers. On the ride from the house, rain hammered the street and every surface. It slowed to a drizzle, letting her breathe easier, but renewed itself after a short break.

The shop opened for business on schedule at ten o'clock, but nobody came. The first hour brought a trio of undaunted shoppers with umbrellas. Mom grew quiet. Only Dana and Elaine's whispering broke the silence.

Taylor remained confident. "They'll be here."

Before noon, the clouds relinquished their wrath and drifted off. Customers bustled through the door the entire afternoon, browsing and buying. Five o'clock arrived with the swiftness of a ski run. At the cash register in the center, Mom talked about artists who had signed contracts to sell their wares. "If this keeps up, I'll need more product."

"I'd call it a phenomenal success." Taylor shook their hands with mock formality.

Elaine bestowed hugs on all and blew a congratulatory kiss as she left.

Mom noted the time, stepped outside, and checked for possible shoppers before locking up.

As Dana ambled toward the back room, Taylor whisked by at roller-skate speed. Hand on the doorknob, he turned to her, pinned his finger to his lips, and ran out the door, letting it shut on its own.

She blinked at the closed door. Where was he going? She opened the door, but he was gone. Was he abandoning them at their best moment?

Mom floated with euphoria through the shop. In the back room, she saw Dana lumped in a chair and asked, "Where's Taylor?" Her eyes hollowed with loneliness while she waited for an answer.

"He"—she paused, glanced at the ceiling, then the door and said—"left."

"Where to?"

"Ran out like he was on fire."

"Ran? As in running away?" A nearby chair kept Mom from falling. "Did he say anything?"

Dana glared at the door again to recreate his exit. Did it happen as she reported it?

"Not even goodbye?" Mom searched through her purse for a handkerchief.

Anger bubbled up in Dana like the time she had punched Carter in the nose, but Taylor was the least bully-like person she knew. Early suspicions had kept her from wanting to meet him, but he had turned out to be so much fun and easy to talk to. Still, she should have chased after him and asked what was going on. Why had he helped them every day, only to cut out at the first sign of success?

"You'd think he'd stick around to have a party with us. It was such a good day."

"Nothing makes sense. It's not like him. He's always been so happy for us." She appeared to be doing a mental checklist, but no answer came. "You saw him leave?"

"While you were out front locking up."

"And he said nothing?"

In answer, Dana tucked her chin in the least perceptible way. "Looked like he was sneaking out when he reached the door. Didn't want me to say anything. Then he ran."

The smell of damp potter's clay hung in the air, encouraging the drabness of the room to fold around them. They sat motionless, too depleted to move.

A thump resounded from outside at the bottom of the door. Someone was there. If it were Taylor, he'd come on in.

Dana froze. Should they call the police?

The sound turned to urgent kicking and pummeling on the door, again at the bottom.

Dana whirled around and jerked it open.

Taylor held two small wrought iron tables, one in each hand. "Stumbled on them at a consignment shop. Refinished them with emery cloth and oil-based paint. Will they do?" He presented them to Mom.

"Can these be what I think they are?" Tears ran down before she could control them.

"Not quite the reaction I expected." He put his arm around her while she blotted her cheeks.

Smiling again, she placed one table under the sink's supporting structure for an exact fit. "The other can go in the bathroom for the flower arrangement I have in mind."

He waited while she dabbed her eyes a final time. "We have reservations down the street. Shall we get going?"

Without hesitating, Mom threw her arms around him.

It was the first time Dana saw her mother kiss Taylor.

The shop ushered in a new life. If Dana didn't go to Mary Jo's after-school, she walked to My Mother's Pottery, where she finished her homework or helped by cleaning up.

Taylor became a frequent visitor to the house. On weekends, the three of them had dinner out together and often a movie if Dana didn't have a sleepover somewhere. Sometimes, he hosted a meal at his house; other times, Mom cooked dinner at home, followed by a board game that three could play.

Contentment and purpose settled on Dana and Mom for the first time in more than two years.

The closing of school after sixth grade meant another flight south for Dana, but it sparked no anticipation. Only Dad and Kaye's five-month-old baby boy JJ roused her curiosity. Even so, she asked, "Don't you want me to help in the shop, Mom? I can tell Dad you need me here."

"I'll manage. Taylor will drop in on Saturdays. It's the busiest day."

She wanted a week, at least, to pal around with her friends; but Dad had bought the ticket months earlier. Maybe he and Kaye would treat her with the same friendliness they'd reached at the end of the Boone trip. It was her only hope.

After a goodbye hug with Mom a few days later in the airport, Dana trudged to her gate and received a cheery greeting from the stewardess at the plane's entrance door. The seat beside her was still empty when the door shut in preparation for takeoff.

Her mind, liberated to wandering, rested on one of her mother's pet topics. "Every day changes your life¾what you read, what you hear, what you do. You might turn an idea topsy-turvy to uncover new insight or find a new way to do something more easily or tackle a task you didn't think you could do. Everything you do becomes an episode—or part of one—to add to your life. It's how we become older and wiser."

How much wiser would she be at the end of summer? Would she have new adventures like last year to share with Mom? Dad didn't make any promises but wanted her to see the new baby. What she wanted was another short visit, not one for the entire season. She projected herself to the return flight home when she could think back on her visit and remember baby JJ and her bedroom in the remodeled house. Resigning herself to the present, she felt a remarkable lack of enthusiasm. Of course, her stay in Western North Carolina meant a new experience because she'd never been there—except for the Boone visit—but when she weighed it against spending summer at home among friends, home won hands down.

She shut her eyes then, wishing for time's elusiveness to dissolve summer. If this were the return trip, she wouldn't have to imagine how it fit into her future. But one thing was certain. Turning twelve-and-a-half in July, she'd be closer to age thirteen than twelve when she went home. And within a few months, she'd be a teenager. That had to be different from anything she knew—like this summer, in ways she couldn't envision.

CHAPTER 13

LAURELSVILLE, NORTH CAROLINA

SUMMER 1974

After landing at the Charlotte airport, Dana spotted Dad; but something about him was different. "You're wearing glasses?"

Large, horn-rimmed frames—more rectangular than round—rode above his eyes, leaving the bottom frameless and clear.

"The doctor says I've impaired my vision with my work."

"I almost didn't recognize you."

They snaked through a larger crowd than what she'd experienced a year ago. A new terminal offered more modern accommodations, including a moving walkway. In the parking lot, she hurried to keep up with Dad as she looked for the Chrysler 300. He directed her instead to a dark green Ford station wagon, faux wood panels spanning both sides. At the back, Dad unlocked a fifth door in place of a trunk with an automatic window and deposited her duffel bag, bigger than a suitcase, onto a flat space large enough to hold several bags of luggage. He led her to the passenger side, where he held the door and watched her buckle up before he shut it, the way he did for Mom.

He jockeyed himself into the driver's seat. "What do you think?"

"The car, you mean?"

"Sure. The station wagon."

"It's so big . . . and long. Where's the Chrysler?" She ran her hand across the slick dashboard in front of her.

"I traded it in for this. We needed a bigger car for JJ and with you being here for the summer."

She recognized his flat-mouthed grin. Was the source of his pride a new son, a new car, or her visit? "Is it hard to drive?"

"Smooth as anything and handles like a dream." He stopped to pay the parking fee and sped to the airport road leading to the main highway and home. "It has a lot of new features, like automatic locks. I can control all of them from the driver's seat." To demonstrate, he pressed a button, producing a sharp click. "Good for JJ's safety when he learns how to handle doors for himself."

Did he care as much about Luke's safety as a toddler? Mulling it over, she made no attempt to talk, even though the drive to Laurelsville would take two hours. Conversation for that length of time was impossible. They needed Kaye to fill the empty spaces.

It seemed he'd read her mind. "Kaye stayed home with JJ—his naptime when I left. She didn't want to disturb him." He glanced at her. "She thought you and I might enjoy the drive home together."

"Umm." Her single nod to listening. She had loved having Dad to herself when she knew him better. The few days last summer in Boone represented the longest span with Dad in two years, but they didn't have a single moment alone except on the Tilt-a-Whirl and the swinging bridge. Even then, she was sure Kaye strained to see every interaction from afar. The visit of her eleventh birthday—the good one when Dad understood her a little—carried the record for the best time together. She wadded the sweater she had brought because of Mom warning about the plane's air conditioning and threw it in the back.

As she settled into the seat, Dad noticed something. "You're wearing your mother's necklace."

"She gave it to me."

"Glad she did." He cleared his throat. "I wanted you to have it, but it wasn't mine to suggest."

"I wear it every day." She touched the familiar wings.

"Maybe your daughter will wear it in the future. Who knows?" Keeping his thoughts from going any deeper, he gave it a quick sideways glance. "Those are diamond chips adorning the body."

"I know. Mom told me. And it's real silver and gold."

"Did she tell you anything else about it?"

"That you gave it to her. When you were dating." She didn't dare ask if he gave it to Mom because he loved her. No sense in getting off on the wrong foot. "People say how pretty it is when they see it."

"It certainly is."

Several minutes passed. Silence persuaded her to find a topic. "Why did you name the baby JJ?"

He coughed up a laugh, his first since the airport. "I held out for Jesse Junior, even though Kaye said it's confusing to have two people sharing the same name in one house." His eyes swerved toward her for a second. "She finally gave in but kept saying he was 'Jesse all over again.' She called him JJ, and it stuck."

Had he wanted Luke to be a junior? She didn't ask, but thinking about him triggered the blue boat. "Did you ever do any work on Luke's boat? The one from Uncle Barn?"

"Some. Not a lot. I'll show it to you."

Her hands cupped the imagined boat and its splintered wood. "Will it be like new?"

"Have to create a whole new boat. It was nothing more than a hull."

"But can you do it?"

"Eventually. Too many things are demanding my time—finishing rooms in the basement and other projects Kaye wants me to do."

She fell silent. He must have had some spare hours before he met Kaye. What did he do in the evenings when he had lived in the apartment? The boat should have been his priority.

Dana dozed off and roused herself when they left the highway. In half an hour, they ascended a hill to Stone Mountain Lane in Laurelsville and slowed for a ranch-style house on the left. It faced the Blue Ridge Mountains, where each peak nudged the other like giants vying for the best spot on the horizon.

Dad left the car in the driveway, grabbed her bag, and directed her ahead of him on a flagstone pathway. They passed rhododendrons that hid chairs and side tables on a long front porch with burgundy support posts and shutters accenting the wheat-colored exterior.

By the time Dana climbed the stairs, Kaye was standing at the door holding JJ. Her hair was shorter than last summer in a gingercolored, bushy style. Maybe the sun had lightened it.

"Say hello to your baby brother. Isn't he cute?"

In a one-piece summer playsuit, the baby churned his chubby legs in constant motion like an older child pedaling a bike.

When Dana offered her finger, his little ones curved around it.

"He had lots of fuzzy blond hair when he was born. Later, red hair—rustier than mine—grew at the back of his head. Had a full swath, but it fell off. Whoosh! Completely gone."

Dana's veiled inspection found, to her relief, that nothing about him reminded her of Luke. She gave a little tickle to his tummy.

JJ gurgled and squirmed.

"I'm relieved you're here. I can use some help with him. He's getting more active every day. Needs an eagle eye watching him. Constantly. We think he might crawl early."

"I haven't been around babies much. You'll have to show me what to do."

Dana's dragonfly caught Kaye's eye. "Ooh, what a beautiful necklace. I've never seen anything like it."

Its uniqueness attracted attention. "My mother gave it to me." She didn't look at Dad, who was busy transporting her bag down the hall.

Kaye called out, "Show her around, Jess, why don't you?"

Dana passed three doors to where Dad waited at the end and steered her into the room at the corner. "Here's the biggest change—your room, the new guest room."

Windows to the west allowed plenty of light in the afternoon and gave a wide view of the backyard. A small television set rested atop a low bureau on an inside wall. Bragging rights. She couldn't wait to tell Mary Jo.

JJ's even brighter room was directly across from hers. Circus animals pranced and clowns turned somersaults across the wallpaper.

"So many doors," Dana said on their return up the hall when she noticed one half-open and stairs going down. "Is there a basement?"

"It's not finished down there. There's a recreation room that needs more work and my workshop. Not much else. Here, I'll show you." They descended center stairs that divided one spacious basement room into two. At the flick of a wall switch, light flooded the bare room of painted cinder block at the left. "A possible in-home office. Someday."

The large paneled room on the other side boasted a new television set inside a cabinet. That got Dana's attention. "Wow! What a big TV!"

"I bargained for a twenty-one-inch screen, but this twenty-three enticed me." He opened the cabinet doors to show it off. "I don't indulge myself much. Decided to give in to this one." A gray suede couch and three plush earth-toned chairs created a seating area in front of the set. "Fixed this room up first to watch my games."

She followed Dad through a small room more like a short hall, big enough for a new washer and dryer, noiseless and clean. The doorway at the end opened to another cinderblock room painted white and a workbench and tools off to one side.

"This is my work space when I'm home." He lowered his voice.

Was it a secret? It was too nice to be a basement. At home, a concrete floor and walls of stone formed a single Spartan room accessed through an outside entrance. It housed a washing machine and, until recently, Mom's pottery wheel and shelving. Not a single window. Years ago, Dad had attached a fluorescent light fixture overhead, but it wasn't pleasant like this.

Up the stairs again to the main hall, he gestured toward the closed door he had skipped earlier. "The master bedroom and our own bathroom."

"It's nice. And modern." What else to say about the sharp contrast to the house built in the 1930s where she and Mom lived?

She re-entered the living room and looked left into the dining room separated from the kitchen by a long countertop. Sliding glass doors in the dining room gave access to the deck. Again, Dana compared the two houses. From the kitchen at home, she stepped through an ordinary single door to a four-foot-square stoop.

Kaye, carrying JJ, joined them in her fresh-pressed style of last summer. The cuffs of her lightweight denims matched the blue print in her short-sleeved top. The closet in the master bedroom held many more.

Dana wished for one like it. Just one.

"Get the walker for me, will you, Jess?" She locked a baby gate across the stairs to the patio below. "We'll barbecue outside and eat here on the deck tonight. Can you believe it's the season's first cookout? JJ has kept us busy. It'll be a good start to your visit." Her chatty talk accompanied them as it did on their trek through Boone. It came with ease, furnishing a counterpoint to Dad's quietness. "Do you barbecue at home?"

"We . . . uh . . . don't have one." She shot Dad an awkward look as if he had control of what came from Kaye's mouth. "Mr. Hamlin invited us to one at his place in honor of summer break from school."

"He celebrates the end of school?" Dad chuckled louder than necessary. "Didn't know he had children."

Dana bristled at his amusement. "People who work with him do." It wasn't a complete lie. That it had been a private barbecue with Mom and Mr. Hamlin wasn't anyone's business.

"JJ keeps us on a schedule." Kaye sighed. "Can't run off on a quick trip like last summer."

So much for hoping for an outing to write home about. Dana already missed Mary Jo and the other girls who had big plans for backyard slumber parties in their families' camping tents. At the horizon beyond the deck, another projection of peaks edged the western sky, a place for camping and real adventure.

CHAPTER 14

Time limped along to the first Friday in August. A few more weeks and Dana would be home; but if Dad even hinted at flying her back early, she would have packed in two minutes. She resigned herself to clearing the breakfast dishes, a routine that became her exclusive duty after offering to help the first few days. But it gave her something to do, and she preferred doing it alone, anyway. She looked up as Kaye crossed the kitchen, carrying a naked, wiggling JJ. The gait of her bare feet suggested purpose.

To Dana's mystified expression, Kaye laughed. "He's ready for his tubby, but I forgot to deliver a message from your dad." She slid the deck door aside. "After you finish here, you might tidy up that mess in the yard." The farthest corner of the surrounding stockade fence was the only place not fully landscaped. A clay slope kept anything from growing. "See the pile of crushed limestone? Rake it uphill for a better look. Anything's better than loose soil." Her voice lilted to the level reserved for asking favors.

An Eastern yellow pine in the next lot towered over the corner, shading the hill. Its branches draped across the fence and into the yard. Dana was grateful for it in the hotter-than-usual mountain temperatures.

Dragging a cultivating rake across the rocks took strength and didn't work well. Her hands hurt from pulling out the trapped stones. When gloves didn't help, she flipped it upside down, prongs curving like badger claws in the air, and used the straight side underneath. The job became easier, but the heat didn't let up. Sweat streamed from her head. Her eyes burned. Squeezing them shut, she bent to blot the rivulets with the end of her shirt. Luke was right about salt in sweat.

Satisfied with the stones' layout at the top, she returned to the pile below. Some absent-minded hacking brought angular shapes from layers of pine needles accumulated over many years. "Seashells in the mountains?" She said it aloud, but no one heard.

Raking the needles, she turned up shells, rocks, and coral and ran her fingers like a blind person over the new finds. On her knees, she pawed deeper, unearthing a cone shell spiraled like a screw, an inch or two long. It would complement the Cape Cod shells carried in Dad's cap during their last vacation with Mom.

To abandon those thoughts, she became a merchant arranging her natural wares for sale but soon switched her career to professional groundskeeper at a public park.

Then, the best discovery of all. Two broken geodes appeared as brown knobs, rough as walnut shells cut in half. She flipped them over. Inside, miniature mounds and valleys of lumpy white coating glittered like sprinkled sugar, petrified. In the larger one, white changed to a purple hue deep in its center.

A few drops fell—likely sap from the pine. It continued sporadically until it became rain after all but not bad under the tree's parasol of fringed branches. More content outside than in the house, she stayed as the landscaper caught up with her creation until someone called her name.

"Where are you, Dana?" Kaye leaned against the doorjamb, balancing on her hip an active JJ who pulled a handful of his mother's hair and squealed.

Dana picked her way with reluctant steps toward the house, palming the geodes.

"You've heard the saying, 'Too dumb to come in out of the rain'?" Kaye tittered. After no response, she tried to retract it. "Just kidding. Doesn't mean anything, really. It's what kids used to say."

The words brought less effect than Luke's taunting. But Dana used the same diversionary tactic that worked with him—she changed the subject. "See what I found." She opened her fist to reveal the treasures.

Hugging JJ to her with one arm, Kaye held them to the light. "Where'd you get them?"

"Where I was working." She looked at the corner where she spent the entire afternoon as if her stepmother wasn't aware.

Kaye's approval grew while she turned them over. "A good start for a rock collection. Right, JJ?" She buried them in her shorts pocket.

Dana witnessed in slow motion Kaye holding the glittering pieces until they fell out of sight at the last second. She had to declare her wish, now or never. "I wanted to keep them as a souvenir." She reached into her own pocket for a stray sliver that might have caught in a seam.

"They can be shared ownership. JJ will adore them when he grows up. He already likes them. Haven't you noticed?" She smiled. "Here.

Take him for a while. I'm worn out, and I need to check the freezer for supper."

The geodes stayed hidden in Kaye's pocket.

At the dinner table, Dad gave a prolonged accounting of an accident at the mill. When a worker caught his hand in a machine, a fast-thinking man shut it off. An ambulance took the injured man to the hospital. "I don't get it. I schedule safety training sessions and conduct them myself to make sure everyone complies. And I emphasize safety above everything."

"I know you do, Jess."

He ladled another dollop of mashed potatoes. "We were working on a long safety record, too. This ruins it."

"You could use the accident as a training example of what not to do."

"Sure thing." He speared another pork chop from the center platter while he mentally sifted through anything overlooked at the plant. "It means a Workers' Comp report, too."

"Let personnel handle it." Kaye entreated JJ to eat another bite.

"They will, but it's another thing I'd rather we didn't have to attend to. In the end, everything's on my back."

Quiet reigned except for JJ's babbling.

Dana stopped eating. "How's the man's hand?"

"He'll be fine. Didn't lose any fingers, but his hand will be bandaged for three to six weeks. They'll keep evaluating." His head bowed, thinking. "Nobody can operate the machine without certification. I'll have to move people around. They're not cooperative about switching."

He passed the serving plate to Dana. "Another chop?"

"I'm full." All the same, the remaining slivers on her pork chop bone tempted her to eat it down to the last whisker of meat the way she did at home. She promised Mom never to do it in public. Kaye and Dad's house didn't fall into the public category, but it didn't qualify as home, either.

"What did you do today?" It was the first he'd asked all summer.

Dana stuttered. "Worked outside under the pine tree." At his silence, she continued. "So hot out there. Hotter than home." She wanted to tell him about sweat burning her eyes but didn't know if it was a proper word to say in front of Kaye. "Perspiration leaked into my eyes before I knew it. Hard to believe it stung that much."

He stared at Kaye. "Don't you have a headband or scarf you can give her to wear?"

Shocked at his directive, Kaye attributed it to his mindset from work. "I . . . yes. I'll find something."

"Be sure she gets it."

She rose to stack the plates. In her flustered state, she forgot to leave the job to Dana.

Dad excused himself while Dana joined Kaye, who struggled to keep her banter cheery. "Thank goodness for dishwashers! I told your father when we had the kitchen redone to be sure to leave a space under the new countertop for a built-in dishwasher."

"It wasn't always here?"

"Nope. I told him, 'You have the latest equipment at the mill. I need the latest at home, too.'" A forced laugh lurched from her throat.

The dishwasher's electric hum joined the sound of sloshing water, excusing Dana to take the stairs down to Dad's workroom. The smell of fresh sawdust from a toy box in progress reached her as she neared the room. When he finished sawing the board, she waited for him to talk; but he stayed quiet, intent on his task.

After several minutes, she dredged up her courage. "I found a couple of geodes today."

"Did you?" Turning his head meant he was listening. "Where?"

"Out by the hill where you wanted me to spread the rocks. I can show you if you want to see." When no reaction came, she added, "Tomorrow, when it's light."

"I know where it is." He chose a screwdriver hanging on the wall and laid it on the workbench. "Did you finish the job?"

"Rearranged the whole pile."

"Kaye told me you spent a good while on it, even in the rain." His face relaxed.

Did it reflect what Kaye might have told him, or was he making fun of her, too? "I found the geodes earlier. Hunting for more of them under the tree kept me from noticing the rain."

He rummaged through a drawer for a tape measure. "I estimated an hour at most." He used a wide pencil to mark another board for the lid.

Her impulse to lay her hand on his arm wasn't as natural as with Mom. "Dad, I wanted those geodes to add to my box of stones and shells at home. I don't have anything from here." A plea tucked itself between the words. Was he listening?

"Didn't you stash them with your things to take home?"

"I wanted to, but Kaye claimed them for JJ."

He shrugged and took his time measuring another board. "You found them in her yard, after all."

"But it's your yard, too, isn't it?" Her voice shook before she regained control. "Dad, it'll be years before JJ knows a geode from a lump of cement. He's not even one yet."

"Go upstairs and see if he's ready for bed. Kaye can use the help." He reached for the pencil stowed over his ear.

"Why did you ask me to come here?"

"Because you're my daughter." He marked another board and reached for his saw.

She spun around and darted through the laundry room. "Say what you want," she shot back as her feet hit the stairs. "I'm nothing but a slave doing jobs nobody else wants to do." The distance between them helped her say it, but she wasn't sure he heard. She stormed up the stairs, heat prickling her neck.

The sawing began again.

CHAPTER 15

Alone in the guest room—the solitary place Dana could be herself—she scanned the magazines and books on the shelf, trying to cool down. Three books from home found space in her bag during packing. *My Friend Flicka,* from a pile at the library's used book sale, wore green crayon scribbling inside. She bought it because it was the only one. *Favorite Bible Stories* with glossy illustrations had come from Grandma and Grandpa as a gift in first grade before she could read it on her own. Turning to the stories, especially David and Goliath or Daniel in the lions' den, brought memories of Grandma reading to her. It helped her pretend family had come with her to Dad's.

Looking at *The Wind in the Willows* gave her the cozy feeling of sitting on one side of Mom, Luke on the other, in the wide rocker when she was too little to understand most of it. She would fall asleep before the evening's chapter finished, and Mom carried her to bed. Reading it for herself, she found that Toad's impulsivity hinted of Luke's behavior. It was true when Toad convinced Rat and Mole to join him in his canary yellow caravan, drawn by a horse jauntier than a typical draft horse. But when Toad saw the motorcar, soon to become his new passion as well as his downfall, he'd outdone Luke.

The vocabulary proved to be above her level; but she persisted, slogging through and learning a new term: *impromptu*. Her lips puckered like a kiss to pronounce it. When she found the strange words *pettishly* and *cellarage* as well as animals called dabchicks, moorhens, and stoats, she needed Mom's help. In all, it created a challenging read.

She usually persevered in finding definitions by placing a dictionary beside the book because a single page might stump her more than once, but not tonight. It took too much energy. A letter to Mom would be a good way to end the evening. But what should she say? Nothing new to relate except the accident at the mill. Finding the scrap copy of an earlier one, she sank into the pillows to read it again.

Dear Mom,

Well, I know everything there is to know about taking care of babies now, including changing diapers, using wipes, baby powder, etc. I've even given JJ his bath. He can sit up in the tub, but I have to watch him every second. Tell everyone I'm available as a skilled babysitter when I get home. Diaper-changing expertise has to be a bonus.

The house is a modern one. I guess it was Kaye's to begin with. They added two extra bedrooms—one for JJ and a guest room where I'm staying for the summer. It has bookshelves and a Zenith television with its own remote control! Imagine that.

Dad's been working on the basement, little by little. For starters, he has a rec room (his workshop is down there). More to go to keep him busy.

We barbecued on the deck my first night here. We haven't done it again, but I'm sure we will soon.

They live outside a town in the county and have only rural mail delivery. I'll stick this in Dad's mailbox before the mailman comes, and he'll take it to the post office.

Let me know how the shop and classes are going. Say hi to Mr. Hamlin for me. Do you like working in the shop better than his office?

Love,

Dana

As short as the letter was, it took a couple of days to complete. Mom must have expected her to write at least once a week or more to use the ten stamps, a whole dollar's worth, in her bag. She had made several attempts to write more early on but ripped them into pieces too small for Kaye to read and threw them away. No need for Mom to think she wasn't enjoying her visit. The truth—hard to explain in a letter—would be easier to tell on her return home.

Her time there hadn't been a total waste. She considered her new babysitting capabilities an asset, but she'd already reached a high level of expertise. What more could she learn in another month?

Seeing an unmailed letter underneath, a much longer one to Mary Jo, she laughed out loud as she read it.

Dear Mary Jo,

You're going to be jealous when you read this. I've learned more new things than you can dream. First off, I know how to change diapers. Easy, except when they're poopy. And they're always that way when it's my turn. Phew. I use a gazillion wipes to keep from getting it on my hands. All I can say is I'm thankful for wipes.

I'd hardly unpacked when Kaye asked me to take care of JJ at home while she tackled the tough job of shopping. I haven't been out once since I've been here, even for groceries. I don't know if there are other shops near the grocery store; but each time she comes home, she's bought a cute thing for herself—and not from the bargain basement where I get my school shoes. Yesterday, it was sandals. They had wooden soles and a wide strap of natural leather over the top. I'd wear those any day, but my feet are already bigger than hers. She's tiny. I don't know why she needs another pair of shoes. She goes barefoot in the house and doesn't go outside except for shopping. Meanwhile, Dad's hammering away downstairs to make himself useful. How did they live before I arrived?

I almost forgot. One night, we piled in the car for an ice cream run. Yay.

The neighbors are couples, young and old and in between. No children. I don't think there are any kids in this housing development except for JJ. He's always fun to talk to. Seriously, though, he likes my music. That's a good thing.

Dad and Kaye have found lots of chores for me to do outside, but don't feel sorry for me. When I'm outside by myself, I can be me. I don't have to put on my happy face for them or worry about saying the wrong thing. You've said I'm a hermit, and I'm beginning to think you're right. I'm happiest when I can hibernate in my room, the guest room here, and read in peace and quiet.

Please write! I crave fascinating reading material, and I want to know how your summer's going. But spare me the details of slumber parties and other fun. I'm already dying to be home. Pray for summer to be over quickly.

Aren't you wishing you were here? I'd love it if you were.

Your friend,

Dana

She started adding a P.S. but inserted it unfinished in *The Wind in the Willows* on page seventy-one, her secret number, marking the year Luke died. At home, she stored letters or notes to herself on the same numbered page in Dad's old books he had left at the house. One of them, an anatomy book, displayed a human skeleton with layers of muscles and organs on thin, crisp paper. Unfolding them, one by one, disclosed the heart and lungs beneath the ribs. She'd argued with Luke about whose turn it was to have it next. If he were here, she'd let him keep the book forever.

She turned to the television because it required no thought or effort. The screen hummed to life while she perched on the bed, clicking from one show to another; but nothing held her interest. Before long, she gave it up.

Atop the bed's fluffy comforter, she sat cross-legged, her feet under her knees, and smeared creamy lotion on her hands and arms from a tube Mom had given her. She worked it around her fingers, embedded earlier with grit from rocks and the geodes she wished she'd hidden. Life offers a never-ending series of decisions, sometimes complicated and cloudy but clear afterward when it's too late. She needed a do-over.

Sleep didn't follow the final snap of the light switch. No one else shared her problem. Not a peep from the baby's room. Complete quiet. She rolled over and sat up to roam through the stars. The clear night sky showcased its upside-down dipper. Dropping her line of sight to the yard, she could see diagonally past the deck to the slope. Something flickered on the ground. She strained to see. Among the shells and stones, its twinkling emitted a brilliance beyond its size. A firefly?

Years ago, Dad often took her outside after dinner and gave her a jar to catch fireflies. He joined in, springing into the air and clapping the lid on fast to trap them inside. When they were pleasantly tired from running about with several captured in their jars, they carted them inside to the kitchen counter. Dad shut off the lights and hung around so they could see the on-and-off flashing like tiny flames in the containers. The next morning, though, the lids were off; and the fireflies were gone.

When she asked about it, he winked at Mom. "They must have worked the lids loose in the night."

After he left for work, Mom confessed to letting them go. "You can do it again. The best part is in catching them, isn't it?" She had a way of getting to the truth then, too.

Dana pressed her nose to the nearby window to see the spot still glittering. It wasn't a firefly. It didn't move. She sat on the bed, lingering, not quite ready to tuck herself in. Before she knew it, her hands rested on the windowsill. Did she dare risk going outside to investigate? Still not sure, she turned the knob slowly to ease the door open. Snatching her purple flip-flops from the floor, she rallied the courage to go ahead and left the door slightly ajar.

Hugging the wall kept her from alerting creaky boards in the middle of the hall. Years of playing "sneak" with Luke came in handy. He had showed her how to walk on her toes without using her heels and commanded her to follow. When they crept up on Mom, it always worked. But when they used the maneuver to close in on a squirrel or robin, it never did.

Placing one bare foot before the other made slow progress. What if Dad or Kaye saw her? At their bedroom door, she held her breath. Next came the opening where the living room and dining room joined, then a dozen steps to reach the glass doors. If they caught her there, she'd have no alibi except the truth that she'd never tell in a hundred years.

The lock gave a metallic click as it unlatched. Every muscle tensed. When no sound came from the house, she moved the door sideways, tiptoed across the deck and down the stairs to the yard, then turned around to make sure no lights came on. She wriggled her feet into the flip-flops, securing them between her toes to approach the pine's canopy with practiced stealth.

The moon's ashen light kept the glimmering slivers in sight. Shadows from the tree hid them temporarily from view; but within a few steps, streaks of light splayed out again. It coaxed her while she adapted her gait from smooth sidewalk to bumpy limestone and reached the spot beneath the branches. At last, on hands and knees, she claimed her prize.

Beyond her best fantasy, it was another geode, more elliptical than the others. In the hollow of her hand, its jagged, deep, purple crystals glistened when she slanted them into the moonlight. How had she missed it earlier?

When no other luminous spots presented themselves, she prowled back to the deck. A noise rustled from the sticker bushes. She turned, eyes wide, pulse beating high into her throat. At the sound of movement against dry leaves inside a bush, a mockingbird stirred in its typical haunt. Her silliness at being afraid made her smile.

Her dread of the door latch remained, but the slot gave off no sound. Reversing her earlier trip, she barefooted through the dining room and into the hall. JJ whimpered in his sleep. She scurried on silent feet in case Kaye came running.

Edging through the bedroom door, she sat for a while on the bed in the dark and held the geode. It fit perfectly in her hand. Giving it a final squeeze, she opened her pajama drawer a few inches, reached in, and buried it under the clothes. The coolness of the bed sheets soothed her. Sleep took her after what felt like hours.

In an episode of part-dream or hallucination, white and silver masses of light swam from the back of her head, curving around on both sides, converging at the center of her vision. Like fragments of geodes riding the air, geometric figures morphed into new ones before fading away.

The twinkling horde lured her inside a massive area of shining pieces. Mirrors leaned against each other from multiple angles, reflecting hues of blue, pink, and gold. The more she watched, the more they multiplied. In the rotating kaleidoscope of colors, each mirror revealed an amorphous shape in its center. She squinted to sharpen the most prominent image.

A monster glowered. "These are mine." It taunted her, repeating the phrase over and over.

Doubling her fist, she smashed the nearest one with a force beyond her waking strength. Tiny shards exploded, flecking her hair and piercing her exposed skin with red flecks like active chicken pox. Then blurring together, they coated her skin in a rosy flush.

She awoke and sat up, shaking and bathed in sweat. A sip of water from the glass on the bedside table helped her sort dream from reality. It took a while before sleep found her again, after a prayer to keep the hideous nightmares from following her home.

CHAPTER 16

Awake the next morning, Dana tried to bring into focus a figure standing in the doorway. "Dad?"

"The sun gave you a mean burn yesterday." He could tell, even from a distance. "We'll get something for it after breakfast. It's ready and waiting."

Pulling a robe around her, she shuffled behind him to the table.

In contrast to his distant manner of last night, he held a chair for her like a waiter in a high-end restaurant. "You were in a deep sleep."

He'd never given her this kind of attention at breakfast, but she wasn't awake enough to think much about it.

Breaking the yolk in the first egg of three on his plate, he divided it into four equal sections. "I'm taking the afternoon off to thin the cannas at the side yard. Are you up for joining me?"

She took his invitation as an apology for the night before. The eggs tasted better than usual.

"Let's do it this afternoon when Kaye returns from shopping. I'll sharpen my tools this morning so we'll be ready." He mopped the leftover yolk from his plate with a last bite of toasted rye bread. "I have some sunburn ointment you can use. You might want to wear a long sleeve shirt, too." Seeing her red face, he added, "And a hat."

Working beside him meant a chance to say what she had intended last night.

As expected, he met her in an old pair of khakis, riddled with holes and stains but fresh from the laundry. He never wore jeans. Mom said he thought the khakis set him apart from the workers at the mill.

Dana traipsed along while he pushed the yard cart to where cannas grew along the side street on a berm parallel to the fence surrounding the yard.

He jabbed a pitchfork multiple times into the soil beside the wide swath of half-blooming flowers. "They're bound together. This will detach extra roots so we can pull them out."

The tubers sank a foot or more into the dirt, exposing additional roots growing from the main one. Long feelers intertwined like locked fingers.

On hands and knees, she discovered cream-colored ones thicker than Dad's thumb and longer than his hand; but others, black and shriveled, entwined themselves in a death dance from seasons ago. Some branched into two legs like a pair of pants, heaving from the soil after prolonged resistance. The dead ones didn't break from handling, but the live ones snapped like carrots.

The tubers developed into a close family, bending to make room for others, but a few twisted themselves around weaker ones and kept them from thriving. Left on their own, the inseparable live and dead ones crowded out the necessary earth for all of them to grow.

"Kaye says they grow less tall every year and don't flower as long. Used to stay brilliant into fall." His gloved hand reached under a fat tuber like an automatic tool and removed it from the ground.

The slightest vibration moved the air. On blurred wings, a hummingbird tasted the flowers' nectar down the row. She stopped to take in the close-up view of its tiny body and elongated beak.

Dad paused, leaning on his pitchfork.

Her face relaxed at his appreciation for the littlest of birds.

They returned to their work after it zoomed straight up and whirled away.

Thinning the cannas became a puzzle in backward order¾taking the pieces apart instead of making them fit. When she tugged on a sizable clump, a scarlet-topped stem popped through a hole with the rest. It joined the growing refuse pile.

Dad noticed. "Kaye doesn't want us to destroy the blooming ones."

"I didn't mean to." If Kaye thought it was no-sweat work, why didn't she do it? She mumbled again. "Not an easy job." After yanking out an ancient dead piece, sunken in on itself as dry and dark as old rubber, she spoke to a sympathetic plant. "It seems like Kaye does the easy jobs and pawns the crummy ones off on everyone else."

"I understand if it seems that way to you."

His rare admission perked her ears.

"I know you put in more than your share." He looked at her, unwavering for a moment. "Don't think of work as a burden. It strengthens you." His attention returned to the task of digging at the roots while he talked. "Kaye worked in the office at the mill before JJ, as you know. Because she did, we have money to redesign the house. Out of the question without her help."

A pungent, moist smell rose from the rich earth. "Phew. This smells like the bathroom of every dog in the neighborhood." She pinched her nose.

"It's because of rotting organic material. These roots are ancient." He almost smiled but instead wiped his glasses with a handkerchief from his pocket and continued where he left off before bringing up Kaye's contribution to the house. "I used to think my old man didn't value me except for the work I did on the farm. He started showing me at age ten how to repair machinery, and it appealed to me. I caught on fast. My troubleshooting by age fifteen was better than his."

Dana's glove flew off in a wad of tubers destined for the pile. Braving the smell, she reached for it. "Whatever happened to him? I know he died a long time ago, but you've never really talked about him much."

"He died after my high school graduation. Mother wasn't well and sold the farm to pay for medical expenses and back taxes. Her sister in Minnesota took her in."

"And you didn't go with her?"

"No one invited me. It may have been a matter of not having a place for me, but I didn't want to move far away. I hired out at the mill then."

"Where did you live then when the farm sold?"

"Rented a room on the second floor of a house in town with bathroom privileges. The landlord allowed the use of a hotplate and part of a refrigerator shelf. I mowed the lawn in exchange for Sunday dinner. Not a bad deal."

Happy with the success of her questions, she pressed her luck further. "How did you meet Mom?"

"A few years later at a street dance in Tannersberg, where I lived in an apartment." He warmed to the telling of his story. "I worked as a regular at the mill for about a year. When a machine malfunctioned one day, I got it running again. The shop manager promoted me to mechanic and boosted my pay."

"Wow. What luck!"

"Wasn't luck. Truth is my old man gave me my future livelihood without realizing it. You never know where life is going to lead you." He plunged into silence.

The sharing of his early life stopped while she was holding her breath to hear more.

Recovering, he returned to the present, swiping the back of his glove above his eyes. "Let's load the cart and walk it down to the pile where we dump these things. I'll show you. It's on the land of a neighbor who says we can use it."

His return to efficiency didn't encourage her to ask further.

He bumped the loaded cart around the back fence through the yard next door. At the bottom, the ground descended toward a park-like area where neighbors' yards joined in a gently rolling lawn, dotted by a few pine trees and deciduous species of pear, apple, and black walnut. In the clearing, the burn pile rose from dead bushes, limbs, and clippings piled over three feet high. Beside it, dense woods took over. Dad flung handfuls of roots and tubers onto the mound. Turning the cart upside down discharged the rest.

The clearing ended as far as a football field away in a line of trees, ideal for hiding a stream. She squinted to bring them into view. "Let's go see the creek. There has to be one."

"If there is, I haven't heard about it." He viewed the land's downward trend. "If you're thinking of a pristine waterway, you'll be disappointed. Creeks here contain more plant growth and moss than those in upstate New York. What you'd call icky. And bears can startle you at any time."

"Bears? Real bears?"

"They've scrambled onto neighbors' decks here. Attracted by bird feeders or anything edible."

"Do they ever stop by the pile?"

"Haven't seen any." He peeled his gloves off and stuffed them in his pocket. "But it's good to be wary. And not stay too quiet. Animals won't stick around noisy people." He put one hand on the yard cart to steer it home. "Let's go. I'm sure our dinner's waiting."

She trailed after him.

"This part of the state has its share of black bears."

"Like the ones in the zoo at Grandfather Mountain? Remember how the cub tried to catch the splashing water with its paw?"

"In a zoo, they're around people. They're different in the wild and not exactly cute."

She took it as a warning.

Dana and Dad regaled Kaye at dinner with descriptions of their diggings and their trip to heave the rotting scraps. It was not appetite-enhancing, but it made for lively conversation, especially when he chuckled.

The mood carried over to the next day, too. Kaye prepared a bread-and-egg concoction, a new take on French toast for a meal she called brunch. "Eat up, everybody. Enough for seconds and thirds here. I didn't know the recipe made this much."

"It filled an entire cooking sheet." Pleased with his droll observation, Dad fixed his eyes on the main dish.

"I began with a small one but switched. Too late when I saw how much it made." She winked at Dana. "Want to help me make Irish stew this afternoon? It's an old family recipe. I bought fresh vegetables at the farmer's market."

"Sure. I do lots of cutting and chopping at home."

After everyone finished eating, Kaye took a washrag to JJ and persisted as he tried to twist away. She held him out to Jesse. "Here, Daddy. Take your boy for some male bonding."

Dad's entire being wilted. "I have a box seat downstairs for the game—Oakland A's and the Twins at Minnesota. What if Catfish pitches another perfect game? Don't want to miss it."

"Well, what better chance to explain the intricacies of the game to him? You need to start him early if he's going to win a scholarship." Single-handed, she began to clear the table, confident he couldn't resist her teasing. "Don't laugh. Catfish is a home-state guy from Hertford."

Giving in, he folded JJ into the crook of his arm, a gentle basketlike hold against his side. "C'mon, Catfish. Let's see what that right arm can do."

Dana imagined him carrying Luke the same way.

If most of their times together were as lighthearted, Dana would have celebrated. But whenever she and Kaye began to see eye to eye, something ruined it. This time it was the cake, the day after their brunch.

In the waning part of morning, Dana was swinging and swooping JJ around on the deck as he giggled with the tempo of a button-activated toy.

"Put him in the walker, will you?" Kaye called from the kitchen. "You've heard about my friend Marla? I'm taking JJ to play with her little Cassidy. How about making a cake for your dad while we're away? Use this cake mix." She plunked the box on the countertop.

Dana smiled because she knew Dad's favorite long before her stepmother entered the scene. "Chocolate cake with chocolate frosting. As always."

Kaye kneeled to a lower cupboard and placed a rectangular cake pan on the counter next to the mixer, along with a heavy glass bowl. "Eggs are in the fridge. You'll find everything else in the cupboard by the oven." She wasted no time whisking JJ out the door.

It had all happened so fast. Dana stood alone in the kitchen. What if she made a mistake? She imagined Kaye's inimitable pout emitting sympathy but concealing the opposite.

Getting on with it, she greased and dusted the pan, slit the package, and emptied the whole thing into the mixing bowl. To measure the oil and the water, she bent close to the counter to check the levels in the cup.

Her imagination took over, seeing liquids that poured into the mixture as a waterfall roiling the brown soil below to create a muddy pool. The beaters became a typhoon that grew wilder as she advanced the dial. The spatula, another rogue wind in the storm, swept the waves of batter from the sides and toward the center of the maelstrom.

She halted her fanciful visions to concentrate on making a great tasting cake the envy of Kaye.

Before emptying the mix into the pan, she double-checked the directions. Where were the eggs? She removed three from the carton and broke the first as Mom did with a sharp rap on the mixing bowl's rim. The second shell, instead of breaking into two distinct halves, squashed into small bits of shell joined by the white membrane underneath, except where the insides leaked through, golden and gelatinous, down the side of the bowl into the mix. When it stopped dripping, she threw the shell in the garbage and washed the goo from her hands.

Activating the beaters blended in the first eggs with one to go. Breaking the third was easier, but half the shell tumbled into the batter. The beaters crunched, turning the shell into smaller and smaller bits. She turned the dial off and tried to pull the pieces out, but they were too small and too many. An inspiration came. Let the beaters grind them up completely. It meant a little extra egg in the recipe. Nothing more. So logical.

While the cake baked, hot water filled the sink for washing the bowl, utensils, and splattered cabinets. She scrubbed away, pleased with a job to do until a juice glass, slick with soapy water, slipped from her hand onto the counter. The top shattered into fragments. She gasped. What should she do?

After examining the remaining, intact portion, she calmed herself enough to look for the other pieces. A shard blending into the backsplash behind the sink fit precisely from the rim to a jagged break.

She could imagine what Luke would say if he had been there. *The quaint-cut glass is an irreplaceable family heirloom. You smashed it to smithereens. Kaye won't be cheerful about it.*

Her anxiety-heightened search of the floor revealed nothing. Draining the sink, she spied another small half-moon sliver lying there shining and alone. Its smooth top filled part of the broken rim. She couldn't find the missing curved chip in the sink strainer, the counter, or the floor. Dad's flashlight, borrowed from his workroom, shined on every section of the floor and beneath the cupboards. The chip stayed hidden.

From the garbage can, she removed items from the top—empty cake box, inside package, other eggshells that weren't too slimy—and buried the glass and its pieces deep inside. No need for anyone to make a fuss.

After dinner, Dana cut the cake into generous squares to serve on dessert plates.

Kaye gave wholehearted approval. "You must be a professional baker! I can't wait to taste it."

Although she said nothing, Dana's inward pride responded.

Dad's first bite crunched between his teeth. "Did you add nuts to this, Dana?" He turned his piece over and saw tiny splinters of eggshell across the entire bottom. He saw her tears and shoveled in another bite. "It's delicious!" He kept munching.

She fled to her bedroom and shut the door on her failure. So much for showing off to Kaye. Luke used to say mistakes can lodge in the brain and never detach even in old age. There he was again. He turned up when he wanted, but it made her miss him even more.

After a few moments, Dana could hear footsteps approaching the guest room. Wiping her tears, Dana looked up to see Dad with Kaye and JJ beside him.

"Can we come in?" he asked. Immediately after her response, he flew to her and wrapped his arms around her.

Kaye patted Dana's head with her free hand, unable to get any closer. "Your father ate his entire serving, eggshells and all."

"Don't feel bad about it, honey." He tightened his embrace. "It's the best cake I've ever tasted. The best because you made it."

Dana wasn't crying about the cake anymore. Whenever she dreamed of hearing Dad say the right thing, it sounded close to what he'd just said.

CHAPTER 17

The rest of the week passed uneventfully until Friday morning when a jingling phone interrupted a breakfast of fruit and coconut coffee cake. Dana and Kaye stayed at the table while Dad delayed a second helping to answer it, greeting the caller with familiarity.

"Who do you think it is?" Kaye listened without shame of eavesdropping.

Dad continued. "She's fine—the babysitter extraordinaire." A pause. "He's into the rolling stage." Another pause, but shorter. "Here she is." He held the receiver out to Dana. "It's your mother."

Dana placed it to her ear like a long overdue hug. "Is anything wrong... Wow! When... After I'm home... Good... Are you telling everyone else... Umm... Bye. I love you."

She stayed on the line as if she wasn't finished after Mom disconnected. "Wait. Tell Aunt Elaine congratulations for me." After enough time for a typical reply, she repeated, "I love you," and hung up.

Signaling a quick break, she ran to her room for a minute alone. The reality of having a stepfather sometime in the coming year took hold of her. She heard herself saying to her friends, "This is my stepdad, Mr. Hamlin." How should she introduce him? She couldn't call him Taylor.

Dad and Kaye were still waiting when she returned, but she didn't want to share the news. Thank goodness the best white lie already masked the truth. She simply had to convince them.

They sat upright, looking anxious. "What's happening?" Dad set his cup down to give her his full attention.

"Aunt Elaine is getting married."

"What fun!" Kaye clapped her hands. "A wedding!"

"They haven't set a date yet. Later this year, I guess. They hope to find rings this weekend." She carried her plate to the sink and rinsed it to end the conversation.

Not satisfied, Dad kept talking. "You mentioned something that will happen after you get home."

She found a spot for the plate in the dishwasher. "Mom's throwing a shower."

"Who's the guy?"

"A teacher. At her school."

Kaye followed her with the silverware. "Have you seen him? Is he cute?"

Dana's mind did a cartwheel to describe with ease the teacher who had designed Mom's shop sign, but she stopped short of saying anything about his eye.

"I must know him." Dad turned sideways in his chair to see her beside the sink.

"He's new this year." The lie dug itself deeper. "We don't see them much."

"Your mother sounded overjoyed. Enough to call you." Dad scraped the crumbs of his coffee cake.

"Maybe she wanted an excuse to see how everything's going since I've been gone. She doesn't call for fun. Long distance is expensive." She dashed from the kitchen. "Have to take a shower."

Her mind raced. Did Mr. Hamlin want her as his stepdaughter? What house would they live in? Would it be his big one with a television set in her bedroom? She'd be a hit among her friends. One question led to another, enough to make a list of them to ask Mom.

In the shower, Dana saw pink lines running from her wrist to her elbow. After soaping and rinsing under the shower longer than usual, she dried off and stared into the mirror. A crimson rash spread at the side of her chin.

In the kitchen, she showed the marks to Kaye.

"Has to be poison ivy." She stayed at a distance. "You know, there's a saying: 'Leaves of three, let them be.'"

"I'd recognize it in a minute," Dana countered. "It has shiny leaves. I haven't been around anything like it. But I ripped out an ugly stalk with my bare hands." She held out the underside of her wrist again as proof. "Looked more like a root. The top had two scrunched up leaves, rough and crumpled, more brown than green. Not shiny. Is it poison oak?"

"Don't go near JJ. I don't need him catching it." Kaye wrinkled her nose.

"I can work outside again today," Dana volunteered. "Plenty of clippings need to go to the dump area."

"Don't fuss with the kitchen," Kaye said. "I'll finish up. But be careful. You don't want any more of that stuff."

"I'll wear gloves."

Sorting through a drawer under the counter, Kaye found a red and white print bandana, edged in a wide red border. "Here. Your dad wants you to wear this."

Definitely a fashion statement. She didn't see the need for it.

"It's clean." Kaye noted Dana's red tee. "It'll match your shirt."

Holding it, she crossed the deck to the yard, thinking of an easy place to lose it.

In his robe after showering, Jesse poured a final cup of coffee while Kaye ran the broom around the kitchen. A curved wedge of glass skidded from under the refrigerator.

"Whew! What's this?" She held it up close. "Hey," she called out to Dana, who was heading for the shed. "Do you know anything about this?" She raised the missing rim from the cut-glass tumbler like a detective finding a clue.

Hunching her shoulders, Dana descended the steps with a deliberate gait and didn't turn back. Of all times for the missing piece to show up.

Kaye spun around to Jesse. "JJ could have eaten it off the kitchen floor."

"Not likely. He's either in the playpen or with Dana."

"What's that supposed to mean?"

He deserted his cup of coffee on the counter. "I have to go."

Kaye followed him but checked the living room for JJ, who was content in his playpen. "This isn't working as we intended, and poison ivy makes it worse. Don't you think it's smart to send her back home where she can be under her mother's care?"

He hauled his shoes from the closet and jerked open the sock drawer. "It's not as terrible as you think. I've never given it to anyone else."

"She carries JJ around constantly. It's on her arm where she holds him."

"Won't be carrying him today. She'll be working outside. You heard her."

"I can't have her do any kitchen stuff or handle laundry. We'll all be itching." She opened the closet to decide what to wear. "And I thought you wanted her here to help me. Some promise."

He lowered himself to the bed. "You invited her here to be the unpaid maid?"

"I thought we both agreed to some babysitting help."

"I don't understand your inability to cope with one little baby." He worked one foot into his shoe. "Plenty of women have two or three toddlers to take care of single-handedly. How do you think they get their shopping done?"

His words silenced her like a slap.

"And because she's here with JJ while you're shopping, you haven't gone out of your way for her at all."

Kaye turned on him. "I didn't see you taking her anywhere. Dana is your child, not mine."

"I was counting on some female bonding. I thought you'd cherish her for no other reason than being my daughter. Am I asking too much?"

"When did you bond with her? During the Catfish game?" Her voice broke.

He gritted his teeth. "All I want is a civil discussion." He turned his head away from the sound of sobbing.

"This isn't what I bargained for." She collapsed on the bed, more than an arm's length from him.

"My life isn't what I asked for, either. Neither is Dana's. And there's nothing we can do but take it." He finished tying his shoes. "You didn't hear her the other night, after you confiscated her geodes, about being a slave."

"What do you mean, 'confiscated'?"

"She found them. You took them." His eyes narrowed on her.

"It's my yard."

"You'd never know they existed if she didn't find them."

"I'll give them back, then." She wrenched a tissue from the box. "She feels like a slave?"

"That's what she said. I didn't make it up."

"I've been teaching her everyday jobs to help her grow up." She dabbed a tissue to her eyes, trying to keep her mascara from running. "What did you say to her?"

"Nothing. She ran upstairs."

"You see the problem. I don't know what to do with her. She's quiet. I'm not always comfortable around her, Jess." She faced him. "You aren't, either."

His jaws tightened.

She returned to the closet for the blue diaper bag used for day trips.

He hoisted himself up, found his wallet on the dresser, and shoved it into his rear pocket. "I can't change the world this morning, even if you want me to." He looked in the mirror for an uncharacteristic final check. "You don't have to trouble yourself today. She won't be with you."

"I'll make sure of it. I'm going to Marla's." She charged through the bedroom door, the bag swinging on her shoulder.

"Go, then."

She reached the hall but stopped. "I'll leave a note on the counter for her to make a sandwich from food in the fridge for lunch."

"I think she can handle it."

"JJ's not safe with her around." Footsteps slapped the hall, followed by her final, piercing remark. "It's okay with you if he eats glass."

"Go before you fall apart."

CHAPTER 18

Dana held the combination lock in her left hand while the other whirled the numbers around to thirty, back to two, and forward past zero to seventeen. Swinging the shed door open wide, she lugged the yard cart to the gravel bed outside. For entertainment, the shed became a monster. The door was the monster's mouth, regurgitating the cart from the contents of its stomach. Closing the gaping jaws, she hung the lock's curved hook in the opening of the wide latch, where it dangled like a loose tooth.

The monster fantasy kept her from seeing a certain shape on the shelf. Recalling it moments later, she did an about-face. There, high above the workbench, rested Luke's sailboat. A mast and sails rose above the hull as on the day it tipped into the storm drain. Sanded and repainted, the hull showed no digs or dents. But it needed more work.

Moving through a fog of grief for the boat—for Luke and for herself—she returned to the cart. Pulling it behind her, she struggled as it clunked up each railroad-tie stair. Still, the effort was easier than pushing or carrying it. Too bad it didn't have the bounce of Mom's wheelbarrow at home. Level ground inside the fenced yard reduced the strain.

In the garage, the engine of the smaller car started up, the Ford Pinto Runabout Kaye drove during her pre-Jesse days. Dad took it to work because the station wagon held JJ's baby seat.

No sound came from the bigger car driving off yet. Dana didn't risk a peek into the garage for Kaye to suspect her of spying.

Too late to talk to Dad about the boat, she told herself it didn't matter. She'd be on her own today and grateful to work with no one to answer to. But while she heaved clippings into the cart, the boat nagged at her. The cart became her mind, filled with wrath instead of clippings. Sure, Dad slaved over a toy box for a baby too little to use it but hadn't finished the final repairs on the last memory of his lost son. What a discovery while she and Dad were getting along again.

Anger burned as she bulldozed the overloaded cart across the yard. She tried to wedge a brick beside the fence post to keep the gate from clicking shut but found it impossible to do while holding the cart. The gate swung free until the first breeze slammed it closed.

The cart thunked down the stairs, followed by the sound of her sandals treading the pulverized stones at the bottom. The day's work called for sneakers. She'd get them later, after Kaye left. Stabilizing the cart by the shed door, she placed a step stool near the work shelf to claim the boat. Additional tiny sails of thin cotton, starched as stiff as canvas, lay beside coiled pieces of twine like miniature hemp ropes to hold the sails. A great job as far as he went, but it didn't justify the years of having it. He never showed it to her even after his promise on the trip from the airport.

One side of the boat reflected brighter blue than the other. Maybe he was trying to find the most durable paint. She cradled it, a mother with a found child, and gently stowed it in the cart's tool tray.

Her original plan to use the boat to keep Dad home had failed. Now, it belonged to her, at least for a short while. The cart, like a carriage for a prince, conveyed the once stately sailboat into the valley below.

The burn pile's debris had grown larger overnight. Resting Luke's boat on the ground, she emptied the clippings at the pile, tossing them upward to make the mound even higher. When the cart was empty, she folded her garden gloves inside the tray and left them there.

The clearing provided the shortest access to the elusive creek by cutting across its center, mowed in the recent past to keep weeds down. Some fast-growing species already shot up to a foot or more in places. The thickening line of poplars ahead, interspersed with competing tulip trees, birches, and a mix of pines, shrouded lower growing bushes. They obscured any possible view of water, but only temporarily. Tall grasses whispered in anticipation as she passed.

The air's heaviness brought runnels of sweat from the top of her head. One hand wiped at them while the other held her treasure. Energetic bugs hopscotched from one stalk of weeds to another. Never mind if mosquitoes whined in ominous proximity, nothing would keep her from returning the craft to its natural home. Boats were made to float as balloons were made to fly, their single reason for existing.

The thought brought her efforts full circle. She called it "a tribute to Luke" and delighted in the new name.

Her fingertips brushed the dragonfly necklace, warm from the sun's rays. She wondered what Dad had said when he had first given it to Mom. They hadn't dreamed one day their daughter would wear it when she visited a Southern creek far away.

A generous mass of Joe Pye weed bloomed at the meadow's side, where it dodged the mower. Bees and butterflies visited prolific blossoms in hues of rosy pink. When she tried to think of an accurate color to describe them, mauve came to mind. In saying it, her upper teeth grazed her lower lip at the end.

It was the color of Mom's flared skirt in shades of purple, bleeding to red when she twirled.

Dad called it rhubarb.

"It's not," Mom mouthed to her. Back then, her parents enjoyed teasing each other.

A rustling noise cut the memory short. She halted as her heart skipped a beat, remembering what Dad had said about bears. Other sounds continued as usual. Bees hummed in a low din over the wildflowers. A tractor growled from far away. Chittering birds sounded like small children on the playground. Nothing signaled distress or imminent danger. The cheeriness in their twittering encouraged her to turn her head enough to look up, hoping to see a couple of wrens flitting around their nest.

Instead, a gray squirrel with bulging cheeks frisked across a piece of rotting fence. To see if it carried a nut, she leaned into the shade of a tree. It spied her and froze in its tracks. She didn't move. Keeping her in view, the squirrel took a crab apple from the pouch of its cheeks and, holding it with both claws, chewed the ball of fruit in a quick arpeggio. Unwanted bits of stem and peel rained down on the fence in a few seconds. The remaining fruit fell while the tiny creature stayed immobile, its steely eyes locked on hers. Its cheeks bulged and jaws shifted to savor bites already taken. Had it been a contest of the winner being the last to move, the squirrel would have won.

She scoffed at her fearfulness and skipped along, lighter on her feet than before, to the untrimmed growth among the trees that possibly hid a shallow, trickling stream.

A new world opened on a gurgling ten-foot-wide creek, the neighborhood's best-kept secret. An empty bottle at the edge denied the area's supposed isolation. Or it may have tumbled along in the current from upstream, closer to the houses.

A tuft of grass on the other side, too tall to stand up on its own, bent toward the water. A few of its long strands flowed with the current, giving the stream its very own Rapunzel with willowy, flaxen hair. The organic smell of rotting plants, reminiscent of digging the cannas with Dad, reached her nose.

Balanced on snarled tree roots above the water, she stooped to release the boat in a less-than-ideal setting for a launch. Wobbling, it followed a thin line of current before swaying, changing its mind, and nosing toward the bank, where it floundered, trapped in entrails of grass at the edge. To rescue it, she leaned over, supporting herself with one hand on a moss-coated rock. Holding it safe again, she surveyed the water's path below for a better spot. She had to watch for rocks and tree roots blocking its cruise that would prevent her from running beside it.

Her trek grew tedious beside the creek that meandered outward and obscured anything beyond the bend. Persisting in her search for a long run, she stumbled through a thicket of mountain laurel before pushing through some swamp maples growing close to the edge. Stepping around each one kept her near the water as it continually glided away to an unknown destination. Amazing how it kept going.

Along clearing, where momentum wasn't as lazy as before, compelled her to stop. In a subtle change, the creek widened. Rivulets glittering in the sun gave new roughness to the current. She shaded her face to look downstream, determined for the boat to ride the water again.

The high pitch of a mosquito, shrill as metal on thin wire, stopped as it lighted on her cheek. She slapped it. Her hand drew back, wet and shiny. In the heat, the stream's water tempted her in spite of its color. It wasn't muddy but a smooth, clear, green-brown, revealing the creek bed and moss beneath the current. She resisted. The day's plan didn't call for wading.

Her sandals dug into the ground close to the edge to settle the boat in. Yielding to the current, it bobbed through ripples over barely visible rocks. Then, steady, it ran with new speed.

Jumping over weeds and mounds of earth, she followed; but the boat skimmed faster than the first try upstream. When it veered out of sight, she kept running, hurdling low-growing plants and detouring around bigger ones.

Winded and tired, she spotted it at the far side, caught in a pool. It rotated like the red top Luke pumped for her, blurring the design to a streak.

The creek spread out too wide for her to reach the boat. She scampered downstream, seeking another crossing.

Her reward came at a fallen, rotted tree, spanning the water to lichen-spotted rocks on the opposite side. She worked her way around the upended tree roots snaking in all directions until she planted her foot on the trunk, the bridge to the other side. The creek—wider now and deeper, too—wasn't threatening.

Luke would have devised a plan for both of them to fall in. She unintentionally accompanied him again, but this time on a creek bank. He commandeered the log to demonstrate. *Sit on it like this. Flip over with your belly to it. See?* Eager for the thrill, he finished his instructions. *Hold on till you feel the current. Then turn and slide slow into the water.* He howled at his feet rising in the water. *C'mon, Dana. Last one in's a chicken!*

She marveled at his intrusion on her adventure and the way he showed up at his whim. His enthusiasm always encouraged her to follow.

At the center of the log, a large indentation marked the site where a limb originated; but in rotting, it widened into a natural foothold. Easy. The next step took her to a slick spot. She drew back to the rotted furrow. Attempting it again, she tapped for solid footing. From there, she hopped to a rock more substantial than the end where multiple branches splayed over the bank. The maneuver succeeded, but she landed off balance and stepped on the branches. The boat, meanwhile, had broken away and flashed under the log at that minute. The sight of it startled her. The brittle branches cracked, tossing her into the water. Splashing in the hip-deep creek, she felt one sandal slurp into the muddy bottom. In an instinctive move, she sank into a reclining position, feet in front. Down the creek she glided at last, arms curved as outriggers, keeping her buoyant. It felt good. Liberating.

"Luke, I wish you were here." But this was her journey. She wasn't tagging after him today.

How long she floated, she didn't know or care. Setting her mind free, too, she became a boat with sandals for rudders; but they were positioned in front instead of behind her. Luke never let a mistake like that pass without leaping on it. He'd also announce with glee that the sandals needed to dry before she wore them again.

She drifted along, passing the woods and feeling the water slick by her skin, sensations that replaced her thoughts about the sandals. How to return upstream became her new concern. What a silly idea. No fear of getting lost because the creek showed the way, although a winding one, back to where she began not far from the burn pile. Easy enough to retrace her steps.

A ripple in the current tugged her along as she paddled in the center of the stream. In a few minutes, she'd work over to the side but not yet. She shut her eyes to avoid looking into the sun high overhead, giving warmth in contrast to the water's coolness. At a whir of air, she opened her eyes again. A dragonfly, a real one, hovered over her head, a helicopter in the heat. It came closer for a place to alight.

"My head's not a landing pad!"

Her arms held her afloat, keeping her from batting it away. It zoomed low once more before tiring of the game. Soaring off to the side to visit a new attraction, it grew smaller and smaller before it vanished.

An unidentifiable sound filled the surroundings, growing louder. A waterwheel? Dad, on showing one to her, had explained how people had used them to grind grain; but it didn't produce that noise. The river hosted a dissonant choir, swelling with each chorus. The creek gained new depth and swiftness. Amid the growing agitation, she couldn't touch bottom. Now what? The current's pull was stealing her against her will.

The roaring became reality. The creek and a larger river crashed together beyond hallucination, beyond believing. Raucous, boisterous sounds bellowed in turmoil. Foaming with wrath, it dragged her under. Spit her up. Plunged her deep in the rapids. Thrust her down a sluice where counter current propelled her upward.

Her head parted the water into the sun's glare. She gasped. Sucked the air hard. Braced for the next heave or tow, her single goal to keep her head above water.

The sun, like a guardian, kept her aware of the surface. She fought for it. Knees and elbows smashed into obstacles.

She washed farther downstream, a helpless leaf, wriggling to stay afloat.

Again, the rapids flexed their muscles. A surge gulped her under. Lifted her over rocks. Dropped her into a hollow, tapered as a trough. She lifted her chin for life-giving air.

Ahead of her, the boat crested high caps of white water. Luke swam beside it, plucked it, and held it high. *I've got it, Dana! Don't worry. I've got it.*

Seeing him brought adrenaline-pumping but not enough for her to conquer the current. Soon enough, the water ceased its earlier opposition as it widened into a small, elongated lake. The ride became smoother, yet fast and deep. She wanted to lie back in her earlier back float with arms as flotation devices, but her body wouldn't obey. She stayed face up and forward as the flow took her.

The strangest thing happened. The lucky penny entered her mind, even though she'd lost it so long ago. It wasn't what she needed. She prayed then, the most sincere and desperate prayer of her life.

After a short respite, the water's pace quickened again. A din of renewed turbulence rose from the other side of the widened river, where a split tapered away but didn't catch her. She breathed air.

The act brought a rush of reality. She called for help—or thought she did—but the voice sounded wrong. Was someone else caught in the river?

CHAPTER 19

Kaye's hands trembled on the steering wheel as she replayed her argument with Jesse. The short drive that Friday morning to Marla's on the south side of town gave her some relief, even though weekend campers brought heavier-than-usual traffic. Parking the Ford wagon in the driveway, she pulled a tissue from the glove compartment and pressed it to her forehead before unbuckling a wide-eyed JJ from his car seat. She waved toward the porch at her friend.

"Coffee's on." Marla held the door for her.

"Sorry to barge in on your day. I'd suffocate if I stayed there another minute."

"So it sounded." Marla crossed the kitchen to where a happy Cassidy sat, rubbing gooey traces across the highchair tray.

"Did I tell you she has poison ivy?" Kaye dumped the diaper bag on the floor.

"How do you know?"

"Showed it to me this morning. She had no idea, but I did." Holding JJ on her lap, she hunted for a rattle in the bag. "I've lost my babysitter, maybe for the rest of summer. She may as well go home. I told Jess as much, but he didn't want to hear about it."

Marla wrangled Cassidy into his walker. "Is it that bad?"

"On her arms and chin. Enough to be dangerous for JJ."

"Those things are short-lived." She scrubbed the after-breakfast mess with a soapy sponge. "What's she doing now?"

"Cleaning the yard for Jess."

"You don't have to worry about her, then."

"Worry isn't the word. I want her out of my hair."

Marla handed her a steaming cup. "Let Jesse cool down the same way you like your coffee. It'll blow over."

They kept an eye on the babies in the playpen while Kaye's story came out in disjointed segments, including the broken piece of glass and Jesse's accusations of her as an uncaring stepmother and incompetent mother.

After a light lunch, they took a two-block trip to the park. In the sandbox, the little ones found new objects to play with and taste, including sand.

"You might know"—Marla half-frowned as she rescued Cassidy—"they're not ready for this."

They pushed strollers around the park's perimeter until the babies fell asleep. On a bench away from traveled sidewalks, Kaye recounted the morning's happenings uninterrupted. Neither one could imagine the dangers threatening Dana at that time in another county of Western North Carolina.

In the sun's lengthening rays, Marla found an idea to cheer her friend. "Stay with me for supper, why don't you? Vance won't be home. He's traveling again. You can feed JJ from Cassidy's supply in the pantry. Let Jesse see how it is to come home without dinner on the table."

That sealed Kaye's decision. "It's time for him to be in my shoes." She lifted her chin. "I don't care if I ever get home."

The grandfather clock struck seven when Jesse met Kaye finally arriving home with JJ. "Where's Dana?"

"How should I know? I wasn't here." She threw the diaper bag on the couch. "I didn't know you wanted me to be her babysitter."

"Listen to me, Kaye. She's not here! I've checked everywhere. The bedroom, downstairs, the yard. There's no sign of her." Looking at the counter, he said, "See there? The note about making her lunch is still where you left it."

Kaye shifted JJ to hold the paper bearing her own handwriting. The little one reached for it with a chubby hand. "Where do you think she is? Hiding?"

"She stopped doing that at age three." He shot her a scowl.

"Where's the cart?"

"I thought she put it away. The gate's shut." Shock ran through him.

She handed him a wriggling JJ, and they took the stairs in multiple leaps to the shed. The lock hung unfastened on the hook.

He flung the door wide. "Not here."

"You didn't see it anywhere else?"

"Not in the yard or side, cannas, or anywhere." In saying it, he knew he hadn't been everywhere after all. "I'm off to the burn pile. Call the neighbors." He gave JJ back to her. A resolute stride carried him by the shed's graveled entrance and across the lawn.

In the middle of Kaye's third call, Jesse sprinted up the hill with the empty cart's wheels skipping the ground. He left it below the stairs and dashed into the dining room.

Her eyes met his. "You found it. Think something happened?"

"Everything's undisturbed."

She hesitated. "No sign of a struggle?"

"Her gloves are in the bin by the handle. Seems she placed them there on purpose and not in a hurry." He raked his hand through his hair. "No hint of anything. No scuffling, footprints, tampering with the cart."

"Nobody in the neighborhood saw her today, but they're on the alert. And Shane's coming to help." She sent a kiss toward him. "I need to get JJ to bed."

In a daze, Jesse propped himself against the counter. When she rejoined him and put her arms around him, he turned to stone. "Why weren't you home today of all days?"

Her hands fell limp. "You know why."

"She did all that work and went to the pile alone."

"I didn't hear you object to leaving her here."

A thump at the front door ended their exchange. He detoured around her to answer it.

Shane Webber towered an easy foot over Jesse. Under rogue wisps of dark hair, he took one look at his friend and bear-hugged him. "C'mon, brother. I'm here to help you. She'll turn up." He threw his arm around him and guided him toward the table. "Did you call the police?"

A bolt ran through Jesse. "Kaye called the neighbors. That's all."

"I'll do it. My bud, Kenny McDonnell, is on the force."

Kenny, on patrol nearby with partner Bobby Ray Lambert, arrived in minutes. Big men like Shane, they stood a whole head above Jesse. Kenny, the heavier of the two, wore a shirt straining its buttons.

Shane clapped a hand on his shoulder. "Thanks for coming. As I said about my friend here"—he turned to Jesse—"his daughter is missing."

At their successive nods, Jesse offered them seats at the table. Kenny asked questions while Bobby Ray filled out a report with name, age, and kinship, followed by a description of height, weight, color of hair, eyes, and clothing. The last question prompted Jesse to look at Kaye.

"She was wearing a red T-shirt. Remember, Jess? Easy to see. I gave her a red bandana to match."

On asking when they last saw her, Kenny noted their hesitation. "Which one of you left first?"

"I think I did." Kaye sidled near Bobby Ray to see his notes.

"Yes." Jesse squinted, thinking how to make her answer sound true. "I followed after you. Garage was empty when I left." Their heads bobbed together in collusion.

Kenny looked squarely at Jesse. "And Dana?"

"In the yard. I waved goodbye to her before I left."

A time-out sign came from Shane. "These are good people, Ken."

Kenny nodded. "We have to ask. Where have you searched for her? It's part of the report."

"Everywhere. The house, the yard, other yards." He tried to recall more. "The shed, too. Found the cart by the burn pile a few houses down. Neighbors take their clippings and yard debris there."

"Do you have the cart?"

"In the shed. I brought it back."

"That means you touched it."

"Yes." Jesse shot back. "You have a better method?"

"Okay, okay. It's the sort of thing we'd dust for prints if that becomes necessary."

"Not the first thing on my mind at the time."

Shane fell into peacemaker role again. "Nobody's blaming you, Jess."

As part of his thinking process, Kenny's large hand wiped his cheek toward his ear. "Don't do anything else with the cart. Someone can check it." He rolled his head toward Bobby Ray who kept jotting on the notepad. "We need to do a check of the exterior." To the others, he said, "Now, if you'll excuse us, we have to call this in so they can notify Search and Rescue. We'll be a few minutes." Striding to the door, he glanced back. "And we need a recent photograph of your daughter." They left, grasping their flashlights.

"Should you have gone with them, Jess?" Kaye sat beside him in stunned silence.

"Didn't need me for what they're going to do."

Their waiting time filled with Shane's attempts to convince them everything would be okay.

When the policemen returned, Kenny asked, "You have that photo?"

Dana's school picture had been a gift along with a larger framed one at Christmas. Jesse slipped it from his wallet. "I'd like it back . . ." He faltered and added, "Sometime."

Kenny handed it to his partner, who secured it under a flap in the notepad.

In a cooperative move, Kaye volunteered to show them Dana's bedroom. The policemen thumped behind her. Jesse and Shane took the rear.

Nothing was out of place. No clothes or other items sprawled on dresser tops or the floor. Kenny stood in the doorway without stepping into the room. Instead, he dropped to one knee to shine his light under the bed and stood upright to give his directive: "Don't handle anything and keep the door shut in case a team needs to go through it tomorrow."

Tomorrow? The thought shook Jesse like nothing else. He couldn't spend another day without knowing where she was. His knuckle edged his eye for the first time since Luke's accident.

"Want to go on patrol with us?" Kenny's voice brought him back. "We can cruise by places attractive to teens."

"But she doesn't go anywhere. Doesn't know other kids near here. Aren't any." He eyed Kaye for confirmation.

"You do want to find her, don't you?" The officer's hand rested on the doorknob.

Jesse reconsidered. "Whatever you think will help." He transported himself across the floor in sleepwalker fashion but managed a goodbye sign to Kaye. Before he reached the door, he steadied himself by the wall to ward off a stab of dizziness. His body functioned as an empty shell with a hollowed-out inside. He feared the growing darkness lurking beyond the porch as he trailed the officers.

"I'll ride along, too." Shane moved to the porch but waited like a guardian to be last to leave. "Take it easy, Kaye."

Pacing slowly, Jesse returned, his manner and confidence shriveled.

Hiding shock, Kaye asked, "Anything?"

"They'll keep looking. Canvassing homes between here and the burn pile."

"I'm sorry, Jess. For all of this." She stifled a sob.

He stayed inside the front door without moving. "You don't know what it's like to lose a child." His gruff whisper carried to her range of hearing.

Was it a testimony or an accusation? "We're going to find her." She approached him warily, but he stiffened. Her hands hung at her sides.

"There's nothing more we can do tonight." Then, softly, she said, "I'm going to bed." She looked back. "You need some sleep, too, Jess."

Staring at the floor, he saw Luke and heard the burning words.

"Dad, we haven't been fishing in weeks. Summer will be over." The floor became a lake. Its ripples flooded over, blurring his view. When it cleared, the waves smoothed near a hospital gurney where Luke lay. If he was speaking, the sounds emerged indiscernible as a foreign language. Ripples invaded Jesse's sight while Dana appeared beside her brother. Both lay under water that had grown placid and calm. Dana said nothing; but her face, turned toward Luke, implied secret communication.

He collapsed into an overstuffed chair. Like a man in a willing execution, he let his head fall into his arms.

CHAPTER 20

Amid images of Dana raking stones and pulling tubers from the ground, Jesse slept fitfully. The cart frolicked, dangling leggy roots over its sides, while Dana's gloves alternated between flying in the air and mingling among the contents as they rode toward the burn pile.

He awoke at six in a damp T-shirt. Showering, he surprised himself by praying for a miracle to bring her home.

JJ whimpered. At his full-blown cry, Kaye stirred herself from bed to instant action. She gave JJ a bottle in the playpen while a cast iron pan heated on the stove.

Jesse dressed faster than his usual efficiency, planning the next step. "The police said a detective would be here sometime this morning, but I want to catch him first at headquarters. And I need to call Rachael."

"Hold off on your call for a while. Dana can't stay missing for long. We'll find her." The coffee pot gurgled in competition. "If we tell Rachael now, she'll never allow her to stay here again."

"And that doesn't suit you?"

"Don't pick a fight, Jess." She returned to the stove. "I'm afraid, too, but we have to stay positive."

He about-faced toward the wall phone.

She shoveled two barely warm, basted eggs on a plate with toast, set them on the table, and carried JJ on one arm, the bottle in hand, down the hall.

After a phone call, he found Kaye dressing JJ. "She'll be on the first flight here. Invited her to use Dana's room." His tone of voice dared her to counter him. He knew she didn't want to take in his ex-wife despite the circumstances, but he heard what he wanted to hear.

"It's the least we can do."

He agreed. "It's only decent."

Jesse checked at police headquarters for any news since last night. The Search and Rescue team from the local fire department had been out since dawn or earlier. Detective Benson would meet with him when he returned at ten. No one disclosed Benson's intention to stop by the mill to confirm Jesse's exact hour of arrival at work on Friday and to ask the assistant foreman if he had noticed anything unusual in his manner or actions.

The person at the desk added that in questioning neighbors or touring the town mall and bus station, they hadn't yet found anyone matching his daughter's description.

Efforts were ongoing, but the bus station in the heart of town was most unlikely. She couldn't get there. Underneath it all, the overwhelming question plagued him. Where was she? Why did she volunteer to do yard work, empty the cart, and run away? It made no sense.

Balking at the idea she'd gone away willingly, he returned home to knock on doors of neighbors he didn't know, even though searchers had already been there. No one had spotted any young girl at all.

What if someone had run into her by the burn pile and talked her into a visit for a glass of cool tea or lemonade and what? Kidnapped her? Tied her up? The possibility of an attack from a stranger grew in him. He took his idea to Detective Benson. It had to be the only answer. "I want the houses searched!"

Benson calmed him. "It's not out of the question. Nothing is." He guided the irate father toward his office. "We're here to help you. We want to find your daughter as much as you do." He pulled out a chair next to the desk. "Looks like you could use some coffee."

"You might be right." Jesse dropped his defenses and relaxed his muscles.

The detective brought in two mugs and found a clear space for one beside his visitor's elbow.

Reclaiming his mind from afar, Jesse swiveled around to keep Benson in view across the corner of the desk bearing permanent rings from past coffee cups.

"What occurred at your house before your daughter's disappearance? The very last thing. Any kind of trouble?"

"Nothing I can think of." His robot stiffness returned.

"According to the report, she lives with her birth mother in New York. She's visiting you and your wife—her stepmother—for the summer."

"Correct."

"Any problems between them?" He palmed his hands to his face to wipe his eyes and forehead. "Let me rephrase. Can you say she and your wife are compatible?"

"Enough."

"Think she ran away?"

"Not possible." Jesse dismissed the thought. "It's not in her nature. She keeps herself busy. Takes care of her baby brother and helps around the house and the yard."

"Does she enjoy doing those things?"

"I think so." His hands curved around the mug. "She's diligent. Has been since she was little." His frown lines smoothed. "Enjoys having goals. Like me."

"Was anyone else at home with her?"

Jesse jerked upright in the chair. To detract from his action, he slapped his hand over his shoulder and kneaded the top of his back.

"Something wrong?" Benson had seen strange reactions of office visitors. He waited.

Jesse shifted his torso sideways, flexing his back. "Muscle cramps. Probably the stress." He rolled his shoulders to smooth the kinks in his neck on both sides. He hoped the stall would avoid what he didn't want to talk about. "My wife took our baby to see a friend in the afternoon. Dana enjoys being alone once in a while. I came home first."

Benson scribbled on a notepad. "What's the friend's name? I'll need to talk to her."

"For what reason?"

"Routine. We interview everyone in contact with the missing person's family members."

Jesse blinked. Missing person. Overnight, Dana had become a missing person. To Benson, still waiting, he said, "Name's Marla Sentry. My wife can give you phone and address."

"I'll need it." He wrote on the notepad and pocketed it. "Know any hiding places your daughter might hole up in?"

"She's never been a hider. All the same, I combed the house and the yard, calling for her. And through the neighborhood." His splayed fingers prowled through his hair as if to help his memory.

Benson mulled everything over. "Had a baffling case a couple years ago. A family reported a ten-year-old boy missing after school. He'd argued with his father that morning about a chore he'd forgotten."

Jesse shifted in his seat.

"Turns out, he holed up in the neighbor's overgrown forsythia hedge after school to avoid punishment. Everyone called, but he didn't answer. Later at night, officers probed the neighborhood with flashlights; but an older brother found him when he coughed. A canteen and bag of cookies kept him there. Prepared to stay for the long haul."

"Some story." Jesse shook his head and peered hard into his empty mug, hoping the dregs would form a map to find her.

"Keep thinking. Sometimes the smallest recollection can be the best clue." Benson held out a pack of cigarettes. "Smoke?"

"Don't touch the stuff." He raised his palm outward like a stop sign.

"Mind if I do?" At a consenting shrug, the detective inhaled deeply and blew an idle stream of smoke to the side to let his visitor jog his mind.

Amid the tempting smell of tobacco, Jesse sat in silence, a shift from a few minutes ago when he had insisted on a search of nearby houses.

"Does your ex-wife know your daughter's missing?" Benson's voice found a deeper note, muted and soft to match the ascending smoke.

"I'm meeting her plane in Charlotte tonight."

"I have to interview her, too." He tapped the ashes on the tray. "And your wife, of course. They might recall something she said or did recently. I find mothers are usually better at this than fathers."

Jesse gave a half smile.

"Sheriffs and police departments in adjacent counties and towns have been notified and sent a copy of your daughter's photograph." He produced a print from the one Kenny had brought in last night.

"That's good." He reflected on how stupid that must sound with Dana gone missing. He mashed his elbows on the arms of the chair. "What about using dogs?"

"We've worked in the past with a hunter from Black Mountain who has great hounds. I plan to call him after we're done here." Benson sat forward and bent the cigarette into the ashtray. "I also need to drop by your house after lunch for a follow-up. Will anyone be home?"

"I'll be there." He hoisted his body, suddenly heavy, from the seat.

"And your wife?"

"She'll be there, too."

Rising to his feet, Benson made a final request. "Think about what your daughter likes doing at home or when she was younger. What games did she play? Does she prefer being outdoors? Those things are important in helping to find her."

"I'll keep those in mind." Jesse jerked his head forward as an interim goodbye. "This afternoon, then."

As he drove home, Benson's final words haunted him. What did he know about Dana? How did she spend her time? What had she and Luke done in their summer hours? If the detective probed into what he knew about her, he'd realize this father knew little about his only daughter.

An unintended bang from the kitchen door announced Jesse's return. "Saw Detective Benson. He's coming this afternoon for a follow-up check. Requested time to interview you."

"What does he want from me?" Kaye's voice took on a jagged edge. "I spoke to the police last night."

"He wants to talk to Rachael, too. He's hunting for any habit that might give a clue about what happened."

"You should know a couple of guys came to check out Dana's room while you were gone. They took her pajamas, pillowcase, and hairbrush—for the scent, I guess. What else will they take?"

It sounded to him like collecting evidence in a murder investigation, not a lost-child case; but he didn't share that with her. Instead, he brought up the plan to bring in dogs.

"Are you having as much trouble sorting this out? Did we do something wrong?"

He saw her empty eyes and took her in his arms. "I'm sorry about the argument." He wanted to be sincere; but the apology was forced, like everything else these past two days.

She pressed a finger to his lips, pretending it over and done.

Arms still around her, he kissed her on the cheek. "You should know I didn't tell Benson about our quarrel. Didn't want to sidetrack him. Has nothing to do with Dana."

She pulled back to listen.

"Benson suggested the possibility she ran away. Ridiculous thought, isn't it?" He looked at her for affirmation. "I don't think she heard us. Do you?"

"She was already outside."

"I think so. We weren't loud enough for her to hear." His arm wrapped around her waist. "Benson doesn't need to know. It's an unnecessary complication."

"Anything I should do while he's here?"

Relieved at the sound of her normal voice, he said, "Forgot to tell you, Marla's also in the interview group. He talks to everyone who's been in contact with family members. Might tell her not to mention the argument. If she knows about it."

"He'd better do it soon. She and Vance are taking the baby to Knoxville tomorrow. His father's birthday. They'll be back late Monday night."

"May go today after he sees us. But Marla can't shed any light. She doesn't know Dana at all."

"You're right." She heaved a long sigh.

"It's the least of our problems, isn't it?"

Benson arrived as promised in the afternoon. Jesse introduced him to Kaye, who was at that moment leaning over JJ in the playpen. "Hey there, sport," Benson boomed. "What a handsome little fella you are."

Kaye edged away. "Do you want to look around?" Before he could answer, she informed him about the men who were there earlier.

"I've spoken with them; but I still need a quick house tour, including your daughter's room."

"I'll do the honors." Jesse led him through all the rooms, including the basement, watching him with covert glances for any unusual reaction.

Heading back to the kitchen, Benson said, "I'll need fingerprints from each of you."

"What for?" Kaye bristled. She blamed his request on officiousness; but in truth, she knew nothing of detectives or the law.

"Don't go too far. I can do it at the kitchen counter." He removed an inkpad and papers from a kit. He pressed Jesse's fingers, rolling them one by one on the pad before placing them on the squares allotted on a page bearing his name. "Ever been printed before?"

"Can't say I have."

He repeated the process with Kaye, who stepped to the sink upon finishing to soap her hands with dish detergent and slather them with lotion. "If you'll excuse me, it's time for his nap." She swept JJ from the playpen and skittered down the hall.

That gave Jesse a chance to lead the way outside to the yard below the deck. He beckoned toward the shed. "Where we keep the cart."

Benson noted the lock but knew it had been dusted earlier.

The two men began their trip to the burn pile in the afternoon's heat before the sun began migrating westward.

The detective eyeballed every direction from the pile. "Nice view of Rathskill Mountain from here."

"It has a name?"

"Everything has a name here. Native Americans called this area 'Dry Ridge.'"

"Why is that?"

"Ever see how it rains buckets in town but not one drop in your yard?"

"Sure. I've called Kaye from work during a downpour when she couldn't report as much as a drizzle here."

Their eyes roamed over the pile. Two mockingbirds hopped about on a nearby sticker bush. "You say everyone in the neighborhood brings their clippings here?"

"Not all, but many."

"Who owns the property?"

"People in the brown and yellow house, three doors away. They own several acres here. Keep it manicured like a neighborhood park." A black butterfly with blue spots arose in the humid air.

"Nice neighbors." Benson studied the house along with those nearby. There's not much beyond here." He foraged through his pocket for a cigarette and lit it with a pass of his lighter. "Not too long ago, these houses were new."

"Kaye's been here for four years. I moved in after we got married two years ago."

"She owned it?"

"You might say so. A gift from her ex-husband, Brad Parlon. Did you know him?"

"Name's familiar."

"The marriage lasted a year. Lived in an apartment during construction, but before they moved in, he left and gave the whole thing to her." Jesse pulled his hands from his pockets, needing them to finish the story. "She paid the mortgage every month, but the down payment became the real gift. Sizable, too."

"Lucky for her. Out of a sense of duty?"

"Someone else caught his eye. He owned half the cotton mill at the time. She stayed on as head of personnel. I came from New York as a manager. Met her my first day here."

"A fortuitous meeting, then?"

Jesse's raised eyebrows answered. "Parlon sold his interest in the factory and relocated to South Carolina."

Shading his eyes, Benson confessed to the remaining miles he had to go with the day's work and took the lead back to the house. Once inside, he faced a question from Kaye about the feasibility of having Rachael stay in Dana's room.

"It's cleared. Nothing else to see there."

She disregarded Jesse's glare as they approached the living room under a fake cloak of calm.

When Benson asked Kaye for Marla's contact information, Jesse left him with Kaye for a private conversation. On Jesse's return, Benson asked, "Do you make it a habit to leave your stepdaughter alone for an entire day?"

Jesse locked eyes with Kaye to see who chose to answer first.

She volunteered. "She watches JJ while I dash out shopping."

Benson shook his head. "I'm looking for something more helpful than that."

Kaye breathed out a sigh. "She had poison ivy. Planned to take her with me, but I didn't want JJ getting it. She stayed home to finish some backyard cleanup. That solved the problem." She rose from her chair. "It's not like she's a little girl. Nearly a teenager. Our babysitter, after all."

Satisfied, Benson prepared to leave but stopped at the door. "Let me ask, did she keep a diary or notes of any kind?"

Jesse twisted the knob and edged the door open. "Don't think so. As I've said, she's not the secretive type. Good to be aware, though."

A surge of weariness left them shaken, sitting at the kitchen table. Neither wanted to mention Dana. Kaye was first to find a distraction. "I can make fresh coffee if you want a thermos for your ride to the airport."

"Sounds good." He envied her energy to move while his own flagged. "Want to bring JJ and come along?"

"Probably best if you meet her alone. You'll want some time to fill her in." Her eyes softened, looking at him. "Can you do it, Jess?"

"I have to." Neither looked forward to seeing Rachael.

"Take the wagon. It's filled up."

"Thanks. I will."

She popped the lid from the coffee canister on the counter and, finding it empty, reached to an overhead shelf for a new can. An electric opener whined, springing the lid to release the familiar, sharp aroma. "Smells better than it tastes." She measured the grounds. "When does she land?"

"Around 6:30. I may stop with her for a bite of supper in case she didn't eat."

"Be careful. I don't want to lose you, too." She spoke above the sound of the running water.

"What does that mean?"

"Never mind."

He lacked the will to ponder her comment further.

CHAPTER 21

"Did you tell Pastor Connor?" The question came from Rachael to Taylor at Millingford Airport on Saturday afternoon.

"He's going to spread the word everywhere today and from the pulpit tomorrow. I'll be there, and I'll be praying one long prayer while you're away." He stopped with her by a set of seats. "Call me as soon as you land and as often as you can. I wish you'd let me fly with you. I can arrange for hotel rooms there." He added as an afterthought, "I can still make a reservation for you if you'd rather not stay at Jesse's."

"It's best to be at his location for police to reach us. I hope she'll be found by the time I get there. I'll bundle her up and bring her home."

His arm draped her shoulders where they sat beside the departure gate.

"Different scenes keep running through my mind, but I have no idea what's near the truth. Where could she be?"

When loudspeakers crackled the boarding of her flight, he held her as long as he dared. "Go with God. Come back to me and bring your daughter with you."

During the flight, Rachael sat alone, thinking about everything Jesse told her. *Please, God. Where is she? Help us find her.* To keep fear from taking over, she prayed to regain hope but, more important, for Dana to return safely. Those two requests became her prayer until arrival.

At the gate, Rachael identified Jesse by his shape and deliberate way of walking. Neither had changed since he was her husband-to-be. When their eyes met, she didn't see the scowl he had worn long after Luke had died. A new unrecognizable despair took its place.

She spoke first. "Any news?"

"Nothing. Spent time at the police station. Search and Rescue is looking." He took her suitcase. "I can tell you everything over supper if you want."

"I need to hear every detail." As she stepped off the escalator's last moving stair, she spied a payphone and said she needed to make a call.

Jesse stepped away to give her privacy. He matched her pace as she rejoined him and continued toward the exit. "Do your parents know?"

Her answer came as a nod. "I closed the shop and left a message with Dana's picture on the door. Everyone at church and the whole town knows."

"What can they do?"

"Pray—the most important thing."

He quickened his step as he headed for the exit door.

At the parking lot, she expected to see the Chrysler 300; but he stopped by the side of a Ford wagon. He'd traded the car she thought he bought to replace Luke. He was moving on.

A few miles past the airport, he turned on a side road that passed a small industrial area. A rectangular structure's stone-clad entrance emulated a huge figure guarding wire-strapped piles of stone and slate on skids. Another building, erected for the purpose of selling tires, drew attention to a colossal truck tire elevated on a grid of metal posts and cross braces. A diner of ordinary size appeared next door, their destination.

Over dinner, he described his anguish on arriving home and not finding Dana.

Rachael took in every word, although she'd heard the whole telling of it earlier. "Wasn't Kaye there?"

He alluded to Kaye's visit to Marla's place. "Dana didn't want to go. Volunteered to work in the yard." He waggled his empty fork. "We worked on a project together the day before, digging some roots. She planned to finish and cart them away."

"Must have been great fun for her."

"She volunteered," he repeated. "Didn't have to. Could have stayed in the house to read or watch TV. It's the only time we left her alone." When she said nothing, he kept talking. "We wanted to take her by surprise to the big amusement park in Charlotte. Near the airport. Colossal attraction. They're calling it a 'theme park.'"

"I'm not criticizing you, Jesse. I need to find my daughter."

"So do I." He rearranged his plate and silverware, tipped the glass, and replaced it in its original spot. "Want to hear about the police?"

She folded her napkin in preparation for listening.

The first meeting at the police station and Benson's follow-up conversations came out in bits and pieces, including the suggestion she'd run away and how ridiculous it sounded.

"How do Kaye and Dana get along?"

"Benson asked, too, but you know Dana. She gets along with everyone. And JJ. Lugs him around on her hip like a big sister who has always been here. She's incredible." He signaled the waitress for the bill. "You'll meet Benson, too, tomorrow. He'll want to hear anything you can tell him that I might not have thought of."

She listened as he answered everything but her question.

After getting settled, Jesse started the car. "Do you think Dana ever got over losing Luke?"

Her look stabbed him. "I haven't. Have you?"

He backed the Ford from the diner's parking lot and headed for the highway. "What I mean is do you think it will keep her from going on with her life?"

Resigned, she lowered her voice. "She still misses him. His name comes up often."

With changed tones, they spoke at last of Dana like they were an old, married couple headed for home, where their daughter lounged comfortably on the couch, reading.

When their conversation lagged, Rachael viewed a landscape offering little variation between the flat lands and small towns beyond Charlotte. The miles fell away while dusk approached. A mountain range in the distance suggested their destination wasn't far.

His mind went back to Luke. "Summer makes me think about Luke always wanting to go fishing. Remember?"

"Of course. It was his middle name."

"I can't forget how he wanted me to take him. I never got around to it. He took off by himself on his bike, afraid of summer being over before he'd get to go."

She held the dashboard in sight, listening.

"Did he ever tell you he begged me to take him?"

"No. Must have kept it to himself."

"I've wished a hundred times for another chance. I'd take him every weekend."

"I'm sure."

"You can bet I'll do better with JJ."

Her eyes locked on the window toward the last rays of light rimming the mountains in the darkening sky.

The words pranced about, unleashed in the air, too late to be smothered out of existence. The open car window tempted them to the outdoors, but they stayed. His hand flipped to the radio to pump sound into the pervasive quiet on the other side of the car.

She sensed he needed some benign chatter—a talent he'd never been particularly good at—to carry them to Laurelsville.

A vocal rendition of "At Last," playing on a blues station, interrupted the silence. "Dana said Elaine is getting married."

The seatbelt kept her from jolting out of her seat. "When did she say that?"

"Yesterday morning, after you called."

"That's what she told you?"

"Word for word." He seemed puzzled. "Was it supposed to be private?"

The shock wave hit her. Why such an outlandish lie? Didn't Dana want her to marry Taylor? Did the engagement have anything to do with her disappearance? Pulling her thoughts together, she turned to Jesse again. "What else did she tell you?"

"The lucky man is a teacher at Elaine's school."

Tears brimmed, despite her efforts to check them.

"What's wrong?"

Truth wasn't an option. "It was the last time I heard Dana's voice."

"I'm sorry. I wouldn't have mentioned it if I'd known it would bring this on."

"I need to think." Why did Dana hide their engagement and cover it with a story about Elaine that got more complicated by the minute? After a while, she asked again, "Those were her exact words after she hung up?"

"I'm sure."

"Can you go over the whole day again in detail? Don't leave anything out."

"Breakfast as usual. We were finishing when you called. After she hung up, she told us about Elaine, left to take a shower, and showed the poison ivy on her arm to Kaye."

"Poison ivy? Were you ever planning to tell me?" She swiveled around to see him better.

"I didn't think of it." Then lower, he added, "In light of everything else."

"What did you do about it?"

"I think Kaye gave her my prescription cream."

"Then what?"

"She skipped outside. I saw her in the backyard when I left for work. Said goodbye to each other."

"That's all? Nothing else?"

"Nothing else."

When they reached the house, Rachael strayed behind Jesse from the garage into the kitchen. Swollen eyes kept her from seeing Kaye clearly for the first time. She accepted an offer for tea but withheld an apology for her sad appearance. While the tea cooled, she obsessed over finding Dana. "I'd like to see the burn pile."

Kaye's mouth flew open. "But it's dark!"

"I know." Rachael appealed to Jesse. "Do you have a good flashlight or two?"

In response, he left for his workroom and promptly returned with one in each hand. He led the way, shining his light to show her the stairs from the dimly lit deck to the patio. She followed the flight of steps to the gravel below. The depth of the blackness thrust itself upon them. In the city, uncountable light sources foiled the night; but here, no streetlights or other illumination offered aid. Matching their low spirits, heavy clouds obscured the stars and moon.

He aimed a thin ray from afar at the lock. "The shed." No reason to go there.

They retreated in the overpowering gloom, their two narrow shafts of light insufficient to cut through any of it.

Rachael's flashlight slipped to the ground as she braced herself to keep from falling. Her hand reached for Jesse's arm but withdrew. "I didn't know." Then, in a strangled whisper, she said, "What if Dana's out there in this?"

"I try to push it away, but the thought keeps coming back."

Her throat closed in the murky surroundings that enveloped them. Grieving and hoping—but not touching—they wanted to reach out for their lost daughter.

He pressed the fallen light into his pocket, took her arm, and used his single beam to guide her back up the stairs.

Once inside, she turned down any offers of anything else to eat or drink. Kaye showed her to Dana's room and backtracked to the hall linen closet to hand her fresh towels.

Later, after showering, Rachael left the bathroom in her robe and heard Jesse and Kaye in the living room. Stepping closer to the doorway, she listened.

"You don't understand. I'd rather not see her again and know she's alive than live with the thought of anything happening to her."

"What could you have done, Jess?"

"Insisted she stay inside or left work to be here." His voice grated, raspy as a split reed. He shuffled like a sleepwalker until the walls trapped him. "I never should have brought her here."

Rachael heard a different Jesse from the one she knew and peered from the doorway.

"Am I being punished?" He folded himself into the empty corner where two living room walls met and raised both arms above his head, one hand over the other, on the ninety-degree angle where the shadows deepened. His head bowed as if a lead weight pulled it lower and lower into darkness.

Seeing his shoulders heave forward in broken breathing, Kaye flew to him. "It's my fault, too. I let you down, let her down." She pried him from the corner, flung her arms around him and hugged her head to his chest, weeping while he cried into her hair.

Rachael retreated into Dana's room and shut the door.

CHAPTER 22

Rachael spent her waking moments in the guest room praying and reading her Bible. If she had her way, she would have been in church with Taylor and Dana beside her. After breakfast, she made a request. "Can you show me the burn pile? We finally have daylight."

Jesse deserted his coffee and headed for the sliding door, Rachael behind him. "Back soon," he said to Kaye over his shoulder. "Benson's giving us an update later."

Outside, they descended the stairs to the shed. "Here's where we keep the yard equipment. I gave her the combination to the lock once, and she had it down pat. I'm sure she brought the cart out first thing." He turned to look at her. "You know how responsible she is."

From there, they crossed the yard to the south and veered west behind the yards of three neighbors to a rough footpath, curving around overgrown brushwood after the third house.

Rachael surveyed the scrub growth several yards from the pile marking the final stop for area homeowners' outdoor leftovers. "You looked here?"

"Sure. After I went through every corner of the house, I came down here to the trees and this." He stood by the pile and scanned the clearing in front, where they saw a couple of far-off houses through the trees. "Spoke to the neighbors, too, but police have combed the entire area."

"What's down there?" She threw her arm against the sun to make out the end of the clearing. A line of poplars soared like sentinels preventing trespass.

"Possibly a brook of some sort. Haven't been there."

"A place to attract Dana. She loved the run-off creeks at the lake."

Jesse knew little about Dana's way of entertaining herself while he and Luke were busy fishing. He remembered Benson's comment about mothers.

"I need to see it." Her new purpose directed her toward the creek.

Jesse had no choice but to follow.

She reached the bank, inching along to memorize every bend and ripple in the water. "It's shallow. I don't see this as a dangerous place. Do you?"

The sound of voices wafted up the creek. Jesse and Rachael began to seek them out when they heard hallooing.

Two rescue squad members, Travis and Gip, presented themselves. Embarrassed to meet the lost girl's parents, they mumbled something in sympathy. "We're with the squad today, and we're standing by for the canine-assisted search." Gip shook their hands in turn.

Jesse matched the man's firm grip. "If it takes place, when do you expect them?"

"Between nine and ten." Travis also leaned over to shake hands, stuffing them both into his pockets afterward.

"What's it like below?" Rachael shaded her eyes once more, looking.

Gip observed the flow of the water. "Locals call this Trundle Creek because it's shallow and narrow here. Runs into the Rathskill. It's wild. Grows deep and wide at what's called the Conversion."

"Can we go there?"

He drawled an explanation. "Far ways down. More mountainous, too. You'd need a whole afternoon by foot. Faster by boat, but I don't recommend it."

Put off by the man's candor, Jesse turned to Rachael. "Benson is supposed to check in today. We should get back for his call."

"Further searches will include the whole area." Travis extended his arms wide to show they were going all out to find their daughter but dropped them when he ran out of words.

It didn't matter. Dana's parents were already retracing their steps.

Rachael and Jesse were waiting on the front porch before nine o'clock. Rescue squad members, including Travis and Gip, milled around their trucks and gathered equipment. A wiry man in his fifties bounded across the yard with a pair of dogs. Benson puffed behind him. He caught up, raised an arm, and introduced the man. "Rowe Wainwright."

The hunter tipped his cap to Rachael and Jesse and hung his hand outward to the hounds. "Gunger and Molly." His dark eyes, accustomed to searching, looked out from a weathered face. He anticipated some measure of appreciation—or, at least, acknowledgment—of his fine animals.

Jesse cocked his fingers toward him as a greeting.

Rachael trudged beside Jesse and the others to the south side of the house, where everyone came to a halt by the shed.

Stepping into the shed's alcove area away from the others, Rowe conferred with Benson. The hunter bent low toward the hounds to give them a whiff of something, and the whole group took off.

Everyone followed Gunger and Molly, whose speed meant the pursuit of a definite trail. The hounds hesitated at the burn pile, turning one way and another before stopping at the side where Dana might have emptied the cart.

At some unseen signal, they took up galloping again, creating a path to the creek where they followed beside the current. They stopped farther down from Jesse and Rachael's earlier trip by a mossy log spanning the creek. They trotted across it but sniffed out no scent on the other side. Snuffling back across, they nuzzled the ground every few inches as they stalked along the bank but returned again to the center of the log.

"Ends here." Rowe stopped. "Must've gone into the stream."

"It's not deep." Rachael trailed her hand in the water, imagining Dana there earlier.

Rowe agreed. "Not enough for a decent swim."

"Might have waded and climbed out." She waited for confirmation, but no one spoke.

"Take them on down the creek and see what they do," Benson directed.

The hounds headed out in an effortless lope.

Rachael, Jesse, and the rest of the group tarried beside the creek, weighing whether to follow or wait as the dogs neared a thicker tangle of growth.

Gunger and Molly barreled forth again. Rowe followed, traveling in the natural gait of a man who has spent more of his life outdoors than in. Younger rescue squad members hurried to catch up.

Needing no further prompting, Rachael chased after them. She didn't care if she charged through a mile of thorns. Her daughter was out there.

Jesse ran, too, and reached for her arm without thinking.

She sidestepped around a tree and raced ahead of him again. *Please be alive!* No other possibility existed.

They followed far behind, hearts racing and cheeks burning. Dodging bushes and trees, they battled undergrowth that animals bounded over with ease.

The hounds chased around an outward curve by the river where the forest camouflaged them. Soon, Rowe whooped and swung a red rag over his head. The dogs frisked beside him for a handful of treats. He rewarded them before returning to the group. "Stuck in an outcrop of raspberries." He handed the bandana over to Benson, who, in turn, showed it to Jesse. Gunger and Molly circled Rowe as he reached into his pocket again.

"Must be the scarf Kaye gave her to wear. Let's ask her." Jesse reached out for it, but Benson dropped the bandana inside a brown bag before anyone else handled it.

"Nice work!" Benson slapped Rowe on the shoulder. "Let them run on down. See what else they find."

Rachael wanted to go, too. She didn't care how far, but Benson advised against it. "You're not dressed for it. Snakes and other critters live here. You don't want to run into one, with or without the dogs."

What, then, had Dana encountered?

At the house, Rachael, Jesse, and Benson occupied the deck, while rescuers continued in the far distance.

Kaye immediately identified the bandana. Not knowing what else to do, she offered to serve coffee.

Jesse turned to the detective. "What do you make of the location where the dogs found it?"

"Might have lost it anywhere in the area and wind carried it to the bushes. Dogs didn't pick up any other scent nearby."

"Think she took a dip?"

"Anything's possible."

Rachael cut in. "If she and Luke were there together, they'd end up in the creek; but I don't know if she'd go in by herself." Her hand gripped the deck railing. "She might be lying helpless, injured, unable to walk. A broken ankle or broken leg." In front of everyone, she admitted her worst fear but one that called for Dana being alive. Her mind allowed no other possibility.

Hearing someone conjure up a scenario of a loved one in great pain—but alive—wasn't new to Benson.

"If it's true, what are her chances?" Scenes of bears and other animals invaded Jesse's imagination.

"A bunch of 'ifs,' but we always have hope." Benson stretched his hand across the railing to the creek they couldn't see. "This is the third day, but it's more like forty-eight hours. We've found people lost out there much longer." He strained to hear the hounds' baying again from acres away. "Finding the bandana puts a light on everything. Makes sense to explore further down the river."

He sat, thinking, before offering an explanation. "The creek runs well beyond city limits. I'll have to yield the jurisdiction to Virgil Fairberne, the sheriff in Laurel County. We don't have the same resources as highly populated parts of the state; but his deputy, who pilots a single-engine plane, has helped in the past." He sighted in on the horizon where it might materialize to prove his statement. "County pays his expenses and a fee, but his real reward comes from finding people."

The smell of fresh-brewed coffee wafted to the deck. Kaye entered with a tray and showed Benson the phone on the kitchen wall on his way out. She poured a cup, mixed it to Jesse's liking, and handed it to him. "Tell me again where they found it."

All the while, Rachael regarded Kaye's demeanor, serving coffee as the friendliest waitress on earth. Did she care about finding Dana?

After a prolonged conversation, Benson returned. "Fairberne says the pilot can go out today if the weather holds. If not, then tomorrow." He waited while Kaye filled his cup. "Here's more news. We're expanding the search for volunteers on foot if efforts of police, sheriff, and rescue teams—including dogs—don't find her. There's a meeting at the Methodist church tomorrow night. Seven o'clock. You ought to be there in case we can't answer everything on our own." His hand reached into the pocket that held his cache of cigarettes but fell away. "A piece of advice: it might be rough because people who have done land and water rescues will advise on specifics for volunteers to hone in on. You might want to hang at the back."

A pattering sound on the aluminum deck roof increased to the persistent rattle of a rainstorm. Rachael took in the changes in the weather. "Would an earlier rain have washed away any trace for the dogs to follow?"

"It's likely," Benson said.

"It held off for us." She sighed. "Has to be a sign we're going to find her." Silently, she added, "Alive."

CHAPTER 23

A white-hot sun dominated a clear sky in Laurelsville, burning off any moisture from the previous day. Jesse and Rachael, on their way at the Laurel County Sheriff's office on Monday afternoon, didn't allude to what they might learn when they arrived there.

Not at all chatty like Benson, Sheriff Fairberne towered over them in a uniform jacket that hung at his sides over an expansive girth. Belying a rough exterior, his eyes bore the look of sympathy—or perhaps weariness—from cases delivering a devastating outcome.

Aware of that possibility, Rachael did her best to dismiss it.

The sheriff tipped his graying head to them. He nudged his thumb toward a stocky man in his late forties, whose sandy hair met a darker color of rust in his trim beard. "This here's Deputy Trey Garvey. Flies a single-engine Piper Comanche. Booked uncountable manhunt hours over the past ten years." His shoulder turned to the other man. "Grady Shonemeyer, the naturalist who accompanied him this morning. We like to have another person trained in search skills."

Jesse eyeballed them to see if they met his personal standards to search for his daughter.

Neither offered a verbal greeting but tilted their heads in keeping with the sheriff's manner of communicating. Unfolding a map on a table, the pilot directed Jesse and Rachael to come in close. "We flew over Laurelsville, across the Stone Mountain neighborhood and runoff creek to the confluence at the Rathskill River. Followed it from there over rough water to Highstep Falls and beyond." A damaged, misshapen fingernail traced their route on the map. "Took several passes parallel to the river. Then into thicker, wooded areas." He relaxed his arms and gestured to Grady to take over.

Thirty-five-year-old Grady, small-framed but muscular and sporting a ponytail, pored over the map. A flat slash of a mouth allowed his lips minimal movement. "We observed no unusual signs. The survivability rate for people caught in this part of the Rathskill doesn't register well. It races from Hilltop Mountain, hits a wall of stone, and curves downward in a collision at the creek. Like a Boeing 747 crushing a Cessna." His fist skidded off his other palm.

He disregarded Rachael's choking sound. "A few cabins still exist in the forested areas below. Most are deep in the mountains and no longer inhabited. The water's cold, even though this isn't the coldest time of year. Still cold enough for someone in it."

Fairberne flattened his hand on the map and held the two men in his gaze. "You found nothing of the girl, then? No sign at all?"

"That's it, sir." Grady answered for both men.

"I can make another pass if you think it will help," Trey offered. "We'll be at the church tonight, but I'm on standby if you need me."

"Can you tell us more about where the rivers connect?" Rachael tried to recall the name. "Has anyone ever made it past there?"

"The Conversion itself is as rough as it gets. The noise level there is enough to scare you. Over the years, few have made it through. We've lost fishermen there and kids swimming on a dare." He stopped when he saw Jesse's look of horror.

Rachael turned to him. "We haven't found her yet. There's still hope."

Kaye chewed the inside of her cheek before Jesse and Rachael left for the pre-search organizing meeting at the Methodist church in the evening.

More than once in the past two days, they had left her at home to care for JJ rather than cart him to the police department or other places involved in the search.

She studied their actions as they walked out the door, knowing the seriousness of finding their lost child could bring them closer together. Although they weren't looking at each other, she thought about their companionship when alone. It added up to Jesse spending more time in his ex-wife's company than hers.

Her worst worry about Dana's disappearance centered on her squabble with Jesse. Was it the reason Dana left? Or did it distract her from being wary of someone who might lure her away? Guilt weighed on her, especially as she tried to imagine the depth of Rachael's anxiety for her missing child.

Today, a new alarm rang in her mind, one involving her own future. When she had married Jesse, she knew he didn't earn as much as her former husband; but having someone faithful who loved her was more important. Now, an unutterable fear threatened her reason for marrying him. She promised herself anew to keep a sharper eye on both of them.

Joining a line of people to the church basement, Jesse and Rachael surveyed the room to locate seats far from the center. They recognized Shane, Kenny, and Bobby Ray in the crowd.

A hand on Jesse's shoulder turned him toward Benson. "Lots of volunteers are here. Grady Shonemeyer is going to conduct the main part of the meeting. You may have met him. He's been holding others like this in towns along the Rathskill." He excused himself from a brief attempt at small talk when he saw Grady in front of the room.

After everyone was seated, Benson held high a flyer with Dana's picture on the front. "If you know of additional places to post these, extra copies are on the side table. Most businesses have them already." His brief history of search efforts covered police in the neighborhood, canine search near the river, and the plane for an aerial view. He introduced Grady, listing the credits of his outdoor expertise, including a decade of tracking in Western North Carolina.

Grady assumed a humble stance during the applause. "I trust you've had a chance to go through the pamphlet distributed at the door. Stop by the table if you didn't receive one. Now, if you'll turn your attention to page three for a comprehensive search list, I'll review and leave questions for the end." He ruffled through a sheaf of bundled pages. "According to the report, the Foster girl wore a red T-shirt, denim shorts, and white sandals." He pronounced the items slowly. "Be on the lookout for clothing or shreds of hair on bushes, trees, or undergrowth. Stay alert and be aware of your surroundings at all times."

He checked to make sure everyone was following him. "Also, note any evidence of camping or areas of matted undergrowth.

Someone—even someone lacking good intent—may have found her. Let nothing escape your attention."

A hand shot up in the middle of the room. "So should we expect to find a live person or a body at this point?"

Every muscle in Rachael's body tensed as Grady answered. "We're hoping for the girl to be alive, conscious or unconscious. Tomorrow's groups will include the area above Highstep Falls. Down below will be a different kind of rescue." He scanned the room for more hands, keeping his manner as serious as a professor answering students' questions on the economy.

"How long does it take for a drowning victim to surface?" A collective gasp echoed through the room.

A whisper caught Rachael's ear. "Where do these people come from?"

Grady continued, unfazed, in seminar mode. "Depends on a number of factors, including water temperature. That's territory for people trained in water search-and-rescue." A cough came from a listener, but the entire room's attention stayed on the speaker. "A logical directive is to look downstream from where the person went into the water. In this case, the dogs lost her scent in a shallow runoff creek. The absence of clothing or shoes on the bank leads us to believe she didn't take a swim, but she may have tripped or waded in for whatever reason. She also may have emerged. We don't know. Earlier investigations from there to the Conversion disclosed only the bandana. It either blew off; or she dropped it, and it caught in the bushes. It's proof of her presence there. Somewhere."

Sounds of discussion hummed through the room.

Grady signaled for quiet by holding one arm out, hand raised, like a pastor giving a blessing. When the talking abated, he began again.

"We will begin at the runoff creek. Line up from the bank outward into the woods and walk with the current, in sight of each other. Don't deviate from the plan."

Someone yelled out, "What time?"

"Six thirty, sharp." A visual sweep of both sides of the room showed no objections. "Assemble at the police station for more instructions and carpool from there. We want to be at the creek no later than seven. We'll traverse the yard past her father's house and four other houses through cleared acres. The search by the creek begins where the clearing ends."

When the meeting broke up, Jesse headed for the door to keep from having to talk to anyone. As he held the car door for her, he said, "I'm not ready to go home yet. I need to get away."

"What do you want to do?"

"There's a small place on the other side of town that serves light fare. It's quiet, and the lighting's subdued. You can have some tea or whatever you want."

On the drive over, Rachael mulled over the meeting, searching for something positive. "I'm impressed by the number of people willing to give their time."

"Sure, but there's been no sight or sound of her. Doesn't that bother you?" His hands tightened on the wheel.

"She can't answer if she's lying out there unconscious. May have hit her head."

A sound between a grunt and a sigh came from his side of the car.

"Don't give up. I haven't."

Even though she wanted to believe what she said, they rode to their destination bundled in their own pain.

Once inside, he chose a dimly lit side booth and ordered two glasses of apple cider. Neither alluded to the meeting's new horrors. They ended up talking about Dana and how she kept up with Luke and his wild antics. Their conversation centered on her past, avoiding her future.

During a lull, Jesse rolled the glass between his hands, seeming to try to summon the courage to speak about his fears, even after their years of shared life.

Sensing his half-attempt, she waited but gave up on second-guessing him. "We should get back if we want to see the volunteers at 6:30. It comes early."

The drained glass reflected his empty eyes. He paid the bill. She didn't ask if he often stopped there alone.

To Rachael's amusement, Kaye met them in an apron, appearing to have puttered in the kitchen the entire time they were gone.

Kaye's greeting sailed toward Jesse. "Shane called for you after the meeting." Her voice stayed flat, perhaps to keep from accusing him. "About 8:30."

"It's too late. I'll talk to him tomorrow." He locked the door behind him.

Rachael wanted to say they needed a place to think afterward; but the explanation belonged to Jesse, who offered nothing at all.

Kaye's cheeriness prevailed. "How was it?"

"Rough." He gravitated toward her, threw his arm around her shoulder, and guided her down the hall toward their room. "It's a good thing you weren't there."

Rachael, following ghostlike behind them, observed the less-than-candid partnership between Jesse and his new wife. When she reached the guestroom door, she heard Kaye call out, "Good night," followed by a muffled, "Where've you been?"

She shut the door and heard nothing else.

CHAPTER 24

Although search-and-rescue teams in the county and neighboring ones were still active, the expanded search with volunteers in Laurelsville began on Tuesday morning. Against a leaden sky, a mass of clouds in a wide waterfall shape disclosed a heavy downpour miles away. Rachael began to wonder if it ever stopped raining in this part of the country. "What do you think of Benson's request that family members not accompany the volunteers?" She had no one else to ask but Jesse.

"May be the usual practice."

They suspected Benson didn't want them there. Five days had already passed since Dana's disappearance. Each additional hour worked against finding her alive. That knowledge was too desolate to discuss.

Searchers filed by, while Rachael and Jesse watched from the deck. No one waved. Many wore backpacks like a group of scouts going camping.

She left her coffee cup on a side table to keep the group in view beyond the curve. "Let's go as far as the burn pile to be closer. No one will know."

In truth, he wanted to be there, too, eyeing every stem and leaf of plant growth and the base of every tree and bush again.

In minutes, they found their feet ahead of their minds on a path beaten into the grass by rescuers and volunteers in a search growing more desperate each day. The air brought the sound of people calling, too far away for their words to be distinct.

The huge mound of clippings had become a new fixture in Rachael's life. "The dogs sniffed all around the whole burn pile area, didn't they?"

"They did." His lips pressed together for strength as he took stock of the area for a hidden sign to lead them to Dana. "Where is she?" Caving in to his feelings, he turned from the pile and Rachael's eyes.

Seeing his state of distress, she folded him in her arms, the way she'd held Luke when he had a skinned knee.

"I was wrong." The words came from the fathomless place that contained them for too long.

She stepped back.

"About Luke. It wasn't your fault. He didn't get to grow up. I took my anger out on everyone—on God, on you."

She listened.

"It's too late to undo everything. I have another family."

"We've all moved on."

"No. You don't know. I've been thinking how my future hopes for Luke have to be fused into a double dose of love for Dana. She's been shortchanged, like you." His voice cracked again. "Now I don't know where she is." His eyes fastened on the horizon. "Let her be alive."

She needed to calm him, give him faith again. "Pray with me."

Bowing his head, he listened.

One of her hands rested on his shoulder while she prayed.

As the sun broke through the glass doors, Kaye saw Jesse guiding Rachael by the elbow over rough ground. She kept them in sight until their shadows dwindled to nothing. She raced down the hall to ensure JJ still slept, allowing her to follow them. She took the steps two at a time and darted through the adjoining yards, fearing JJ might awaken in her moment of absence.

At the bend, she detected movement and something else through the trees. A spot of indigo—the color of Rachael's top. She lurked near the foliage of a nearby yard, as silent as a cat stalking its prey. What she saw made her gasp. Rachael held Jesse in her embrace.

She spun around and fled for home. Breathing in short bursts, she ran flat out and made it up the deck stairs. The kitchen air pressed heavy enough to choke her. She collapsed, head in her hands, to sort it out.

Should she confront them when they returned? With no sign of Dana, holding off was the only thing to do. But their image confirmed that Jesse's ex-wife was trying to woo him back. Or did he initiate it?

The sounds of volunteers became muffled in the distance. Seeing no reason to tarry in the field, the broken couple plodded toward the house.

Streaks of mascara were drying on Kaye's cheeks when she handed them the *Laurelsville News*, a weekly newspaper bearing the day's date: Tuesday, August 13, 1974. Jesse unfolded it to see Dana smiling at him from her school picture under a large headline. He read it aloud:

MISSING GIRL'S SCARF FOUND

The first piece of evidence in the investigation into the disappearance of 12-year-old Dana Foster came Sunday when a canine search team found a bandana beside Trundle Creek in the Stone Mountain neighborhood.

Detective Jed Benson, spokesman for the Laurelsville Police Department, said the girl's stepmother confirmed it as the scarf she gave Dana on Friday. The girl was reported missing that evening.

"This is an important find for us," Benson said. "The dogs traced her from the home of her father and stepmother, Jesse and Kaye Foster, to the creek. The trail turned cold when it reached the water."

The search team followed the stream for another quarter of a mile and found the bandana in thick brush. It carried the scents of the missing girl and her stepmother. Foul play has not been ruled out.

The missing girl, 4'11" with dark blonde hair and blue eyes, was wearing a red T-shirt, denim shorts, and white sandals. Anyone who saw a girl matching the description should report sightings to Laurelsville Detective Benson or Virgil Fairberne, Laurel County sheriff.

Foster failed to find his daughter in the house or yard when he returned home from work on Friday and called police.

The girl, who lives in Fenton, New York with her mother, had been visiting her father and stepmother for the summer.

See page 5

After finishing, Jesse turned to a page with shots of the creek bank, where Dana had allegedly strayed. "It looks like they interviewed Benson late on Sunday or Monday morning. The rest came from the police docket."

"Why is it being reported now?" Rachael asked.

"It's a weekly." He flung it on the table. "Written Sunday night before layout and sent to the printer for today's distribution. Depends on their process. Notice there's nothing about last night's meeting."

Retrieving it, Rachael read what it said about Dana.

Kaye's tearful eyes shifted from one to the other.

Jesse stopped thinking about the paper in Rachael's hands to focus on his wife, who didn't speak as she stayed, unmoving, near the table. Unusual for her. "Afraid this implies we're uncaring parents?"

"No one asked us. Not a single reporter called." Kaye wiped at a dark smudge on her face. "The story implicates me. Ask Benson who he thinks might be involved in 'foul play.'" Quietness overtook her.

Rachael took advantage of the temporary silence. "I'm going for a walk."

"And still no sign of Dana." Kaye was crying openly, seeming to pay little attention to Rachael as she shut the door. "Did something terrible happen? Or did she run away because she heard our argument?"

He walked her to a chair and sat in another beside her. "I keep asking that, too, but I don't have any answers."

༄

When Rachael headed out the door minutes earlier, rain stopped her. She dallied on the porch while the kitchen voices diminished to a mumble, allowing her return to Dana's room to wait it out.

She thought about reversing the charges on Jesse's phone to tell Taylor about the news story but held off, hoping for a report from the search people. It would be better to talk to him tonight when he wasn't busy. Sporadic rain fell until Jesse alerted her from the hall.

"I'm off to give some thoughts to Benson." Jesse held the rolled-up newspaper.

She accompanied him, toting her umbrella.

On the way, Rachael wondered what they could accomplish with another visit, especially one to please Kaye.

At Benson's desk, Jesse stabbed the accusing words. "What about this?"

Though Benson saw it earlier, he read it again and pushed it aside. "This suggests I made a shady connection to the bandana." A tail of smoke rose from a cigarette in an ashtray. "Whenever there's a missing person case, family members become suspects; but I'm not suggesting any of you were involved. The bandana is our strongest proof of where she must have gone. Whether she got out or not is the next big question. We need to keep scouring the creek area and the river below."

He processed his thoughts by recounting what they already knew. The dogs tracked her to the creek, lost the trail there, and found her red scarf in the bushes without any other sign of her. Aerial and ground searches brought nothing.

Below the Rathskill Conversion, Highstep Falls remained a specter.

A man in uniform beckoned from the hall. Benson made a timeout sign to show his visitors he'd be back.

On his return, he relayed a report from Grady. Some volunteers gave up in the rain, despite their ponchos. The most stalwart among them built lean-tos and vowed to make it to the falls, even if they had to stay overnight.

"The final group insisted they saw a double rainbow, something he hasn't spotted in a while. Grady said, 'Be sure to tell her folks. I'd guess they're in need of a sign. They struck me as believers.'"

Benson added his own reassurance. "Grady's not a trifling guy. Gives me reason to think we're going to find her yet."

Rachael's eyes rose to the sun breaking through the window.

CHAPTER 25

Wednesday morning brought an unwelcome guest: a feeling of despair. Rachael lingered in her room, trying to dismiss the sinister cloak that threatened to envelop her. When she finally went to the kitchen for coffee, Jesse flagged her.

Car keys jiggled in his hands as he headed for the garage. "Let's go. Sounds like they found the dragonfly. I'll tell you on the way."

He talked fast as he drove. "A fisherman and his son chanced upon an object and took it to the police station after seeing posters of Dana. Benson described it as a gold and silver bug-like piece of jewelry. In bad shape. Think it's hers?"

In the detective's office, they identified it immediately. Realizing Dana was wearing it on the last day anyone saw her left Rachael breathless.

"Where did they find it?" Jesse passed it to her.

"Not far above the Conversion. Can't say where, exactly. Trundle Creek is wide there. The fisherman told a sergeant on duty how a curve outward in the bank created a small pool. Fish like to hide there. Good for dropping in a line."

Turning it over in her hands, Rachael studied it more closely. Tiny golden legs twisted underneath, one severed in half. Two diamond chips survived. The other eight were missing.

Benson saw her gentleness with it. "Must have been a special necklace or pin."

"Belonged to me. Years ago." New images joined her worst fears as thoughts of Dana kidnapped, injured in the forest, or possibly drowned, returned.

He waited to hear more, but nothing came from either parent. They looked at the damaged piece—not at each other. "Light caught the tiniest glint in the muddy bank where they could see it."

Rachael forced herself to speak. "This means she passed not far from where they discovered it."

"Like the bandana, it's additional proof of being in or near the water—but this time, nowhere near the raspberry bushes." He reached for anything to bring hope. "Volunteer groups are in communities farther south. Team leaders reported combing the areas close to you and continuing down the river." When they showed no sign of relief, he added, "If the fisherman can locate the exact spot, we'll bring in the dogs again."

"Please." She looked straight at him to make sure he heard. "Will you? For Dana and for us?"

As much as she needed encouragement, his reassurance didn't bring what she wanted.

Back at the house, Rachael gave Kaye the dragonfly while Jesse recounted the story of finding it.

Kaye's state of mind in waiting for their return kept her from thinking about the necklace. She'd wanted to go, too, but Jesse would have questioned dragging JJ to a police station.

Rachael reclaimed the dragonfly. "The river must be the answer. First the bandana and now this. I need to go there to see if they missed some clues. It's frustrating sitting here doing nothing."

Jesse volunteered, "Let's do it. We still have half the morning and the whole afternoon."

Kaye's face lit up. "Hey, I'll join you, too." To his quizzical expression, she said, "You never know what an extra pair of eyes might see."

Seemingly oblivious to any hidden meaning, he took the basement stairs, shouting orders like a Parris Island drill sergeant. "Put on long pants and a hat. I'll bring the canteens."

"Let me call Sally to take care of JJ." Minutes later, Kaye dashed through the house, the blue diaper bag swinging from her shoulder and JJ jabbering from her hip while Jesse loaded the folded playpen into the big car.

They returned from Sally and Shane's house after 9:30.

"Sorry for the delay." Kaye's apology sounded sincere. "I needed to give some instructions."

Time collapsed into moments as the three traveled the trodden path and stopped by the burn pile.

"Is this where she left the yard cart?" Kaye glued her eyes on Jesse instead of guiding them elsewhere for clues. It was obviously her first visit there.

Rachael breathed in the humid air, different from the mountains of New York, and waited for his answer to Kaye.

"Near here." He flattened his palm next to the pile's edge. "Left undisturbed like she strolled away." A croaking sound unmasked his fear.

The women tried to keep their own emotions in check.

In the silence, flying insects looped in the air while those less mobile leaped from stem to stem. He slapped a mosquito on his cheek. "Let's go. We need to make time."

In broad-brimmed hats and smelling of mosquito repellent, Rachael and Kaye followed behind to keep from making a new trail in the meadow. Missing all of those protections, Dana risked exposure to weather, bugs, and other woodland inhabitants.

When they approached the creek beyond the thickening trees, Kaye cooed over it without stepping too close. "A cute little stream. And not too deep."

Jesse threw her a frown. "It gets deeper. And wider."

She stopped talking.

He continued beside it as they followed, bumping along and overlooking the subtle way it widened as the current deepened. At the rotted, mossy branch spanning it, he clarified for Kaye. "The dogs traced her this far."

"Did they sniff out the other side, too?" She pressed one foot on the branch and brushed her fingers over the moss.

"They did, but they didn't find anything over there. The water's where she must have gone. What do you think?" He looked to Rachael for the answer. "Think she'd want to swim here?"

"She and Luke did plenty of crazy things." Rachael crouched beside the water. "Looks safe enough, doesn't it?" She used her perception at its most penetrating level to see any new sign. What did she expect? A footprint, handprint, scrap of torn clothing? After a few disappointing minutes, she gazed toward the sky to clear her vision.

Jesse's impatience intervened. "Let's go. We've just started." Following the water's edge, he spoke for his wife's benefit. "We can show you where the bushes caught the bandana." A while later, at the outgrowth of raspberry bushes a few yards from the creek, he stopped. "In here, somewhere."

"Did the dogs track down anything else?" Kaye used the stop to scrape mud from her new white sneakers on a fallen limb.

Rachael thought about the bandana to keep from thinking of anything else. "She didn't wear it into the water. If it was waterlogged, it wouldn't have been in the bushes."

Jesse urged them again. "Let's push on. More to go yet."

As they tramped along, Rachael called out, "Dana! Dana! It's me! Can you hear me?"

The others took up calling, too. They'd pause to listen and resume shouting. It served another purpose. Sound encouraged creatures to run away.

Across the river, a mountain cliff broadcasted its enormous size. The water's flow continued, tumultuous and gaining speed. They attributed its quickening velocity to their own individual panic playing tricks on them.

They fought through dense vegetation. Jesse found a branch small enough to carry and sturdy enough to slash annoying vegetation, parting a way without the hatchet he didn't bring. He led them through sedge and several species of bog plants and zebra grass. Raspberries and chokeberries thrived there as well—proof of bear country.

Constant yelling made them thirsty. They sipped from their canteens and feared their supply running out too soon. They took turns calling until the tributary's bellowing threatened. The roaring hit their ears full on. Their terror was greater than someone coming upon it for the first time—they already knew about it and heard the stories. Fear made them stop when the deeper river splashed high as it slammed around rocks, overtaking the creek with turbulence beyond their worst nightmares. Boulders jutted from the water down river.

"How could anyone make it past there?" Kaye pointed to the largest rocks. "Imagine trying to get to the bank here, especially if she was hurt."

Rachael moaned with the sound of a wounded animal. Seeing the rivers collide, she wanted to shake her fist at the element that stole her son. She refused to surrender her daughter to it, too. It came to her that she was raging against water that couldn't hear her. Still, she knew nothing about where Dana might be or if a force of nature was responsible. She braced her shoulder against a tree and prayed for strength to go on.

Beyond the spray of water from the tributary, the scarp in the background wept from every crevasse and gully. Her body felt like that wounded stone, but her determination grew stronger than ever. "We need to keep going."

"I can't." Kaye leaned against Jesse.

Not about to stop, Rachael said, "This is where the real danger begins. She may have come this far safely, but down below . . ."

Jesse couldn't side with both of them.

Rachael understood. "Wait here." Choosing where to step, she detoured around a copse of mountain laurel blocking the way and doubled back toward the river again. Staying close to the water gave her a clear route. She wanted to screen every inch of bark, every square of soil under every shrub; but urgency moved her onward. Forgetting her own safety, she crashed through the forest, trying to match the hounds' speed while undergrowth snarled around her feet. She thought about Dana lacking safeguards of any kind.

In a hurried step, she tripped on a curved root hidden by seasons of rotting leaves. She fell hard, plowing her hands into wild ground cover. A stab of pain shot through her left foot as it bent under. A viscous substance stuck to her skin from the unusual foliage where she landed. Able to move, she pushed herself up. Cuts marked her hands, and black, root-enriched humus clung to every part of her that connected with the ground.

Jesse used his hands as a megaphone. "You can't go on alone! Too dangerous."

Her foot throbbed with each step as she struggled to get back to them. She hurt all over; but worse, a damaged spirit returned with her.

When Kaye held out her arms in a comforting gesture, ready to help, Rachael didn't respond.

Kaye's ready chatter covered the rebuff. "We didn't know any of this existed. We would have told Dana. What could have tempted her to come to the creek?"

Dealing with injury and frustration, Rachael brushed hitchhiking remnants from her fall. They had failed to bring boots, proper equipment, or first aid. If they'd been so foolish, even with the advantage of preparation, how did Dana fare in a T-shirt and shorts? In surrender, she propped herself against another tree. "Give me a minute." Assurance wavering, she bowed her head.

While Jesse led the way back, the river's wild current carried away their hope. For all their efforts, they found no encouraging signs. They hiked in silence to keep from talking about it.

Above the Conversion, Rachael asked them to stop. "My hands are itching like fire." She plunged them into the coolness of the river, but it gave short-lived relief.

"Let them soak for a few minutes." Jesse splashed water on his face while they waited. "Aeration here makes it clean enough to drink." He refilled all their canteens before they took off again.

As they hiked, Rachael observed Jesse's silence as a way of grieving for Dana, but she couldn't imagine why Kaye made the effort to come along.

"I have to slow down." Rachael raised her pant leg. "I twisted my ankle in the fall." Swelling at the arch of her foot distended over the side of her shoe.

"Take your shoe off." Jesse knelt to help her untie it.

"I don't dare. I'll never get it back on."

Jesse pushed himself up. "You and Kaye stay here while I go for help."

"Don't leave us here," Rachael said. "We need to get back. I'll take care of it later."

The house threw off long shadows from a deep sunset at their return. Inside and finally sitting, Rachael noticed small blisters dotting the palms of her hands.

"What did you land in?" Jesse moved in for a closer look.

"No idea. Lots of low foliage where I fell."

"Could be spurge. Gives off milky sap that sticks to you. Soap and water won't wash it off—over a thousand species of the stuff." He gave her rubbing alcohol and paper towels.

She did her best and limped off to the bedroom. A tug at her shoelace released her foot, blown up twice its normal size. She lay on the bed and propped her foot on two pillows.

Kaye offered her an ice pack, as well as a tube of medication. "It's Jess's prescription for poison ivy. He thinks it might help your blisters."

An ashen line, tinged in purple, ran from Rachael's heel below the anklebone to the center of her arch, parallel to the sole of her foot. It could have been dirt wedged under her sock, she thought at first glance; but rubbing it changed nothing. And it hurt.

Rachael heard Jesse call Shane, who soon arrived with JJ, Sally, and a homemade dinner of meatloaf, mashed potatoes, and green beans.

"Thanks." Jesse's voice sounded tired. "If ever we needed this, today is the day."

Rachael heard the other voices and imagined a thankful Kaye snuggling with JJ and chatting with Sally.

Then, suddenly, Kaye appeared in the doorway. "They fixed dinner for us. Want me to bring it to you?"

"No. I'll eat at the table. If I stay here alone, I might sink under sheets and never come out."

CHAPTER 26

After another restless night, Jesse woke and told Kaye he needed to check in at the mill. His daily phone contact with the foreman wasn't enough. He had to be there to ensure efficient operations. And maybe it would take his mind off the search for Dana that had, so far, revealed nothing.

Wiping sleep from her eyes, Kaye stumbled to the kitchen. While the coffee perked, she saw his pathetic form hunched at the counter, shoulders sagging. "How much longer is she going to stay here?"

"As long as she needs to." The question scratched itself deeper into his mind. "You know Rachael has every right to say, 'I sent Dana here on good faith you'd take care of your only daughter, my only child. I trusted you'd care for her like the irreplaceable treasure she is.' But she hasn't said it, has she?"

"Why do you take her side?"

He sighed and dropped his hands. "I'm trying to balance you out."

"If you think so much of her, why did you leave her?"

"She's a good woman, Kaye, and I walked away. A good woman."

"And I'm not?" Her voice rose in frustration.

"I need you more than ever, and you refuse to hear me." His eyes sunk smaller and deeper. "I wasn't in my best mind after Luke."

She screamed from across the room. "What mind are you in now?"

"Stop, Kaye. Stop. I met you at the lowest point of my life. You listened to me. You helped me climb from my darkness, convinced me to go on. I have another son in there, sleeping—one I never dreamed of having—and he's not like Luke. He's unique, and I love him. And you." He negotiated his way to her. "Please. Help me through this."

Heaving a sob, she let him hold her. "We need each other now. We always will."

Taylor hadn't heard from Rachael. He punched in Jesse's phone number, the one she had given him for an emergency. He strained to hear while a voice on the other end, probably Jesse's wife, agreed to get Rachael. A long wait.

His up-early-and-at-'em fiancée still sleeping at noon? He finally heard her, but not in a way he expected. Her voice confirmed his fear. Unable to make out anything, he broke into her mumbling. "Talk to me, Rache. I need to know what's going on. I haven't heard from you. Any news?"

He made out *found* and what sounded like *dragonfly*. "Isn't it a positive sign? There's been no—" He almost said "remains" but changed it to "trace of her."

To keep her coherent, he reviewed everything from when she last phoned. She began to come around, enough for him to piece together a short but garbled version of yesterday's desperate hike with Jesse and Kaye.

"You can't give up. Listen to me. I'm coming down there. I'll cancel my appointments." He nodded, even though she couldn't see. "I'm off to the airport as soon as I can check the best connection to Charlotte or Greenville-Spartanburg and throw clothes in a bag. I'll rent a car when I get there. It'll be evening or later." His inner planning mode took over. "If it's late, I'll stay in a hotel and find you in the morning; but I'm aiming for tonight."

Sobbing came from the receiver.

"Hold on. I'll be there soon." He made a kissing sound into the phone. "Rache? We're going to find her." He believed it himself when he said it.

Deep in a dream, Rachael was swimming from the bottom of a wide well, struggling in a circle of turbulence, unable to get out. Someone flailed against the other side, in danger of going under. She looked closer. Dana! Every time Rachael reached out, her arms shrank to tiny stubs.

Insistent hammering echoed from the top of the well.

A gasp like that of a drowning person's intake of air woke her. She fought daylight because she recognized nothing. Fear folded in on her again, tempting her to sink back to sleep; but the knocking resumed, even louder, and brought her around. She fumbled toward the sound and twisted the doorknob.

"A phone call for you." Kaye led her to the kitchen.

Working herself dreamlike into her robe, Rachael guided one arm into a sleeve and then the other. Step by step, she reached the handset. She rambled unintelligibly until a few clear words emerged. "Found . . . dragonfly . . . I know, I know . . . can't give up . . . help . . ." She sobbed into the mouthpiece. "Will you?"

As soon as the phone clicked into its holder, Kaye reentered the kitchen. "How about coffee? Or lunch?"

"No, thanks. I'm not hungry."

"What can I do for you?"

"I'll be leaving soon. Possibly tonight." A hand against the wall steadied her. "I have to pack."

"There's no need to leave. Use the room as long as you want."

"You've been more than kind." Floating toward the bedroom, she shut the door, thinking about a way to clear the fog. She pulled the luggage from the closet, opened a drawer, folded one item of clothing, and transferred it to Dana's duffel. One done.

Plenty of summer clothes in drawers and the closet waited to be packed. Turning over each piece among tops, shorts, and socks, she concentrated on her daughter's belongings like rediscovered treasures before stowing them away. She tried to forget the pajamas in police custody.

Deep in a drawer, a hard lump hid underneath a handkerchief next to a tube of lotion. A geode's dark purple crystals reflected different hues in each contrasting angle of light. No surprise that it had attracted Dana. She wrapped it in the handkerchief and secured it in Dana's bag. Reacting to a noise, she cracked the door.

Kaye held out two more shining geodes. "You can add these to Dana's things. She stumbled on them in our yard and fell in love with them."

Rachael rubbed the smooth and rough textures. Uncanny coincidence and timing made it seem that Kaye possessed a type of stealth enabling her to see through walls.

"You say she found them outside?"

"We took them because we wanted to save them in a memory box for her—as a surprise memento of her stay here."

Both women fell silent. A memory box for a missing girl.

Rachael tucked the additional geodes beside the other one.

Jesse said he'd be home by mid-afternoon; but when he didn't show, Kaye called him. "I think Rachael has someone else in her life."

He recognized the mix of gossip and confidentiality that etched her voice. "How do you know? She's said nothing to me."

"A man called for her. She cried when he hung up and went to the room to pack. Says she's leaving soon. I'm afraid she heard our argument this morning. You should talk to her."

"I'm on my way."

Before long, the garage door grumbled and the car eased in. Then he was there, securing Kaye in a hug. "Everything okay with you?" Emphasis on "you." He followed with, "Where is she?"—his real question.

She fluttered her fingers toward the hall. "In the room."

Outside the guest room, he gave a polite hello and waited. "Have time for a cup of tea on the deck?"

Dallying in the kitchen, he kept an upbeat manner, while Kaye prepared coffee and tea and left the two alone on the deck.

"You're packing?"

"Yes. It's time."

"You can stay, you know. We're happy to have you." He didn't know what else to say and added, "The search is ongoing."

"I'm not leaving town yet." She told him about Taylor and produced a snapshot.

Jesse recognized at once the tanned, confident man standing beside Rachael and Dana in front of My Mother's Pottery shop. He didn't want to imagine her with Taylor, yet there they were. Jesse had known him for years, professionally. Yardley Mills hired him as a legal consultant on occasion. Checking the picture again, he compared himself in a size fifteen shirt to the broad build of the man who wore at least a twenty but was balding early. Jesse took pride in his full head of hair. After leaving Fenton, he had encouraged her to find someone else but imagined her loyalty to him would keep her from choosing anyone, least of all a lawyer with money to burn.

Bringing out the photo bordered on impulsivity for Rachael. Making it worse, she blurted, "We're getting married."

What had compelled her to say it—especially thinking of the possibility that Dana might not be there to witness it.

"Didn't Dana tell you?"

"It's news to me. She told us about Elaine's engagement but not yours." He almost shook her hand but kept it idle. "Congratulations."

The engagement phone call and Dana's subsequent lie churned in her mind.

Kaye poked her head through the doorway. "Anyone need a refill?"

"Look." He handed Rachael's picture to her. "It's her friend."

"Ooh. Is this the man on the phone this morning?" Kaye eyed it up close.

"He's flying down. Maybe by tonight."

"They're engaged." Jesse said, still grappling with the thought of Rachael with Taylor.

"Hooray for you!" Not an unusual exclamation for Kaye, but her elation rose like a helium balloon. She returned the photo to Rachael.

"If he's here in time for dinner, we can barbecue. If you think he'd like ribs."

"He might." Rachael held her cup with both hands. "He doesn't know exactly when he'll get here. May be late."

"I'll plan for it in case."

The telephone rang. Jesse stepped inside, relieved for an excuse to exit.

CHAPTER 27

Mountains of Western North Carolina
August 1974

A boy was fishing. He sat astride a tree trunk that extended horizontally a few yards over the river. Its hidden roots, twice as long as the trunk, stretched under a gentle hill that met the water's edge. It was Friday, but it didn't matter much because days in the mountains ran together without a schedule to follow except to check the garden's produce.

The day promised a dinner of fresh trout. He seldom met disappointment in a good catch because no other family lived anywhere near, and fishermen didn't fight untamed woods to throw in a line far down the river when it was easier upstream.

He surveyed the surrounding forest for nuances in every deciduous tree or pine that appeared unchanged to outsiders. Discovering a new seedling gave him deeper satisfaction than if he had planted the seed himself. Unhurried, he pondered the density of a wet year's undergrowth compared to a dry one, absently staring at the bare roots that clutched the opposite bank, groping for water and twisting like wooden sculptures. In shallow times, jutting rocks joined the rapids upstream; but few invaded the smooth depth of his fishing area.

The river's current, rolling beneath his feet and never stopping, brought unending amazement. Mesmerized by its depth and constant movement, he wondered if it affected his hearing. A bird's caw accompanied the rushing sounds but not as sharp or strong as familiar ones. Not authoritative enough to be a crow. He scanned the tree branches, looking for its perch. The call recited again from upriver, not overhead. Listening, he sensed it belonged not to a bird or animal at all. Unable to locate its source, he studied the undulating flow racing toward him.

A bright dot became visible¾surfing, sliding under, and popping up again. He shut his eyes and reopened them. It disappeared. Fixating on the spot, he saw it resurface, a red streak moving fast. Someone was battling the river. He was sure.

"Over here!" He rested his pole across his legs and swung both arms high overhead. Through cupped hands, he barked, "Here! This way!" His arms rose again in a frantic sweep.

It was hard to tell, but the figure seemed to be fighting toward him.

He flung his pole to the bank and edged as far out on the trunk as he dared. Slipping into the water, he threw one arm around the tree and kept the other free. He shouted to the swimmer. His pulse raced as she came closer. "Grab me!" His hand slid under the stranger's arm and around her back with the speed of catching an outfield ball.

Clawing the air, she reached for the tree.

"Put your arm around me!"

She circled his neck in a frantic hold that surprised him.

He yelled toward a cabin up the hill. "Gram! Gram! Quick!" He whispered close to the girl's ear, "Rest a minute."

A plump woman, her gray hair streaked in white and tied in a knot, inched her way down in flat tie shoes.

"Bring the tire!"

The river's insistent power seemed to reawaken the girl's fear. Wild eyed, she rasped, "Help! Help me!"

"I've got you." His arm tightened around her. "You're not going anywhere."

Garbled sounds came from somewhere deep inside her.

Near the water, Gram dragged a rubber inner tube from the bushes and heaved it toward them, holding the rope tied around it.

It landed too short. The boy's legs churned the water toward the tube, moving one arm forward on the trunk every few inches while the other held the girl. When he could grab the tube, he was relieved to see her reach for it, too.

Gram clasped the rope harder when he shouted, "Help me pull her in."

They made slow progress beside the trunk. Midway, the girl's arm grew slack on his neck. He needed her to keep it there and hang on to the tube at the same time. The current's constant force still threatened to pull them down the river. He prayed for her strength to last a few minutes longer as Gram continued tugging the rope. They worked together, drawing the girl in the red shirt to safety.

When all were finally on the bank, Gram said, "Poor thing."

The girl lay crumpled on the ground.

The boy attempted to pull her to her feet, but standing took strength she lost in the river. Lifting her like a sleeping child, he carried her toward the cabin at the crest of the hill, testing the growing muscles of his fourteen years.

Depleted energy left one of her arms pinned against the boy, resting on her stomach, while the other dangled loose, swinging with his gait.

With each step, his burden grew heavier. He stopped. "Give me a hand, Gram."

She helped him drape the girl in fireman's carry over his shoulder, her head at his back, legs dangling in front.

Gram held the door as he hauled the girl through a large main room on the way to a side room, where he lowered her to a bed. He sagged to the floor on his knees, worried about her state of consciousness.

Above her left eye, a bump took the shape of a stone encountered in the river. Blood flowed from a gash on one knee, and cuts and bruises tattooed her arms and legs.

Gram's concern turned to action. "Got to stop the swelling and fix this nasty cut." She turned to leave the room. "Need butterfly bandages from the kit." She called back, "Stay with her."

He thought the girl was coming to because she thrashed the sheets and called out for someone. When he leaned over to hear her better, she put both arms around his neck and wept. He held her a brief time, but sleep overtook her again in pure exhaustion.

"Her arms aren't broken." He looked up at Gram, who returned bearing a tin box in one hand, a rag in the other, and two towels over her shoulder.

"Not the time for funning, Seth Morgan." Gram sat on a stool beside the bed, where she swaddled most of her patient's head in one towel and used the other to pat her dry. Gently, she spread clear liquid above her eye, cleaned the gash on her leg, and applied two butterfly bandages. "Got to cut one side of this wet shirt, or she'll wear it to eternity." The box contained nurse's scissors, angled at the end. "Seth, fetch one of Papaw's shirts and bring it over here." She wagged her head at a closet that stored clothes from when her husband was alive, four years ago. "And another quilt. Need cold water from the springhouse, too, for this lump."

He handed her a thin flannel shirt, hung a quilt over the foot rail of the bed, and discreetly left the room. "Going for the water." His voice resounded from beyond the room. "I'll be out here when you need me. Gotta change out of these wet clothes."

Before long, she called him. "Bring in the leftover soup from the springhouse, too, and fire up the stove. Need it to be ready if she's hungry, but sleep's good for her." Her eyes rested on him. "And for us to eat while we keep watch."

"We can take turns." He thought of all the family watches during his grandfather's last days. "What else can we do?"

"She's in the good Lord's hands, but we still need to pray."

CHAPTER 28

Dana relived her trip down the river throughout Friday night, unable to tell the difference between waking and dreaming. She remembered how water flowed fast around boulders that blocked the way, but she had sailed past them. Luke would have splashed through the current and added his own roar to the churning water. When the Olsons' boat had bucked him off, did he see it as another blast of excitement in his last split second of awareness?

She fought for consciousness to sort out her surroundings, but the room continued its merry-go-round. Each turn brought the changing of a scene. In one, she sat beside Luke in the boat. In another, she battled the river alone, hearing a voice, unmistakably Luke's, saying, *Fighting won't help.*

In a semi-awake moment, she sensed his presence beside the bed. Were they in Heaven together? She called his name. Someone peered at her through a misty film. When he became more visible, she saw it wasn't Luke at all. Dark hair matched dark brows that rose and fell when he spoke. This boy had blue eyes, but that was the only feature similar to Luke's. But if not her brother, who was he? While she waited for the haze to clear, the muscles in her neck and shoulders relaxed, easing her into the enveloping fog.

Hours later, sunlight slanted through branches to frame a motif on the crazy quilt warming her. A sound accompanied the light, forcing her awake. Rapids falling over rocks. Her muscles knotted. As she listened, it became a susurration echoing up the hill, soothing and tempting her to fall asleep again. Aroused curiosity prevented it. She sat up, acutely aware of her swollen leg. Her washed clothes, except for the red T-shirt, draped over the bedpost. She was wearing a long flannel shirt that served as a nightgown.

Easing from the bed, she limped to the doorway. She leaned against it and took stock of the central room. Constructed of logs stripped of bark, it served as living room and kitchen. Three doors, including hers, opened into the main room. No hallways anywhere. Footsteps over the years had obviously smoothed the rough-hewn floorboards. A fireplace occupied the opposite wall. A few paces away, in a small alcove at the entrance, jackets and tools hung from wall pegs.

A boy, reclining on a couch in the room's center, sprang to his feet and offered the overstuffed chair beside him as an invitation to sit. "Apparently, a good sleep was what you needed, lovely lady."

Even when he was bending, he was still tall.

"Do you have a name?" His flicker of intrigue mimicked the way he examined a just-caught fish or unusual bug.

A couple of dry coughs preceded a clearing of her throat. Of all times for vocal cords to fail her. When she finally pronounced her first name, she stopped before adding, "Foster," so they'd know she had a last name to go with it.

He palmed his hand toward Gram, who was sitting nearby. "My grandma, Nancy Morgan. I'm Seth. We're pleased to meet you in a proper manner." A wide grin reshaped his face. "We readied ourselves to draw straws to see who would make a run through the woods for help, didn't we, Gram?"

"It's the spoken truth." Gram, beside a thick-legged pine table, stirred a lumpy mixture in a large bowl. Behind her, a wood-burning stove bulged against the wall next to a smaller table storing two large pans for washing and rinsing hands as well as dishes. "It's late for breakfast, but a bite hot from the oven will do you good." She peeked over her glasses at Dana. "Feeling better?"

"I think so." Soreness made her aware of parts of her body she didn't know about until today. She eased herself onto the chair's flower-patterned slipcover. "What day is it?"

"What day? My goodness."

"It's Saturday." Seth spoke from the couch. "August 10—and it's 1974, if you want to know the year, too. You came here by way of the river yesterday."

Dana considered the facts. "It seems like ages ago."

"It does for us, too, but we're glad you're safe here."

"Not sure of your ailments last night." Gram stopped stirring. "You got a nice long sleep, though. The best medicine." She beamed over her glasses at their unexpected visitor. "Now, tell us how you happened to get down here and about your family."

Dana told them she lived with her mother in New York, as good a place to begin as any, and added the piece about spending the summer in North Carolina. "My dad and stepmom and their baby, JJ, live in Laurelsville." She rubbed the bandages below her knee, but pain stopped her. "Is this part of Laurelsville?"

Seth whistled through his teeth. "Nowhere near, little sister. A long cruise away. Somewhere midstream, you passed the line between Laurel and Edin counties. We're far outside any town limits. We don't get anything here. No mail delivery, no nothing."

"It's how I like it," Gram chimed in. "Always held our own here. A spring and a garden meet most of our needs. In the old days, we kept a cow and a few chickens. Sometimes, fatten a hog." The bun, tied high atop her head, jiggled. "And Seth's papaw brought in a deer or two. Plenty to make it through the winter."

Seth popped a blackberry onto his tongue and offered the pail to Dana.

Instead of devouring the whole bowl, she took a handful and ate them one berry at a time, remembering her last meal of Kaye's coconut coffee cake and eggs.

Seth made sure the berries stayed close enough for her to reach. "What exactly happened?"

She told them how she had fallen into the creek and coasted along without recognizing it as a poor decision at first. The short version of the truth came out, omitting the blue boat. No need for them to think she'd relapsed to five years old, floating a toy in the water.

"See? You have an unbeatable back-to-school story: 'What I Did This Summer.'" He cocked his head for her reaction. "We puzzled at how you swam down here. Most of our visitors don't choose that route."

She tried to hide her blush by stroking a large lavender flower on the cover of the chair's upholstered arm. Again, she reviewed yesterday's events of drifting in a creek, getting caught in a raging river, and being rescued. Hallucination or dream?

"You need to know what's up." The side of Seth's hand blocked the berry juice at the corner of his mouth. "There's no truck or horse or easy way out of here to get you back to where you waded in. Pa left yesterday morning for work at the phone company. Might be gone five days, even a week. Ma is a secretary at the junior high in Edingrove, where our main house is—where we live in the winter—but she's at a church women's retreat. And there's no way of contacting your parents. We don't have a phone. No lines out here."

"Lived fine without one." Gram, in her cotton housedress and bibbed apron tied around her midriff, spooned dollops of blue-streaked muffin dough into a tin. Amid the blasting heat of the wood-fired oven, she placed the tin inside.

"Can I ask you something?" Seth held their visitor with his eyes. "Who's Luke?"

Dana gulped and drew her shoulders back. "How do you know about him?"

"You kept calling for him last night. More than once. Said his name plain as day."

Barely audible words eased out. "He was my brother."

"Was?"

"He, uh . . . " Her lips pressed together, but one word slipped through. "Died."

Seth stifled a sigh.

"What a sorrow." Gram filled the silence. "You poor girl."

"I'm sorry, too," he added. "Long ago?"

"Three years." Dana focused on a wide plank in the floor.

Gram and Seth glanced at each other before returning attention to Dana. In unspoken agreement, neither asked for further details.

After an appropriate pause, he asked, "So your family wouldn't know to follow the creek?"

"Don't think so." Dana blinked to keep sprouting tears at bay. "They don't know I found it." How could she explain the distance? "Far from where we dump our clippings."

"They don't have any idea?"

"They expected me to stay in the yard, working."

He leaned back, thinking. "You won't be walking long-distance for a while. After breakfast, I'll hike up river to see if I can figure out how you got here or if someone out there can get you home." He gave a reassuring smile to show that her dilemma was solved.

As if in collusion, the aroma of blueberry muffins permeated the room. Seth took Dana's arm to help her to the sturdy table and sat across from her.

A closer inspection in the light of day gave him little resemblance to Luke, whose blond eyebrows had blended into his face above a nose slightly rounded at the end. Seth's gaze came from azure eyes flecked with lighter particles. His dark brows, highest where they began near his nose, ran in a line to the outside of his eyes but changed their shape when he spoke. He had grown beyond Luke's stage of development, evidenced by the defined jaw of a boy becoming a man. His nose was distinguished by a slight bump at the bridge. How had she mistaken him for Luke last night?

Gram busied herself between the stove and the table, placing eggs, muffins, and blackberry jam before them. Her expression grew stern as her grandson shoveled his food, but her happiest moments came from seeing him gobble up whatever she prepared.

He caught her stare. "Forgot. This is an occasion for company manners." He placed his fork on the table and lifted it in exaggerated politeness to the eggs on his plate.

Gram brushed aside his silliness as she bustled by the stove. "I'll pack you a lunch for later. You might be gone all day."

"Depends on how rough the going is."

From a peg, he lifted a darkened canvas backpack, scarred by numerous expeditions. Into it went the food package Gram prepared, a canteen, and a hatchet with a leather sheath protecting its head. Jackknife secured as usual in his pocket, he took a quick inventory and slung the straps over his shoulders. "Here I go!" He glided out the door, carrying a rifle.

Dana had seen it earlier where it rested, barrel up, in the corner before the entrance, blending into the cabin's walls. She watched out the window as he loped down the hill toward the river. Without breaking stride, he turned back and gave a mock salute, his arm a moving arc in the air.

When Seth left, Gram turned her attention to Dana's injuries. She unfastened the toolbox lid and inserted a cotton swab into a bottle stamped "tincture of iodine." She dabbed it on Dana's scrapes. "To stop infection. River's clean as it runs, but you never know."

It prickled and burned like bugs nibbling her skin.

Next, Gram took a close look at Dana's eye that had turned black overnight. "Goes to purple next. Happens as it heals." After she dripped clear watery liquid on a ball of cotton, she applied it to the swollen knee.

It stung, making Dana's eyes tear. "Rubbing alcohol?"

"My gracious, no! DMSO. Used it on the animals and us for years. Can't be without it. Takes the swelling down." She capped the bottle. "Now, let me get you a cure for the rash." After helping Dana into the rocker in the bedroom, Gram tore a clean strip of cloth, soaked it in bleach, and applied it to her irritated arm. "Leave it on a bit. It'll sting some, but it dries it up real nice."

"You know this is poison ivy?"

"No stranger in these parts." She filled a basin from a pitcher on a small cabinet next to Dana in the rocker and set a pail on the floor. "Stay put for five minutes. Then, I'll rinse the bleach off you, and you'll be on the road to healing."

"Thanks, but I can finish." Dana recognized the cabinet as a dry sink. Mom treasured the one in her pottery shop and called it her one and only authentic antique.

When Gram returned, she carried a pile of clothes. "Seth's outgrown T-shirts." She smoothed the one on top, using her hand like an iron, and ended with a pat. "Had to cut yours. Didn't want to raise your hands over your head in case of broken bones."

"I'm okay. A bit sore."

"When you're done, hang the night shirt on the bedpost and change into one of these. Not too pretty, but they'll do." She laid a short pile of shirts on the quilt on the bed and returned to the main room.

After the calculated time, Dana removed the strips from her stinging skin, then rinsed and dried herself, being careful not to rub. Her clean and dry shorts lay beside Seth's shirts. Settling on a royal blue one, she found the shoulder seams hung a few inches down her arms. It would have to do.

Hobbling back into the main room, she reclaimed her former, comfy seat not far from the worktable by the stove. Gram's easy banter persisted, a relief for Dana, who preferred listening to talking, especially to someone new.

"Wouldn't be here unless Seth was willing to stay. He's a good one to have around. Knows how to do most everything there is to do. Fishing, gardening, bringing in water when it runs low. He and his pa hunt here in the winter, too." She gave a sigh. "He has only one problem I know of. Wanted a brother or even a sister, but it didn't ever happen for his folks. In kindergarten, he drew a picture of his family with a brother and sisters. Even though that never came true, the framed picture is on the bookshelf at the house."

As she talked, Gram kneaded a wad of dough in flour atop the table. "A couple days ago, he picked a supply of apples. This strudel will be his reward." She folded the oblong lump of dough, kneaded it down, and did it again. "Do you know his full name?"

She responded to the shaking of Dana's head, letting the lump rest briefly while she took a breath.

"On the day of his dedication, the preacher held the tiny baby in front of his pa and ma, Nathan and Calley. He introduced the congregation to Seth Jeremiah Morgan." Her attention returned to the dough, folding and kneading.

"A nice name." Dana said it aloud to hear the cadence. "Seth Jeremiah Morgan."

The dough flew in the air, attached at the end to Gram's hands, and back to the floured board. Repetition stretched it thinner and thinner. "Middle name gives it rhythm, like a drum beating." Gram pronounced each syllable slowly, emphasizing the first and third. "Jer-e-mi-ah. Know its meaning?" The dough rested on the board as she met Dana's curious eyes. "Seeker of truth. If it's not a name for greatness, it certainly begs a blessing from the Lord."

There could be worse things on the earth than having a grandmother who saw you possessing the sort of greatness that would eventually become apparent to everyone.

While she peeled and chopped the apples, Gram set the teakettle to boil. At its whistle, she poured a cup for Dana and handed her two leftover muffins from breakfast. "Tea with nettle, from the flowers and leaves." She stirred in a little honey from a small pot. "Good for my arthritis. Won't hurt you to have it for your sore knee and all."

Placing the strudel in the oven, Gram surrendered to the call of her chair and resumed talking about Seth. "God granted me only one grandchild, but He gave me a good one. And his folks raised him up real nice. Why, he hasn't thrown a conniption since he was a toddler." Her fingers prowled through the sewing basket on the floor and grasped a spool of red thread. "He knows how to handle himself in bad situations, though. A boy at school, meaner'n a tied-up dog, ambushed him after class. Seth wrestled him down and pinned him. His time in youth wrestling came in handy. Students saw him talking to the boy afterward and wondered what he said, but Seth doesn't speak about it."

Before Dana could ask more, she recognized on Gram's lap the familiar material of her red T-shirt, battered by the river.

Nothing escaped Gram, including the way Dana took note of the mending task. She continued her tiny, neat stitches. "Sorry about cutting your shirt, dear, but I couldn't leave you in wet clothes. Didn't need to tempt pneumonia in your state."

That opened the way to a question she'd been waiting to ask. "What if Seth didn't catch me, and I kept going?"

Gram held the shirt close, too absorbed on the sewing project to answer. She changed her posture and relaxed but didn't take her eyes from her work. "Thread gets snarled."

Dana wanted to repeat the question but didn't. Gram was holding back.

"Poor shirt. I'm fixing it as best I can." She continued to repair several rips besides the cut seam. "It's a testament to a rough trip."

"I'd never want to do it again." Her hand fell near her swollen knee, not daring to touch it. What was Gram hiding?

"A wonder you got this far in one piece." Gram smoothed the shirt and approved the final stitches. "Hope Seth can find someone."

"Why did he take a rifle? Is it dangerous out there?"

"Never know what you might meet in these parts if you go far from the cabin. The mountains can be unmannerly."

Dana preferred for Seth to stay, but she couldn't deny Gram's delight in having someone to talk to who couldn't run away.

"Did you say you and your mama live in New York state?"

"Yes, ma'am. I've always lived there." Dana looked at her to be respectful and saw Gram still busy with her work. In that moment, she let her gaze crawl up the walls and ceiling beams. How did one man build it all? Someone must have helped at least a little.

"You must have plenty of snow up your way in the winter."

"Uh huh. Around Thanksgiving through spring, off and on. But in North Carolina, Dad says it hasn't snowed except for dustings."

"Doesn't always stay around these parts. Can come down when it wants, though. We near froze to death here once." She shivered to make it seem real. "A bad storm blew in. The decade's big one."

"What was it like?" Relief came at not having to carry the conversation.

"Checking the sky showed us some weather stewing. It let go some rain—not cold enough yet—but falling a little and kind of drying on the way down, innocent-like. Next thing you know, it turned to snow. Fine flakes in squalls. We set ourselves to a card game and saw it snowing heavy. You couldn't hardly see through it. Papaw lugged us in more wood—and a good thing, too. Kept us alive."

"Papaw?"

"Seth called his gramps Papaw when he was a tyke. It stuck with me beyond his growing up years."

Dana found that swinging her leg back and forth helped the stiffness relax. Not wanting Gram to think she wasn't paying attention, she asked, "Did the storm last long?"

"Snow kept on a couple of days and piled up. Folks in town complained about the electricity being out three days running. We didn't know the difference. Used our kerosene lamps when we needed them and turned in early. Windows frosted over solid and thick, but we were toasty warm in our featherbed."

Gram checked the shirt with the hope it still fit. "Don't know how long the fix will stay. Least it's clean. Seth's old shirts should be fine while you're here." She tapped Dana's shoulder. "You're a pretty gal, no matter what you wear."

Dana's ears rang. Kaye had called her pretty last summer during the Boone trip. When she got home again, whenever that would be, she'd ask Mom's honest opinion as to whether she qualified as pretty. Pondering it, she put her hand to her neck for the dragonfly. It wasn't there. She patted it again to make sure.

"What's wrong, dear?"

"My mother's necklace. It's missing." This time, she didn't try to stop the tears.

Sitting beside the sobbing girl, Gram stroked her hair. "What is it, honey girl?"

All the stamina that had left her during the rescue renewed itself as weeping. Broken phrases edged between sobs. "The dragonfly. Mom's necklace."

Gram hugged her harder.

"Did you find it anywhere?"

"I'd a seen it round your neck right away. Couldn't have helped it." Gram took a seat on the couch as close as she could get to her. "What did it look like?"

"Dad gave it to Mom. Before they got married. A dragonfly. Real gold and silver." Why did she add the last part? Gram may not have owned anything of gold or silver, except for a wedding band. "After he left, Mom gave it to me. I wore it every day."

"You wore it while you did chores?"

"I know. I should have taken it off." Her knuckles pressed hard to her eyelids.

"I see you're feeling bad, but my guess is your mama and daddy will be happy you're alive without the necklace. Silver and gold aren't worth as much as you."

"But it's a keepsake. Mom said to think of it as a symbol of Dad's love for me. And Dad wanted me to have it."

"A necklace of love your daddy gave your mama, and they got divorced?"

How did this woman who knew nothing about her father dare to question his love for her or anyone? But as the thought cascaded through her, it mocked her. When Dad had moved far away, he had left Mom; but he had left her, too. This summer marked her first extended visit with him in three years.

Gram peered over her reading glasses and squeezed Dana's hand. Returning to her seat, she tidied the thread in her basket. "Maybe Seth will find it."

She recognized the attempt to cheer her up, but it didn't lessen her irritation at herself. How stupid to wear it every day, especially yesterday.

Then, Gram asked what neither she nor Seth spoke of last night or this morning. "Did you go barefoot into the stream?"

"Barefoot?" Her eyes began to swim. "I wore sandals. They're not drying somewhere?"

"Nothing on your feet when we pulled you out." Gram's voice softened. "River can be a thief when it's wild. Current must have ripped them off." She offered nothing more.

"If it stole my sandals, a tiny chain didn't have a chance." A tear leaked down her left cheek.

"You may not have thought about this, but you didn't swim the river by yourself. God breathed over you every minute and put Seth on the log at the right time for you to be coming along. Your necklace and sandals might have been lost to keep you from attaching to things of this world."

Dana's neck pulsed as she listened.

"I've had many more years than you to learn from the Word. Our most important needs are met when we walk with God. It says this in both the Old and New Testaments. We need to be content in what we have—in the real necessities supplied to us."

Leaving Dana to think on it, she eased herself up. "Let me check the end of Seth's closet." She returned with a pair of black flip-flops and gave them to her young visitor to try on. "Fit almost right."

Although Dana acknowledged Gram's cheery approval, her mind stayed on what she'd heard. Her ride on the river might have ended in disaster.

"The smell of strudel kindles my taste buds." Gram gave a little sniff. "Won't hurt to be tasters before Seth gets back."

"If you owned a bakery, the smell alone would make people line up for blocks."

Gram's face smoothed on hearing her comment, but she shook her head. "Too much time and love in it for selling. Seth's 'preciating of it is enough." She found her potholders and brought the steaming pan from the oven, releasing the smell of hot cinnamon and cloves through the cabin. Apple juice from brown sugar, butter, and flour oozed from the sides.

It couldn't cool fast enough for Dana.

Seth trekked up the river, hallooing and hollering for an answer, though not expecting one. For an outsider, the hike was treacherous but still tough enough for someone who knew the area as he did. He heard the tributaries crashing together to make crossing to Dana's original route impossible. It was as he remembered, although he hadn't been that far in a while.

Resting on a slab of flat rock overlooking the river, he dallied a while to eat a late lunch of two peanut butter and jelly sandwiches, a couple of carrots, and a muffin, washed down by a swig of his canteen. Taking in the rock-thrashing turmoil below, he tried to imagine Dana and her fear in the midst of it. She didn't need to know about recovered bodies, stripped of their clothing by the current's turbulence.

Doubting the likelihood of anyone hearing above the water's roar, he hooted a few more calls before heading back.

By dusk, he returned from his hike. "No one out there. At any rate, I'd have to cross the river somewhere to go on up. I'm not good at swimming upstream. No salmon blood." He pointed to his ribs and made a silly smirk.

No choice but to wait for Pa's return.

CHAPTER 29

Sunday morning leaned through the window to spread its healing brightness, taking away some of Dana's soreness. Did the early sun make the other bedrooms as pleasant as this? She took comfort in the way the light tickled her eyelids to wake her up. It began when one eye crept open to allow a thin, triangular shape to leak through the blur of her eyelashes and make wiggly lines on the ceiling.

When she ran out of optical games, she dressed in her shorts and another tee. Thankful for finding people who treated her more like family than a visitor, she opened the door to the main room that ruled out a fantasy filling her imagination.

Caught up in routine tasks, Gram and Seth started the morning like clockmakers winding the clocks at dawn. A pleasant smell filled the cabin but not the fruity one of yesterday's strudel. Hot biscuits? Her taste buds readied themselves. Cornbread. Full of buttery goodness with scrambled eggs on the side.

Gram joined them to eat. "We're lucky to have us some ducks this year."

If those were duck eggs, they tasted the same to Dana as eggs Mom brought from the Fenton Market.

After breakfast, Gram stooped to retrieve a basket under the table laden with carrots, potatoes, and onions, the garden's dirt still clinging to them. After scrubbing them, she began chopping to prepare stew for both lunch and dinner.

"Want to do some bean picking?" Eyes on Dana, Seth dipped his head. "Can you walk a few yards? The beans are on this side of the garden. Not far."

Gram scraped the cut vegetables into a large pot on the stove. "Might bring in some basil and oregano, too. What this stew needs." To Dana, she said, "Time to bend the knee a little."

Dana didn't need any more prompting to oblige.

They hadn't gone far when Dana saw a wall of pole beans twined around a dozen sharpened tree branches thrust into the ground to serve as poles. The garden stretched longer than her imagination.

Seth lifted leaves, revealing beans growing in clusters of three as big as his hand. "Beans are good hiders. They use these as little tents to lurk behind and make you play hide-and-seek to find them."

She knelt as far as her knee allowed for a new vantage point to spot them. A long bean, bigger than all the others, hung where entangled vines served as camouflage.

"Missed this one a few days ago." He snapped it from the vine and held it out to her. "These little lumps are the seeds. Not as tasty when they're this big. Gram calls them, 'Beans with knobby knees.'" He bit it in two, chewed in dramatic exaggeration, and pulled a wad of stringy pulp from his teeth. "Not bad."

She sucked in her breath. Luke did yucky things like that.

"We cut the not-so-tough ones into pieces for the soup. You'll see how tender they can be when it's ready. Not good raw, though." He flung the wad toward the trees. "Let the critters fight over it."

"Will they?"

"Dessert to them."

She thought Mom's phrase "gift for gab" applied to him. His came from a well of self-assurance, sprinkled through with humor. Not a strong trait for Luke, who may have taken a cue from Dad's seriousness.

A few leaves were turning yellow with brown blotches. "Aphids or gold bugs got to these guys." He ripped off the discolored ones and left the pile beside his feet. One skinny bean remained on the vine. He stripped it with his teeth to demonstrate the ease of chewing the new ones. "Want to try one?"

"I'll wait for the soup." She continued parting the leaves.

"Watch out! A granddaddy longlegs."

Atop a leaf, hair-thin legs in graceful arches descended from a round body.

"They bite." He jumped, but a grin betrayed him.

"Not what I've heard."

"But they can tickle you to death." His curled fingers twitched toward her.

Never again would she believe him.

The wind tousled the tops of trees at the clearing's edge and swept through the woods, shooing lightweight objects into the air. "Feel that?"

She shivered. It renewed the rivers' eerie convergence before the sound meant fear, before she fell prey to its surge.

"Nothing to panic about. It's normal here. Means it'll rain any second."

Thunder growled from afar; but after a long, tumbling brawl, it faded with the grumble of a rebuffed giant.

Seth snapped off the beans as he talked, paying no heed to a possible—even imminent—deluge. "Gramps used to sit on the porch and wait for storms to roll in. 'The best entertainment'—that's what he called it."

The wind gusted again closer to the ground and blew off every leaf not securely attached to its branch. One smacked him square on the forehead and stayed, glued by dampness.

She laughed until the last gurgle stuck in her throat.

"Am I a linden or an elm?" He swayed tree-like in the onslaught before he peeled the leaf off and tossed it to its fate, a hitchhiker without a ride.

The wind blew, cool and invigorating—a change from earlier. As he predicted, intermittent raindrops hit the ground, popping on contact like water on a hot griddle.

"Shall we stay here and take a shower or make a run for it?" He leaned down to throw her over his shoulder the way he carried her from the river. "You're in charge of the bucket." He bent low enough for her to snatch it from the ground and hold his belt at the back with her other hand.

Inside the cabin, Dana saw leaves plastered to the windowpanes. "You aren't the only one decked out today."

He skidded to the other side of the room and pivoted. "Catch!" He threw her a towel.

She dried off, content to be there, wet or not.

Dana took a second helping of Gram's stew, thicker and more robust than soup, and didn't worry they'd see her as greedy because Seth ate four bowls to her two. He couldn't have downed more soup using a ladle, but his prediction held. It was not only tender; it was mouthwatering and made entirely from vegetables.

"If we accidentally pluck a granddaddy with the beans, he ends up in the soup, too. Good protein."

She stirred through her bowl, just in case.

Not hearing him, Gram continued, "He eats with the biggest tablespoon we own, and it's still not big enough." She waited for his next bites and asked, "Did I tell you about his name?"

Dana didn't have the heart to say she had.

"His mama found a name rooted in history. He's destined for more than ordinary."

"Even greater than county marble champion?" Seth held an imaginary marble in his hand. Forced-air sound effects between a hiss and a pop accompanied his imaginary shot.

"Time will tell." Gram gave up on telling her tale and carried her empty bowl to the dishpan.

Seth tipped his bowl and slurped the spare remains. "Don't tell."

Thunder somersaulted long and far, broken at the end by a sharp crack. Dana jumped. The weather, in collusion with Seth and Gram, held surprises. "It's a good thing we're not out there."

He sprang from his chair with incomparable timing. "The porch gives the best vantage for storm watching. C'mon. The clean smell after the rain will clear our lungs."

They dispensed their bowls and scurried to the door.

"My dad told us the smell doesn't come from above. Most people think so, but it's not true." She recited the facts. "It's from organisms in the ground released by moisture. You know, from the rain. Wet air carries smells better than dry."

"I didn't know we reeled in a girl who is half-encyclopedia. Or is it encyclopedic?"

"That's Dad's scientific explanation, but I prefer Mom's."

"Which is?"

"Angels send their sweet scent with the rain." Memories of Luke surfaced. She wanted to think he might be helping them project their sweetness.

With a grandiose sweep of his arm, Seth steered her toward a wooden rocker. "A throne for a person of great knowledge."

Lightning flashed; and a clap of thunder slapped the air, shaking her ribcage. "Wow! Fireworks!" She loved the deep boom from a whole series across the sky.

"Good thing you didn't choose the first week in July for your river voyage. We stay in town for the festivities and fireworks."

A short stint of pummeling rain ended and gave in to the sun.

"Now, it'll be humid as the inside of a pop bottle. I vote we save more pickin' of beans or anything else for morning when it's cooler." He lounged in the rocker.

A quivering caught the corner of her eye. An intricate web, the work of an attention-oriented spider, began its task on the cabin's front logs, stringing across to the side rail and the front porch railing to create a hammock secured at three different sites. Smaller webs swung from every corner and under the roof's overhang to catch bugs, leaves, and seeds. Spiders up north were less industrious in comparison.

Hummingbirds darted around, drawn by the nectar in a group of large scarlet and orange flowers bunched together, like Kaye's cannas but taller. After sinking its long, slim beak into the blossoms' depths again and again, one hovered beside the swamp maple that shaded the cabin. Perched on a tiny branch the size of a twig, it flipped around—360 degrees—sparking laughter from the two watchers who hadn't moved a muscle.

"It's an acrobat." She was glad to find a name for it.

"A circus bird. See, we provide diversions for our guests, as the brochure says."

"Sure. The same brochure I pored over on the way down."

"Not convinced? I held auditions before you began your trip. Went all out to attract birds here. Built a feeder and hung it from a hook on the porch. It didn't make it through the night, though."

"Not even one night?"

"Bears carted the whole thing off and made a mess, to boot."

"You have bears here?" She drew herself back, searching his face for signs he was telling the truth.

"Didn't you hear them knocking at the windows last night?"

"I heard some eerie noises."

"Must have been one of 'em."

"Will they break a window?"

"Been known to. If it's a cold night, they'll climb through and snuggle up under the blankets."

"You!" She slugged him on the arm but not too hard.

CHAPTER 30

The swelling from Dana's bumps and bruises subsided considerably, thanks to Gram, who applied the clear liquid morning, noon, and night. The routine didn't vary. She washed each one, rinsed them in cooled boiled water, and dabbed on the medicine using sterile cotton. "Has to be clean. It'll draw to your insides anything that's on your skin."

Finishing the process, Gram talked about the days of Nate, Seth's pa, and his growing years in the cabin. "Local kids learned their lessons at the schoolhouse up the road through eighth grade. In high school, Nate took to staying in town with a friend's family. Easier getting to school. After his hitch in the army, he married Calley, rented an apartment in town, and hired out for the phone company. Course he never came back here." Long sighs accompanied her story. "When your young'uns grow up, they have their own lives."

"Does that apply to grand-young'uns, too?" Seth sauntered into the cabin at the perfect time to interrupt.

"If they're not the misbehaving kind." Gram almost smiled.

He sidled closer. "Before I left grammar school, Gramps died; and Gram moved into town with us." He provided an explanation. "Winters alone are harsh here. Now, it's a vacation cottage."

While Gram indulged herself in a pensive moment, Dana changed the subject with a question for Seth. "Do any of your friends spend time up here?"

"Pa brings a volunteer whenever he can. They don't enjoy roughing it. Kinda like my ma, but she doesn't have much vacation because she works summers, too." His eyes rolled sideways toward Dana. "With Ma in the office at school, you can guess I've been on good behavior. This fall, I'll be in high school, where I'll be free to be me." He waited for Gram's reaction.

Paying no heed to his remark, she took over the conversation like a relay runner seizing the baton. "Working in town kept his folks from living this far out. For us, easy traveling to town wasn't part of our set up. Papaw mapped it out in such a way. Wanted his space away from other folks."

She rambled on until Seth broke in. "It's been a good home." He turned to Dana. "Ready to take in the countryside now that the nurse has fixed you up?"

Her initial sight of the cabin from the river left a memory of the steep hill, but other details about her rescue drew a blank. She looked to Gram for permission.

Even though the old woman was sad to lose her audience, she chuckled. "That'd be fine. Exercise strengthens you."

"I'll be your guide on the grand tour when we finish here." He left for the springhouse with the water bucket.

Dana wandered as far as the porch to check the morning weather. Unruly tips of pines tickled the sky and cast long shadows on the grass, sheltering the silver blanket of dew with droplets plentiful enough to drink. It hadn't burned off by 8:00.

Seth returned, lugging the water bucket inside and trading it for the dishpan of dirty water that he threw with a great splash next to the porch. Soapy water kept anything from growing in the shallow trench.

His tasks done, they trotted off with energy but slowed to a crawl in the heat, passing the beans and other crops. The cleared space, appearing to be a lush meadow at a distance, became nothing more than scrub grass with uncountable weeds and other earth-hugging species.

A faint droning came from afar. Seth squinted at an airplane overhead. "A Piper Comanche. Nice one. Built a model like that once. Don't see many of those here." He traced it as it followed the river's path. Its route triggered a thought as to why it was there. "Hey, think it's hunting for you?" He bounded to a flat-out run, waving his arms and whooping wildly.

Unaware, it continued a sustained humming like a bird headed to its nest, unable to be distracted.

He jogged to where Dana withdrew by the tomatoes. "Why would a plane fly over today? Haven't seen one in weeks, and it shows up while you're here. More than coincidence, isn't it?"

"Can't be searching for me. No one has any idea I came down the creek. Dad's never gone past the burn pile to prove there's a creek."

"He's probably figured it out, one way or another." When she didn't answer, he turned to see that the happy girl he had left the cabin with minutes ago wasn't there anymore.

"They'll find you eventually. Pa will be along in a couple of days."

"I know. You told me."

Her answer halted his aerial search. "What are you afraid of?"

No answer came to her. She was too embarrassed to say she wasn't ready to leave yet, even though Mom and Dad had to be beside themselves. "Dad doesn't know anyone with a plane."

"He must have called the police, county, or someone. Plenty of resources for finding lost people."

She shrank further into herself.

To bring her around, he switched tactics. "If you don't want to be found, we can hide you in a closet."

Her burst of laughter astonished both of them. His mind-reading abilities were stunning in addition to his other talents, like not being able to stay serious for too long.

When they'd traveled a few more yards, the plane approached again, this time farther off. Seth whistled sharp and shrill through his fingers. "Pilot can't hear over the engine noise. Not sure he can see the clearing."

The unbroken sky looked down without a reply.

"Can't say I didn't try." He waited until it disappeared. "Think your dad is angry because you got lost?"

"He might be. He doesn't approve of doing things for fun. Even for himself."

"Then you're lucky to be a fun-loving person."

"Some fun I'm having at Dad's! I wanted to see him and the new baby—but not for the whole summer. I wanted time with my friends. It's my only vacation until school starts."

"But you're not spending it all at his house. You're spending part of it with us! Where could you have a better time than here?"

"I guess I'm blessed in more ways than one." The thought rolled around in her mind and settled on her trek to the creek with the boat. Her plan to grant the boat its freedom gave her freedom, too. She had never been this free. Being with Seth brought her a new sense of adventure—no abundance of that in her life since Luke.

Pausing to admire the western mountain peaks beyond the trees, Dana shaded her eyes. "What was it like here when your grandpa arrived? Was it a forest?"

"Gramps chose this plot for its natural clearing before he built the cabin. I fire up the tractor sometimes so the weeds don't take over. Keeps the bugs down, too. If I didn't do that, we'd be gawking at Snow White's castle, completely overgrown." He stopped in the middle of their stroll. "Did she have a castle? Or did she live in a more modest dwelling, like a cave, with the seven dwarfs?"

"Am I supposed to be an expert on Snow White?"

"I thought girls were fairytale experts. Are you ready for the quiz on Cinderella and Goldilocks?"

The slant of his shoulders revealed how much he enjoyed being silly, but she gave his arm a playful slug.

"Ow! I'm mortally wounded." He found a long stick and lifted it with difficulty, imitating someone injured. "A splint for my arm."

"That's the stupidest splint I've ever seen." She couldn't believe how easy it was to tease back.

"It's a multipurpose tool." He held it to his mouth like a flute and pretended to play. "And an effective bug catcher." He probed it into patches of growth as they plodded along.

The grass ended where a shallow runoff stream, no wider than a foot, gurgled across their path to join the river.

"We call this the Trickle Down. It runs when there's been enough rain. Goes away when it's dry." He scooped the water and flicked it at her.

She laughed, shielding her face from the drops. "I didn't know anything as inviting as this was waiting out here."

"What? Haven't had enough of creeks?"

"I love to throw things in and see where they go. What's around here that I can use?"

"One of my sneakers?" He started to untie one.

"No, you goof. A twig, a leaf. I need a bunch to compare which one goes farthest."

"You're bound to find them. Try closer to the garden for twigs or fallen leaves." He poked around, looking. "In the spring, when this is wider, frogs live in it. Happiness for me as a kid."

"Wish I'd seen them. Once, we visited Dad's cousin in Pennsylvania. Frogs beyond counting hopped all over in his pond. He showed us how to smack badminton rackets in the mud to trap them for fun. But then we'd set them free."

"Did you have frog legs for dinner?"

"Ick. Are you kidding?" She stuck out her tongue and made a retching sound. "People eat them?"

"They're considered a delicacy. Even in these parts. But you need fat frogs. The teeny ones from yesterday's tadpoles aren't big enough."

"I take it back. I don't want to see them, after all."

"Don't fret. They're not on Gram's menu." Seth bumped along in no real hurry toward the garden. "These weeds need a hack. I'm going to fetch a hoe from the springhouse shed. Stay by the Trickle Down. Okay?" He turned to go. "Enjoy the leaf contest." He saw the crinkled leaves she'd piled up. Off he tromped with his stick. In a few steps, he swiveled about and planted the end with a firm thrust on the ground. "Don't go thinking you can follow it down to the river. Promise?"

"You won't catch me going there again." When Luke had banned the concept of fear, she had to go along with him. His no-fear rule held until her recent rescue in the mountains.

Seeing the leaves surf the shallow current before they pitched under took her back in time to other creeks where she played, content and alone. Once, when the whole family—including Luke—picnicked and fished at the lake, she found a tiny creek whispering into the larger body of water. The miniature plastic horses she'd stowed away in her pocket got a rare bath, cavorting in the water and cantering across it. She hid them to keep Luke from teasing the daylights out of her. When Dad asked what she did during the afternoon, she admitted to throwing twigs into the creek to see if they'd make it to the lake. She accepted his half-smile as a sign of approval.

Amazing how her brain found its way back to an old scene. Did other people have such recollections, happy or sad, when they least expected them? Near a mass of black-eyed Susans, she waited without straying far from where Seth had left her. The air clung to her skin. New York's humid days couldn't compare.

A good distance down the slope in front of her, apple trees bore abundant fruit, where Seth picked the filling for Gram's strudel. A large, black lump stirred under the trees. She gaped in disbelief.

A bear, like a farmer testing the ripeness of his crop, rose on hind legs with forepaws on a tree trunk. It weighed the effort of climbing but settled for grubbing around at the base of the tree. As it moved, its layers of insulated shoulder fur revealed a golden hue underneath. Or maybe the dappled sunlight caught its coat. The buff color of its snout repeated on the ridge above its eyes. Swinging its head back and forth, it nosed everything like an inquisitive child. Snout in the air, it whiffed. On all fours, it lumbered up the hill toward her by the run-off stream. Padded paws swept the ground in a forward-backward motion as smooth as swimming. Whether it saw her or not, she didn't know; but it kept on, not in a hurry.

What to do? If she ran, it might chase her. Should she slowly back off? Dad said fast movements weren't a good idea around animals in the wild.

It stopped.

Her feet, bolted to the ground, refused to move.

The bear stood again to sniff the air, front paws hanging in front of its chest.

She tried to call for Seth with a tight throat and dry tongue. His name finally spun out as thin as a strand of Gram's thread.

From behind her, she heard, "Don't move!"

Seth inched forward, signing with his hand for her to keep still. Sidestepping bit by bit to reach her, he put himself in line with the bear that had dropped to the ground to resume its nonchalant progress. A few yards from Seth, it raised its head and spotted him.

"Get outta here!" Seth flailed his arms, one hand wielding the hoe crosswise like a wizard's staff. "Go!" He stomped his foot.

Dana jumped, too.

The bear turned tail and skated beyond the tree like a frightened terrier.

It was hard to tell who ran faster, the bear down the hill or Dana to the cabin, her sore knee forgotten. She didn't ask if it marked the end of their excursion.

Seth chased behind her and, once inside, locked the door.

They sank into the nearest chairs.

The hoe accompanied him inside to lean on the armrest.

"What's the fuss here?" Gram turned from the stove, wiping her hands while she tried to tell if Dana's sounds came from laughing or crying.

"A bear." Seth stared through the window, returning to his usual self to enlighten Dana about the habits of that furry species. "They want to be around us even less than we want to be around them. Their whole purpose is to find food, but you do want to keep your distance."

"What if it charged us? What would you have done then?"

"Asked it to waltz?"

Dana rolled her eyes.

"Black bears aren't as aggressive as grizzlies in other parts of the country, unless you stumble on a mother with cubs. It was probably a little one, the first year without its mama."

"It looked bigger than a cub."

"They can get to be a decent size in their second year." He relaxed into the cushions. "You can't believe how bears hang around those trees. Saw one last fall on the ground there wallowing around on top of mashed and rotting apples in pure ecstasy. Yellow jackets circled like crazy, and it didn't mind one bit." His hands swirled around his head to imitate the action. "Same place I harvested the apples from the other day. Didn't you see paw prints in your strudel?"

Dana struggled to withhold her smile.

Gram listened as they filled in the details about the bear and how it shambled toward them.

"Thankfully, you didn't carry a catch of fish today. Might've had an unfortunate ending."

"Bears chase people for them?"

"Yes'm. If it wants them enough. You don't want to tempt one."

It wasn't the answer Dana wanted to hear.

Dana and Seth busied themselves for the entire afternoon helping Gram with tasks that kept them in or near the cabin.

Later, after dinner, Seth called from the porch as dusk turned to dark. "C'mere. You need to see this."

Where the hill sloped toward the river, flashes of light swirled upward in the air, winking and dimming in an off-and-on glow.

Fireflies, sparkling like blown Christmas glitter, reminded her of catching them with Dad; but these exceeded them by dozens.

Gram tarried long enough to be polite. "You two enjoy the ballet. I've seen the creatures dance many a time."

"Fulfilling the promise of entertainment for our guests." Seth held his arms wide and bowed for Dana's benefit like a ringmaster presenting the finale. "Where else can you see a show like this?"

Viewing the whole panorama in one glimpse became impossible.

"Ma and I tried counting them by shouting a number when we saw one. Don't know if we counted forty separate ones or twenty of them twice."

Imagining the phosphorescent patterns as reflections from Heaven, she followed a single firefly in the dusk. It blinked off then on in another place. Each group vied for attention with a dazzling display in the vanishing light.

He saw how the light show had taken her in. "It's your own private performance. They're showing off for you."

All the air in her lungs breathed out long and slow to keep from disturbing the entire phenomenon. "I'm going to remember this forever."

Later, alone in the bedroom, she created an image of sitting beside Seth in a double swing instead of separate rockers, his arm draped around her shoulders. The thought soothed her in the looming shadow of pines through the windows while the fireflies illuminated the room with their wheeling and diving, lulling her to sleep.

CHAPTER 31

Dana awoke to a rain-soaked earth. Because a gray day didn't generate the same kind of curiosity as a sunny one, she lay there, allowing internal ramblings to take over. Gram and Seth arose at sunrise whether it was Tuesday—like today—or any other day. She didn't know the exact time, but she straggled last into the main room every morning; and yet they always ate breakfast with her. Did they wait in hunger or eat an earlier breakfast and then another to keep her company?

Their kindness in letting her sleep never extended to evening. Last night, they had said goodnight when the sunset's vermilion remnants rode the edge of the peaks. To be polite, she had plumped herself into the featherbed in the center bedroom early. There was a practical side to it, too. The cabin had one little-used kerosene lamp, and they offered her no candle. How different it was to turn the sheets back under the dimmest rays of light caressing the bed.

She finally knew what going "to bed by day" meant in Robert Louis Stevenson's poem, the one she had memorized from Mom's ancient copy of *A Child's Garden of Verses*. Pencil markings still decorated some yellowed pages from her preschool years when the book's small size, five-by-six inches, had attracted her. Years of use wore away edges of the glued paper on the cardboard-like cover.

The poetry book turned her mind to home and wondering about Mom and Dad. Little did she know they were together at that moment, praying for her at the burn pile while volunteers continued to search for her below the creek.

Voices in hushed tones seeped under the door. Sitting up in bed, she kicked her legs over the edge, letting them dangle until her feet brushed the braided oval rug. She didn't want her new friends to think she was lazy.

Amid the sound of steady—but not pounding—rain, she greeted them in Seth's olive shirt. "I see why everything grows bigger here. If I planted myself outside, I'd turn green."

She joined them by the window to witness the creation of several new running creeks. The sky dumped enough water to give them a visible current, roiling toward the river. Runoffs gushed two or three feet wide, flattening the field grasses. Others gave birth to small ponds bearing thickets of grass like tiny islands. A wide stream curved around the base of a tree, daring anything to stop it, yet splitting in two when the ground level changed.

Gram regarded the scene as a regular occurrence. "This will fill the rain barrels and give us water by the door. The blessing of a storm."

"It'll fill the duck pond, too." Seth made quacking sounds. "We'll get more eggs."

Dana gave a quick peek at the worktable to see if breakfast waited.

Gram took the cue. "Bread's toasting in the oven, and there's raspberry jam from last year's supply. Some fresh berries, too."

"The hills and hollers are trying to impress you this week." He scraped a chair back from the table and swept a curved hand across the seat. "For the queen of the mountains."

She curtsied at the new title.

Gram waited for everyone to be seated and said grace. Afterward, she looked at them with as much pride as if they were both her grandchildren. "Sitting here and looking at you young'uns, I can't help but wonder what God has in store for you."

Seth chimed in. "Can hardly wait. I've always been curious about the future." He focused on Dana across the table. "Don't you feel that way?"

His question shocked her. She didn't project anything beyond Mom marrying Mr. Hamlin or thinking about the summer's possibilities during the flight. "If you gave a penny for my thoughts a minute ago . . ."

He dug into his pocket and held a nickel in his palm.

"I still remake the hours and days before Luke's accident to keep it from happening. But it did, and there's nothing I can do about it."

It wasn't what the other two expected to hear. For once, they were speechless.

Before too long, Gram touched Dana's hand. "Want the Lord to help you?"

Dana's head bobbed in answer.

Heads bowed, the three of them prayed together.

After breakfast, Dana and Seth helped Gram clear the table.

He screwed the lid on the jam and handed Dana an umbrella as an invitation to follow him. The rain died down during breakfast, but a light pattering continued. Outside the door, he turned onto the familiar route beside the cabin to the privy.

Fearing she'd misunderstood his directive to follow, she held back.

He didn't choose the pathway to the left but veered behind the cabin to a broad clearing. A wide mound swelled from the ground. At its front, a single cellar door slanted into the earth. Mary Jo's mother brought washed clothes from the basement to the clothesline outside through a similar one connected to the house.

Leaning down, he gripped a metal ring in the door to heave it up and over to the side. The door yawned open to a short flight of stairs descending into a dark cave. He twisted a flashlight from his pocket. "Our only modern cheat." Its beam brightened the murky blackness below the stairs.

"What is this?"

"The root cellar. Gramps dug it himself and carried in every one of the rocks to line it. Keeps everything fresh." He took the first few stairs and stopped, his head above the opening. "If you ever need to cool off, you know where to go." He turned. "Want to come down?"

"I'm staying here."

"You're not as intrepid as I thought."

She held her umbrella and refused to move.

The shaft of light wiggled as he jogged the final steps.

On his return, she saw his head rising above the stairs. "You'd make a good groundhog. Did you see your shadow?"

"I did, and it told me about a surprise visitor."

In a reflexive action, she ran. Whenever she teased Luke, he'd chase her for sure.

Seth followed her effortlessly to the cabin door. Inside, he was about to pull the checkers game from a shelf when Gram asked if he and Dana would peel and cut vegetables for dinner.

Seeing he looked less than happy, Dana asked about it.

He confessed that indoor food chores, as he called them, were his least favorite thing to do. "I like the outdoor stuff—driving the tractor, fishing, and taking a hike. That's why I come here besides to keep Gram company. No one else is free to do that." He glanced away. "I think it would be different if I had a brother or sister."

Dana rinsed the vegetables in fresh rainwater. "Gram said when you first went to school, you drew a family picture and it included several children."

"She told you that?" He snapped a carrot in two and popped the thin end into his mouth. "It's true, though. I've always wanted at least one. As it is, there's just me."

"It would be fun to have someone else here all summer."

"It's not all summer." He chewed while he talked. "Can be a tug-of-war about coming here. Like you, I want to be with my friends. Gram would stay all the time if she could. Probably makes her feel closer to Gramps. Alternating weeks can work for taking garden produce home. You can't believe how big some beans get when we're gone."

He chopped while Dana peeled until the pot was half-full. "You ready to take on the checkers champion now?"

They played through the pattering of rain with no more talk of siblings.

The sky was still overcast at midday. Gram tugged the door open to shake her dust mop outside. "Not a day for fishing or picking either one."

"Unless you want us to wear rain slickers." Seth snaked one long arm around her. "Come with us, Gram. We'll make it a picnic."

"The gift of joshing comes from your pa and his from Papaw. I tell you, if we lived here year-round, we'd be churning butter this minute. No lollygagging—not even during rain storms neither."

"But we're temporary residents, aren't we, Gram?" He plopped into the rocker and rested an ankle on the other thigh.

"And thankful to be here." She returned to her work.

"But we're here when it's important. Like this week." He checked to see if Dana understood what he meant.

His elfish look seemed to conceal deeply serious thoughts. What if this wasn't a temporary week? Or if today's rain had arrived last Friday to keep him from fishing? Gram's belief about an unseen hand of protection held true.

Rain played staccato on the cabin's old roof. By experiencing it from inside, Dana and Seth avoided another drenching. It stopped as it began: suddenly. They headed to the porch, their haven for idle pursuit. Before long, the sun vanquished the clouds. Wet leaves glistened like mirrors.

"Wow. It's pretty again. What a difference." Dana squirmed in her rocking chair. "Is this the way it is all summer?"

"When it wants to be. But we can have several days—even a week or more—without a drop. Pa says the weather has a mind of its own, but mountains affect the storms, too." He assessed the sky. "Today's temperamental."

They sat in relaxed silence to save themselves from the humidity by not moving. Among people other than family, she would have been self-conscious sitting and not talking at all, but not so with Seth. The new comfort level was a surprise. He could have been Luke, grown another three years older. Yet aside from being a boy and making silly faces, he was nothing like Luke.

An explosive bang of thunder reverberated through the trees.

Dana ducked. "Did it hit anything?"

"Whoa! No warning?" A few drops of rain fell in reply. "The sound of Heaven's Olympic games. The hammer throw against a wall of glass." His fist swung around supporting the imagined heavy weight.

"I think it broke the sky."

The storm set in, pounding the earth. At first, the sun refused to be conquered. Rain as opaque as a dense fog overpowered it in its second assault since morning.

Within the hour, the storm blew away, leaving a changing cloud cover. A rainbow bridged, faint but visible, soon sharpening in brilliance. From a mix of purple and pink on the bottom left, the colors ranged from blue to green, yellow, orange, and red and repeated those hues on the other side. Above it arched another in muted shades. The two originated brightest at the earth and soared high into the air. The space between them remained a gray path edged by two sky-scraping curves of color.

"Gram! Come quick!"

On seeing it, she clasped her hands together. "It's God's covenant to us. Did you ever see a double rainbow press the sky this way?"

Dana had to admit it was unique. "Do you think Noah and his family had to lower their eyes at the glow of the rainbow after the flood? Wish we could roll back the centuries and have a peek."

Gram rested her hand on Dana's arm. "Maybe this one is bringing a special sign for you or your folks. They might could see it, too, and know it means you're safe." Her arm slipped around Dana's shoulder to give her a squeeze.

Dana couldn't speak. Who knew Gram thought about the same things she did?

Gram stood in awe with them, taking it all in. At the next grumble of thunder, she retreated inside.

The top rainbow began a slow fade in the atmosphere. The path below it evaporated while the main rainbow's blaze dissipated, leaving only the colors near the earth on either end. An overcast sky declared itself with ambient light bleeding around the far edges.

A premature evening descended from a painter's brush, dripping a mixture of oils to create gray, deeper gray, then charcoal.

As the light ebbed, Dana could barely see Seth sitting there. "I don't like the look of dark clouds."

"Because you can't see through them?"

She crossed and uncrossed her legs. "Sometimes, I imagine Luke tumbling around in the puffiest white ones, having fun." She expected Seth to think she was crazy, but he took it in stride.

"You think it's easier to speak about him as time goes on?"

"A little, but I've always talked to him since he's been gone." She wanted to say more but cut her thoughts short and added, "I still do. Used to burrow under the blankets for a conversation with him. Is that weird?"

"Nothing can be weird about having a brother. Tell me what it's like. What times with Luke do you still think about?"

She laughed. "Sometimes, he could be annoying in ways you can't imagine."

"Maybe I can. Give me an example."

"He used to chase me with bugs."

"Dead or alive?"

"Both. I learned to pretend they didn't bother me, and he stopped. I never dreamed I'd one day wish he could do that again."

"I could find some bugs if you think it would help." His hand reached for a spiderweb.

She stuck her tongue out.

"Any feats you kept secret from the world?"

The story of the library ledge came first, then the fish pond, and forbidden yards behind formidable fences. She laughed as she recounted her antics with Luke.

After a while, Seth saw she was talked out and eased himself from the rocker to escort her through the cabin door in the dark. It was the latest they'd stayed up during her visit.

In the light of the kerosene lamp, Gram was reading her Bible. She turned a page before she saw them. "What happened to the rainbows?"

"They . . . took us on a pilgrimage."

"What?" Curiosity furrowed her forehead.

He flung his arm toward Dana to include her in the conspiracy, but she had no more idea than Gram.

"We've been searching for the pot of gold."

Instantly, Gram was all in. "Did you find it?"

"I wish we did. If we found it on your land, you'd be rich, Gram." His words spawned a song to the tune of the nursery rhyme, "Baa Baa Black Sheep." As he sang, he moved across the room, twirling Dana, who went along with the unpracticed dance.

Did you ask me if we found some gold?
Yes, Gram, yes, Gram, three bags full;

Enough for new plumbing, and lighting, and heat,
And you will be relaxing in an easy seat.

At the end, they held hands and bowed close to the floor. While darkness crept from the corners, Seth leaped over to Gram and hugged her. "It's a game my friends invented. The person who's 'it' has five minutes to make up words to any song we choose. We scan the rhyme scheme and shout suggestions to help. Ends up as a group effort." Thinking about it, he shrugged. "It's what kids do when they're bored."

"Such foolishness." Against her remark, Gram's shoulders shook until the other two joined in, laughing.

CHAPTER 32

Dana studied the lay of the land through a window until a break in the trees gave a glimpse of a mountain ridge not noticeable earlier. Her gaze shifted back to trees near the cabin with leaves that no longer glistened and didn't stir. The mountain breezes were resting after yesterday's storm. "You'd never know it rained."

"Happens here often." Seth rubbed his stomach to show Gram his appreciation for the blackberry-topped oatmeal earlier. "We finished the berries off. Time to gather some more. We haven't done any picking since the beans."

Gram nodded encouragement. "Go, reap the garden's bounty. Get you some big, juicy ones."

Dana turned from her view of contrasts in the landscape. "Do they grow anywhere near bears?"

"We scared him more than he scared us. He won't be around for a while."

She took a step backwards. "Speak for yourself."

Disregarding her, he snapped a pail from the kitchen floor. "I'll carry the bucket this time. If it doesn't rain." He hustled her out the door like a theater usher showing her to a seat, minus the flashlight.

In his easy lope across the rise and fall of uneven ground, he stepped aside, twisted a tomato from its stem, and took a bite like an apple. He gave another to her.

The tomato's crimson skin held the day's heat like a hand warmer. "Wow! It's almost hot." One small bite sent juice running in a line to her chin. "Mom's garden gives us peppers, tomatoes, and lettuce; but nothing like this."

"We haven't gone hungry here yet. You won't find tastier." From another row, he plucked cherry tomatoes to share.

"Luke liked these."

One smaller than a blackberry slid down his throat. "Suppose God assigned Luke to be your guardian angel, and he's watching you now."

"Is that how it works?"

"I'm not sure, but He can plan anything. Our pastor says He assigns angels to watch over us." Seth, walking in front of her, looked back. "They had to be with you. Maybe they gave you special armor."

The details of her trip—especially the last part—remained fuzzy. "Didn't I go through rapids? Seems like a bad dream now, but I was scared. More than I've ever been."

"You had reason to be, but they're not as bad as what's below here." He said more than he meant to.

"Can you take me there?"

"If you want to see them." He flipped another tomato into his mouth. "Don't believe me, do you?"

"I'm not sure. Never sure, in fact."

"But you do know, even though Luke isn't here in person, he left you lots of good memories. Think of your times together." He was quiet as they walked again, giving her time to mull it over.

The tone of his voice changed. "But remember a gift he gave you. Without a brother like him, you'd accept everything I say as truth."

Like Gram, he shied away from talking about the river below. She could only appreciate how he switched from serious to silly with nothing to alert her except the grin that appeared more often than Luke's ever did.

Bushes in the berry patch teemed with dark fruit. At its abundance, Dana held her arms out wide. "This must be it. They look the same as the ones from my first day here."

Seth confirmed the best place for harvesting by dropping the bucket on the ground. "You mean second day. You spent the first one swimming and getting patched up."

"And being carted around like a ragdoll."

"You were aware the whole time?"

She confessed, blushing. "Partly. But I couldn't move. Never been so exhausted." Her manners prompted her to say, "Thank you. If I haven't said it, I am now."

"It's definitely a new exercise for Gram and me. I think Someone put us here." He seemed far away for a moment, blowing into the side of his doubled fist, thinking, until the bucket caught his attention. "These things might rot on the vine if we don't rescue them."

They fell to their knees to begin the harvest. Plump blackberries left their purple mark. "Will this stain come off?"

"If you lick them for a few days."

"Sure. To make you laugh when I look ridiculous."

"I didn't tell you how to pick these. There's an art to it. If you pull them, they can squish and separate. Hold the stem below the berries like this and snap them off." He demonstrated.

She watched him to make sure he wasn't joking, then copied his technique. Her hands made several trips to the bucket. She noticed then how his lips pressed together in taking the berries from the stem and depositing them in one motion. "Luke did that."

"Did what?"

"Made a face like that."

"This one?" He crossed his eyes and stuck his tongue out to the side.

"You goof."

"Was he your main sidekick?"

"Till Teddy came along." Her mouth drooped, but she continued snapping the berries to avoid his gaze.

"Who's Teddy?"

"His friend . . . the family . . . who had the boat." Then, softer, "When Luke died."

He leaned forward, encouraging her to go on. "What happened?"

"The boat hit a wave and bucked him off the side. Propeller caught him between his neck and shoulder."

Seth shuddered.

"We saw him in the hospital and scarcely recognized him." Tears welled from a previously dried-up source and wouldn't stop, even though she didn't want to cry in front of Seth.

He tugged her beside him on the grass and threw his arm around her. "Nothing wrong with tears. God gave them to us on purpose." He held her protectively while she cried it out.

Her entire surroundings—sky, trees, berries, and all—began a spinning course from her head to the spot on the ground where she sat. Leaning back, she took in Seth's face. It was Seth, after all. Not Luke. She rested her head on his shoulder as the tears flowed. The blinds had opened to the most hidden part of her life, the place few ever saw.

"Promise you'll talk to me about him when you can."

The heel of her hand wiped upward on her cheek.

A cumulus cloud dallied in its journey to listen to their murmurings. "How about one event from the front of your mind?"

Her broken breathing subsided as the voyage of the blue boat tumbled from somewhere inside. She told him how the storm drain stole the best toy of their lives. "We never saw it again, at least not in its original shape."

To encourage her story, he trained his gaze on a clot of berries and continued working.

"Wish you could have seen it and the tiny details in the making of it. Threads twisted and braided like ropes made it a miniature of the real thing."

"Which explains your attraction to boats and creeks."

"Want to hear the rest?"

"There's more?"

"I found out the hull survived when I came across it in Luke's drawer." She finished the story about offering it to Dad, finding it on his shelf, and giving it a final ride.

"The blue boat brought you here!"

"I guess that's true."

"See? It's part of Luke's legacy to you. Think of the escapades he's given you. This one has to be at the top!" His excitement overcame the solemnity of the topic. "Remember about Luke being your guardian angel? Maybe his spirit could be watching over you in a different way from when he was alive."

It was true that Luke had told her to keep her feet in front of her in the swift current—or, at least, she thought he did. That may have kept her head—instead of her knee—from grazing a rock.

Seth checked the pail and realized it brimmed more than three-quarters full. "When Gram sees this, she may want you to stick around longer." He pulled her to her feet and tucked the pail in one arm.

As they ambled toward the cabin, he raised a finger to the sky. "Know this sign? Gramps showed it to Pa and Pa to me. Reach up any time you want. Jesus is always there, and you can imagine Luke beside Him."

"It's a good sign." She copied him. "I won't forget it."

Gram's hands left the folds of her apron as she tarried in the doorway. "Got enough for a pie? The oven's heating." She looked closer at Dana's tear-stained eyes. "My goodness! What's wrong?"

Seth skirted around Dana and answered for her. "Reminiscing about Luke."

The flowered chair enticed her. Dana sat and backed her feet from the extra roomy flip-flops. "Helps me to talk about him sometimes."

At the table, Gram turned the dough in the mixing bowl until it was ready to be rolled flat. "Do your folks ever speak his name?"

Dana spread her toes across the wide planks, like a game, to keep her eyes on the floor while she told how Mom protected everyone by not mentioning him. "And I never saw Dad cry, even once, after Luke died."

"Some people hold it in." Seth was rinsing the blackberries. "Lots of men think a man shouldn't cry. Think about the way he grew up."

"What way is that?" Gram spread the bottom piecrust in the pan, overlapping the edges.

He answered again for Dana. "He grew up on a farm. His father was the type who worked every minute. No time to play, so he said."

Berries mixed with sugar, flour, and butter tumbled into the unbaked crust. Gram recited facts about farms demanding constant care and kids who work on them doing chores before and after school while too many city kids think they don't need to work at all.

Dana protested with upraised hands. "But Luke didn't. He did lots of chores, including the garbage and mowing the lawn. Mom said he could mow the next day. After the boat ride." Her voice broke, but she swallowed and blurted it out. "Dad blamed Mom—blamed her for Luke being there when he should have been home." She looked away again. "Blamed Mom for Luke dying. He was so angry when he left her, but he left me, too. I'm his child, as much as Luke, but he didn't stay for me."

Gram crimped edges of the dough, cut slashes in the top, and placed an edged cookie sheet under the pan to catch any run-over. In rejoining the conversation, she redirected it. "Have you forgiven him?"

"Forgiven?"

"For all you know, your daddy might be letting God into his heart this minute, what with you missing and all. He might have realized leaving you and your mama was a bad decision. But he was hurting then, like you. He didn't know how to reach out."

A single response came from the opening and shutting of the oven door.

The heat of it wafted over Dana. "Why forgive unless someone asks for it? I thought people had to beg for it."

"Aren't any rules." Seth moved toward her but stopped midway. "Some people won't let themselves forgive. They justify it by remembering how someone hurt them."

Dana remembered her efforts to make Dad stay that brought sadness and fits of temper. While she turned them over, rage won; and resentment boiled over. She lashed out at Seth. "What do you know about it? Your father and mother stayed together. Always."

Seth's face and his whole demeanor wore a scowl—something Dana hadn't seen on him before.

Dana had done it again. Her fury spilled over, in spite of Seth and Gram's kindness. What a mess she'd made.

Juice bubbled up from the pie onto the cookie sheet. It hissed while Gram dripped water on the metal to keep the gooey mess from sticking. "None of your fault. If you can forgive, you help yourself, too. Maybe even more than the other person. That's the truth. Forgiving frees you; helps you heal up and move on."

A few steps took Seth closer to give her a piece of his mind. He stopped, unable to move. How could she be so ungrateful? It took effort and a few moments for him to cool down to speak.

Gram beat him to it. "Don't let anger own you. You need to be letting it go." She raised her hand with fingers open in a sign of release.

He knew her advice also applied to him.

Dana bit her lip. How did they keep calm after her outburst? Too late to take it back, she couldn't bring herself to apologize. Gram's words, though, began to sink in. After prolonged silence, she asked, "You mean *I* can forgive my dad even though he's not here?"

Seth finally spoke. "It can be as sweet as that blackberry pie."

"I didn't know..." She turned her attention from the floor, forcing herself to look at him. "I never thought of it that way."

Gram returned the pie to the oven. "Life has given you some rough breaks, honey girl, but you've had a special traveling companion through the whole trip. The Lord wants your thoughts of Luke to heal you so you can feel blessed instead of sad." She made sure Dana was listening. "Memories of Luke are gifts from God."

Seth appeared to be reflective for a moment. "That gives all of us plenty to think about."

After a pause, he drew Dana from her chair and walked her toward the heavenly smell rising from the oven. His face revealed he was about to leave his serious mode. "Now, it's your turn to focus on this. If your father hadn't left, you wouldn't be visiting North Carolina. And you'd be wearing something other than my old flip-flops and T-shirts." A wink crept out, unable to hide for long. "And I wouldn't have fished a mermaid from the river."

She smiled about Luke and his endless curiosity and energy.

The smell of blackberry pie filled the cabin.

CHAPTER 33

While Dana helped with clean-up the next day, her mind went to Mom and Dad again. What did they think had happened? They had to be frantic. A thought came to her about Dad. Did he notice the blue boat was gone from the shed and draw a connection to the creek?

Although she was sorry for what they were going through, being with Gram and Seth seemed to be what she needed. Mary Jo would never believe her.

She looked up to see Seth returning from the spring house.

"Pa ought to be back any day." It was the seventh day since the river had towed her to the cabin.

She replaced the broom in its corner. "I've enjoyed being here. More fun than home."

"You've added spice to our ordinary summer."

Without thinking, she posed an earlier question. "Where would I have ended up if it weren't for you?"

"Probably with some other kid and his grandma."

She reached for the broom to sweep him out the door but yielded to curiosity instead. "I'll spare you on one condition. Explain what it's really like down the river."

"You'll have to wait till next time when we can do some serious backpacking. It's rough territory."

Relieved at her acceptance of his reply, Seth hid the truth about the waterfall a mile away. Since elementary school, he had packed it with Pa, who knew the area best for teaching safety in the wild. Together, they tackled the dense terrain and viewed the waterfall's fearful reality. After a rock-riddled passage, the river exploded over the edge to a brief precipice thirty feet below. Then it hurtled another hundred twenty feet of free fall, roaring to consume all other sound. He heard it in his mind, but Dana didn't need to know. Her last chance came from him on the log. Gram's request for trout for supper prompted him to get his pole that fateful Friday.

Now, he had offered to guide a girl through rugged terrain, who knew little about the river's fickle ways. He shifted gears. "Hey, want to go fishing? Something we haven't done yet."

"You want me to hang around by the river? A place I don't want to see again?"

"Think how strong you'll feel if you stare down your fears before you leave here." He disregarded her half-lidded scowl and charged ahead. "What about some fish for lunch? We've been living on vegetables and eggs all week. If I can have the pleasure of your company, I'll show you where you can be safer than anything."

She didn't budge.

"C'mon. Where's your sense of adventure? How can you reject it when it's been your middle name?"

While she hesitated, she saw him grab the pole by the door, then step outside to prop it against the cabin. The creel dropped beside it.

Through the open door, he said, "Got to dig a few worms. 'Preciate your help."

She knew before he asked that she'd follow as she did with Luke, but Seth offered an invitation instead of a challenge. Inching to the porch where she last saw him, she found it empty. Angry at herself for not grabbing the chance, she debated what direction to take to find him.

"Ready?" He slipped soundlessly beside her, a spade and small pail in hand.

She jumped, starting her pulse racing; but she hoped that scurrying beside him as usual would make her appear unfazed.

A compost pile rose near the garden. His spade sliced in deep to turn it over.

"What black dirt! Darker than the bear's coat."

"It's worm heaven." He emptied a scant bit of moist earth into the pail. On his knees, he dug into the exposed pile with bare hands, plucking worms with ease.

She joined him in her personal contest, grabbing as many as she could in a count of ten.

"Hey! We need enough for a meal, not a whole banquet. Leave some for another dinner."

"You asked for help."

"I did," he conceded.

He swung by the cabin for the pole and creel and handed her the worm pail. "May as well be the caretaker, since you personally selected most of them."

The rushing water grew louder the closer she came to the river. It soothed her to sleep at night; but in the light of day, it made her remember fighting for breath in the river. She stood still to halt the impulse to run.

"I won't let anything happen to you." Seth threw his arm around her. "Scout's honor. I didn't pull you from the river to watch you get hurt again."

Fully awake this time, she heard him and saw the tree lying flat out, almost floating, over the river. The inner tube lay nearby, idle since the rescue.

Handing her his pole, he rolled the tube on its side and plopped it on a bunch of crisscrossed branches at the water's edge. "Here you go, madam. A pillow to rest your bones." He baited the hook.

Many a time, she had watched Luke do the same. "Was it icky to put the worms on when you first learned to fish?"

"Too long ago to remember." He shooed a fly near his ear. "It's what you do if you want to find dinner here. You'll see how enticing worms can be; and if I lose one, it doesn't matter."

He shed his flip-flops by the bank. His feet oozed through mud until he mounted the trunk on hands and knees while holding the fishing pole. He didn't go as far as where he rescued Dana. Instead, he straddled the trunk like a cowboy on his best horse. The pole cut high through the air to cast his line where the current caught the bait and pulled it downstream.

After her river experience, she could imagine herself as the bait. "How did you see me out there?"

"Believe it or not, I heard you."

"You did?"

"Yep. Calling for help. When I couldn't find you, I scanned both ways."

"I don't remember. Was trying to stay above water." Her throat turned scratchy. "I'm grateful you have good ears." She couldn't tell if he was listening because he was intent on fishing again, monitoring the playing of the line. Her eyes traced the pole to his arms and the developing muscles of his shoulders.

Casting again, he glanced over at her and smiled.

Heat moved from her neck to the top of her head. Why did she look at him then? She meant nothing by it; but at that moment, she regretted her fair skin that betrayed every emotion. Luke had inherited the same skin, but she never saw him blush.

The line grew taut, bending the pole to the water. Seth reeled. A speckled trout flashed a few feet above the water, spraying silver across the sun's rays glimmering through the trees. He raised the pole, letting the line come toward him, and closed his hand around the fish. "There's number one! A pan-sized trout." He worked the hook free and dropped his catch into the creel.

"Didn't take long, did it?"

"Rainy weather this week might have helped." He turned, stretching for the worm pail she held toward him to bait his hook. Again, the current tugged his line downward.

After a while, she reached a conclusion. Fishing is boring if you're only watching. A fish on a hook provides one exhilarating second and landing it, if it gives a fight. The rest is a trial of patience. She sat while he added two more to his catch. "Can I try?"

"You want to crawl out on this log?"

She hoped to throw a line from the bank but wasn't bold enough to say it.

"Might want to reserve the risk for your next visit." A clucking sound accompanied the recasting of his line.

His refusal and amusement that went with it annoyed her, but his words, "next visit," echoed his earlier talk of hiking with her. To pass the time, she imagined filling a backpack full of Gram's provisions for lunch in preparation for trekking with Seth down the river one day.

Before noon, he counted eight trout. "Enough for a small feast." He used his jack knife to begin the cleaning process, slitting the belly and ripping out the innards. "Guts for fish to grow by." He tossed them far over the water.

It was no different from Luke and Dad cleaning fish.

"We'll cook these on an outdoor fire today. You're in for a new taste."

"I know. I've eaten trout before."

"On a campfire in the wild?"

It was a debate she couldn't win.

Beside the pot of ready vegetables, Gram washed the trout and dredged them in corn meal, salt, and pepper and drizzled oil on them while Seth built a fire in the pit in the ground. He placed a rack several inches above it, supported by large rocks at its corners. As they waited for the fire to grow hot enough to lay the fish out, a coughing truck engine broke the stillness, rattling beyond the cabin.

"It's Pa!" Seth ran to the road with Dana behind him like small children at their father's return from work.

An older version of Seth slid from the driver's seat. His high cheekbones, defined nose, deep-set blue eyes, and dark brows to match his hair gave Dana a quick comparison. A few wisps of gray at the temples confirmed additional years beyond his son. And he needed a comb after driving with the windows down. His eyebrows arched—like Seth's, but higher—at seeing a stranger.

"We have a visitor this week, Pa. Meet Dana Foster."

"You're the girl they're looking for! Everyone thought . . . " He stopped, seeming to be keeping something back. She didn't need to hear the world assumed she'd drowned. "I saw the flyer at the post office. How did you get here?" He gave a thumbs-up to Gram by the fire.

In a hurried give-and-take between Seth and Dana, they described her harrowing swim and the rescue.

"You're not the worse for wear except for a purple eye." Pa leaned over to pat Dana on the back. "I'm thankful Seth and Gram were here. And that I have a son who likes to fish." His eyes twinkled like Seth's, then became serious again. "Your family doesn't know you're safe yet?"

Dana shook her head.

"No way to tell them, Pa."

"I know. Sorry I wasn't here." His hand swept toward the truck. "We'd best get you to the sheriff's office, Miss Dana, to call them."

Gram intervened. "We're fixing to have us some nice brook trout. Be a shame to waste a fine lunch."

"Good idea, Ma. Let's fill our bellies before we head to town."

"I'm coming with you," she said.

For a moment, Dana enjoyed being the center of attention.

CHAPTER 34

Dana knew her stay at the cabin was coming to an end as she prepared to leave for the Edingrove sheriff's office. She forced herself to switch thoughts.

"I should change into my own shirt." Grinning at Seth, she modeled her attire, stretching the oversized tee sideways from her hips.

"You mean you don't want to keep mine as a souvenir? You'll grow into it and find it appropriate for all kinds of occasions."

Pa remained dazed about the miracle of her rescue. He confessed that it rivaled any he'd heard in all his years by the river. "I'm sorry Seth's mother isn't in town, Dana. I know she'd want to meet you. She's at a women's conference with a busload of friends from church."

"She'll be sorry about missing the fun." Seth, relaying dishes to the worktable, looked at Dana. "Unusual happenings rarely visit us here. You rewrote our history."

Gram unhooked a hand-sewn cloth bag from a wall peg and offered it to her. "Keep this as a souvenir from us. Put your T-shirt in it. If I ever knew I'd be giving it off to you, I'd a sewn your name on it." She chuckled. "Might as well take a couple more shirts. Seth won't be using them."

Everyone readied themselves to go, but Pa headed out the door first. "I'll get the truck started."

Seth placed one foot on a back fender to catapult his other leg over the side.

Imitating his routine came as natural for Dana as it did in following Luke; but this time, a helping hand extended to help her up.

The trip got underway, Gram riding in front with Pa, as they followed tire tracks that cut between the cabin and the garden. The makeshift road pitched down a long grade, woods on both sides, until it reached a one-lane bridge of heavy timbers over a gully protecting a small creek, maybe the Trickle Down. Pa didn't slow down to drive over it.

Dana saw how Seth sat in the corner, his back to the cab and one arm over the side to make the jostling less severe. She did the same. Carnival rides were nothing in comparison.

"Rattles your teeth, doesn't it?" He amplified the jittering of his voice.

The bumpy ride continued to a macadam road and then the highway.

"How long has it been since your last ride in a truck?"

The game with Luke in Dad's panel truck came to her. She told him how they had braced themselves to keep from falling while it dipped and swerved over rough roads.

In reality, Seth's question had nothing to do with trucks. He wanted to distract her from the scene behind her. Against the horizon past her head, a scowling rock face spewed water from a mountain edge—Highstep Falls. The river dropped over sheer stone and down to thick foliage that obscured its landing. The distance kept them from hearing its roar.

When she finished her story, he encouraged her to watch for advertising signs straight ahead of her. "They show the town's not far off. Holler when you see the first one."

Signs touting local businesses popped into view, followed by gas stations with shops tempting travelers to buy candy, gems, and crafts.

They turned up a hill to Edingrove, leaving the highway and Highstep Falls. Old but well-kept homes surrounded them. Sheaves of coneflowers, daisies, and asters, amid mounds of annual marigolds, impatiens, and alyssum, dotted the ground between foundations and lawns. Potted plants added color to a porch step here and there.

Houses wearing peeling paint didn't fare as well, but the view of Main Street appeared pleasant enough. In a few blocks, houses gave way to restaurants and other enterprises, including a newspaper office. Dana noticed an ice cream parlor. Beyond it appeared the brick building that housed the sheriff's office.

Pa braked by the curb but left the pickup running. "I have to park somewhere else. The sheriff has a fit when anyone takes a space reserved for deputies, even though they don't own that many cars. Go on in. Gram and I will be there in a few minutes."

Dana and Seth tumbled over the side.

The sign on the door read, "Edin County Sheriff's Office," and below it, "Sheriff Otis Bramble." The two left the sunny day outside and entered a room with shuttered blinds. They edged past walls of time-yellowed paint, where a woman dozed in one of many folding chairs. A man slouched against the wall.

Sheriff Bramble, distinguished by a close-clipped swath of white hair rimming the back of his head, leaned over the receptionist's desk. He showed no stir of interest when he raised his head to take in the two young people who entered the room. When Seth introduced Dana as the missing girl, he responded, "You the gal on the posters?"

"I'm telling you that, sir. Her parents need to know she's safe."

Without celebration, the man asked for Dana's phone number. "Stay here." He directed them to rows of chairs in the waiting area and returned to his desk in a separate room. A short while later, he stood in front of Dana. "I spoke to your pa. He'll be here as soon as he can." Short on ceremony, he turned to Seth. "You Nate Morgan's boy?" At the expected response, he said, "You need to come with me."

Seth fell in step behind him.

The sheriff lowered himself into a dark leather chair behind his desk while Seth stood without offer of a place to sit. In slow motion, Bramble rummaged through one drawer after another.

Gram arrived in the main room in time to see Seth enter the sheriff's office.

"What's he doing?" Dana asked Gram, hoping his actions came from local lore she hadn't heard about.

"Who knows, but he's taking his sweet time." Gram approached the woman at the desk. "Ma'am, I'm the boy's grandma, and I need to know what business the sheriff has with him." She pulled Dana beside her. "We're bringing in the girl reported missing."

"He'll be out shortly." The woman pointed to their seats. They sat again, poised to hear what they could through the open door.

Pa found them there without Seth. "What's going on?"

"Bramble called her parents and took Seth into his office." Gram's voice rose. "The secretary told us to stay here."

Quick steps took Pa to the door. "What's up, Otis? What do you want with my son?"

Annoyed at being called by his name instead of his title, the sheriff huffed. "I'm conducting an inquiry. I'll call you when I'm ready."

Pa joined Gram and Dana. "He's being officious—his characteristic mode." He passed a handkerchief across his forehead and stuffed it into his pocket. "Dana, let's go call your parents. They might need to hear from you. There's a payphone at the corner."

His polite act of holding the door churned up her self-consciousness. She hoped for a short block.

"This town grew from a lumber camp during the Depression." He shortened his stride for her. "An entrepreneur bought a large chunk of land to extend the town and closed the camp or there might not be a single tree left here today."

The American flag flew in front of an unimposing storefront. "The original post office. Visitors can see historical town photographs inside. Barbershop next door is ancient, too."

At the phone booth, he inserted a coin to let her dial the number. The operator said to deposit another thirty-five cents. He reached into his pocket and handed her a quarter and a dime. The coins clinked and jingled like children's voices chasing each other down a twisting, turning slide.

The phone grew hot and sticky in her hand. It rang four times at the other end.

Breathless, Kaye answered. "Dana, is it really you?"

After a short explanation to Kaye, a barrage of phrases tumbled from the phone. Dana pushed the receiver away but made out two words, "What boy?"

The flag waved like a surrender signal when the action stops. Then what? Does sadness seep in again, or does something replace it?

"Not a good connection. Gotta go." Dana sneaked a parting look at the flag and turned toward the mechanism that rattled the coins earlier. "Be home soon." The last two words, "I guess," sailed in the wind.

Pa remained a few steps away, yet nearby.

Looking past him, she spoke into the air. "Dad and Mom left together as soon as they got the news."

"Good! They'll be here soon! We'll be happy to meet them." He placed a protective hand on her back to guide her up the street.

Back again in the sheriff's office, Pa gave Gram a word of caution. "Keep an eye on Bramble and Seth. I need to leave a message for Calley."

Dana took a seat by Gram, who gave her a hug and said, "Don't fret, honey girl. Going to be fine."

The irregular *whop, whop* of the ceiling fan blades released the single sound in a room that witnessed a measure of grief and sadness over the years.

The sheriff, meanwhile, was filling in the blanks on a page at the rate of a child learning to print. His mind was on something else—his upcoming election. Running unopposed in the past two terms kept him in office, but the coming one meant competition. He needed an event to improve his political standing.

Time passed in agonizing slowness before the sheriff finally spoke to Seth in a restrained tone. "How long was this young lady at y'all's cabin?"

"About a week, sir."

"Speak up, boy. I can't hardly hear."

Seth stepped closer to the desk and restated his answer.

"And you hid her whereabouts?"

"We have no phone or car out there, sir. Pa was in town." One hand hung from his jeans' pocket by a thumb. The other at his side tightened and retightened as he spoke.

"Her family liked to be sick in the head with worry."

"I hiked up river as far as the split but found no one."

"Not one fisherman or hiker? Expect me to believe such a yarn?"

"Not many people out our way."

"The law calls it concealment, boy. You held her without anyone knowin'. That behavior carries a penalty under the law."

"But we didn't!"

"I hereby charge you, Seth Morgan, with kidnapping." His declaration boomed into the next room. He unhooked handcuffs from his belt.

Dana flew from her seat. "You can't! He saved me!"

Gram charged behind her. "No change in you, Otis Bramble, since our school days. Always wanting the limelight!" She jabbed a finger at him. "She's telling you the truth."

The wrinkles in his face crept behind his ears. "Didn't see you here, Nan. Haven't seen you in a dog's age." His tongue clicked against his teeth.

"You need to hear the whole story before you go making an arrest." Gram placed one arm around Seth and the other around Dana. "If you want to charge somebody, you charge me. I'm the one owns the house she's been staying in. My grandson saved this girl from drowning."

He mumbled, "By himself?"

She took him aside. "I helped pull her from the river. Almost unconscious. Full of cuts and bruises. It's a miracle she didn't have broken bones. Why, it's a greater miracle she's alive." A step took her closer to her old schoolmate, where she smacked at the handcuffs. "You keep these things on your belt if you ever want to use them again. Forget those charges, or everyone in the county will vote you out of office."

Aware of others' eyes on him, he fumbled with the cuffs, pretending a malfunction, but didn't know what to do next.

"Otis, if it weren't for this grandson of mine, you'd be telling this girl's parents she's no longer among the living."

The handcuffs fell loose. After an awkward interval, he clipped the metal rings together and tucked them into his pocket, letting the incident fade "out of sight, out of mind"—one of his most-used expressions.

CHAPTER 35

Dana fled the sheriff's office, head down and running full force. She didn't see Pa hurrying beside a man and a woman until she collided with them in the doorway.

Pa announced, "Look who's here!"

She and her mother fell into each other's arms, unable to breathe for a moment. "I'm sorry, Mom." The tears came. "The creek almost won."

"Thank goodness, you're safe." She held her while they cried together before releasing her to her father.

"Dana!" Dad, a runner with the end in sight, tried to calm his heaving chest. He folded her in his embrace and lowered his head to graze each eye on the shoulder of his sleeve. When he spoke, the words issued low and husky. "Thought I lost you, too." He continued to hold her as he never had, pressing out, "Sorry," and "Always loved you."

She processed his words, though few and short, to cherish them forever. Like shafts of sun from Heaven piercing dense clouds, they bathed her in a new light of understanding. It had taken a near catastrophe for him to know and for her to realize.

Mom lingered nearby, allowing them space for their reunion.

Dad reached out and pulled Mom near to Dana. The three formed a circle with arms around each other. For the first time in three years, he prayed the prayer of a broken man, rescued. He gave thanks for the blessing of Dana and her return and, at the end, admitted, "I put myself first." In a cracked whisper, he begged forgiveness. This took the longest. Awareness slowly dawned that the severed pieces of his life could mend together again.

With the phenomenon of an unseen arm sweeping them forward, Gram, Seth, and Pa joined the circle. Each one offered a prayer. Pa said, "Amen," and, "God be with you till we meet again."

When the families assembled on the sidewalk, Dana enjoyed the way everyone chatted together. The first was Seth's pa, introducing himself to Mom and Dad, already having forgotten his initial greeting, "You must be Dana's parents."

He shook hands with Dad, who presented Mom as "Dana's mother, here from New York to help us find her." He added, "My wife, Kaye, and our baby are at home in Laurelsville."

Pa seemed to gain an instant picture of the family dynamic. "I'm honored to be here for your reunion with Dana. You must have been beside yourselves."

"Thank you for saving her." Dad gave him another handshake.

"Wasn't me. I met her today for the first time." He drew Seth and Gram close. "These are the folks who hosted your daughter this week."

Gram beamed. "The Lord's blessing you for sure. Such a fine daughter."

Dad appeared to buzz with energy, but Mom barely moved. Yet if Dana strayed the slightest, Mom shed her exhaustion and searched for her with wild eyes.

Pa offered a suggestion. "Let's find a table at Mable's Diner on Main Street. I haven't heard all the rescue details yet."

Seth grabbed Dana's hand. "Jump in the back with me. Might be your last smooth trip in a North Carolina pickup."

"Please, come with us," Mom begged. "We need to be near her. We're together again, thanks to you. We can't get enough of her. You come with us, too, Seth. We'll follow your father."

Sliding into the back behind her mother, Dana seated herself as she did years ago.

Too late to get the door for her, Seth darted to the other side and lowered himself in behind her father at the wheel. "This is a week none of us will forget," he offered to her parents. "Like a lost time."

Dana's memories resurfaced of sitting with Luke in their respective seats in the car, but Seth didn't scrunch against the other window the way Luke did. Instead, he sprawled over half the seat, close enough to touch her. Besides taking Luke's place for a few days, he led her across the bridge of disbelief to prove she could go on without her brother. Until now, she'd never thought of her unforgettable memories with Luke as blessings. And there was something else. Seth gave her a longing for a future with a new kind of bond.

Arrival at Mable's came too soon, putting her thoughts on hold. The diner, dating back decades, reminded her of an old bus. Keeping up with everyone else, she scurried down the narrow aisle to a booth at one end, large enough for six people, and slid between Mom and Dad.

Sandwiches and soft drinks attracted little attention during the retelling of her story, interspersed with Gram and Seth's added testimonies. He provoked some chuckles when sharing his surprise at discovering a waterlogged mermaid in the river. Although their happiness re-echoed Christmas dinner memories, no one ever laughed around their table with the joy of these new friends.

Though reluctant to break up the cheerful gathering, Dad said, "We're so grateful to meet you, but we need to head for home." He nodded at Mom. "Her friend from New York is arriving tonight."

"Oh, yes! In the excitement, I almost forgot that Taylor was coming," Mom exclaimed. She answered Dana's unasked question. "He insisted. We expect him at your dad's any time."

The clock in Dana's mind ticked ahead to when he might finally reach the house on Stone Mountain Lane. Kaye would gush out the news, to which he'd proclaim his imitable, "Hallelujah!" She pictured them sitting on the deck, Kaye bouncing JJ on her lap while they talked.

Outside the diner, Dana and her parents paused by the station wagon for their final goodbyes. Dana hugged everyone, saving Seth and Gram for last. What to say after living beside them in their cabin every day for a week? It was worse than finishing a book that left her with the bittersweet sadness of longing for more.

Gram folded one of Dana's hands in her old ones and gave it a gentle squeeze. "Seth was waiting for you out there. He didn't know it till you showed up." Her upturned mouth multiplied her wrinkles. "It was no accident. Part of God's plan. This verse can be a keepsake remembrance of your visit."

When Gram's hand pulled away, in Dana's hand lay a tiny card. An inscription at the top in Gram's handwriting read: *When thou passest through the waters, I will be with thee; and through the rivers, they shall not overflow thee . . . (Isaiah 43:2).*

Unable to find words, she threw her arms around Gram again. Aware of everyone's eyes on her, she leaped into her seat and opened the window.

"Hey, little sister." Seth leaned to kiss her on the cheek. "Come for another visit when you can stay." Stepping back, he added, "But choose a better route."

He knew how to wrap those words in love and humor, and that's how she would remember him. Still, her insides churned against saying goodbye.

Digging into his pocket, he unfolded a piece of paper and thrust it through the window.

Two short lines stared up from the page. She read them once, then twice to appreciate what it was—his mailing address.

"Write to me. Okay?"

Her face nearly split from smiling. "I will."

Stepping away from the car, he moved a few paces back to get out of the way.

Once more, her parents occupied the front seat. Dad squared his shoulders behind the wheel, and Mom gave her last friendly wave. A mix of thoughts surged around Dana. It was the last time they'd be together, the three of them, the remaining members of their original family. And although Luke seemed not so far away, he wasn't sitting beside her trying one trick after another to make her react.

The engine came to life; and after everyone adjusted themselves in their seats, Dad shifted the Ford into gear. It rolled forward, imperceptibly at first.

Dana twisted around to face the back window.

Seth kissed his finger and turned it toward the receding car.

Her eyes held him in freeze frame, standing where the car took off, his arm bent at the elbow, hand raised palm out, kissed finger pointing to the sky.

ACKNOWLEDGMENTS

My husband, Gary, chief encourager, first reader and editor, began asking after I retired, "Where is your book?" Without him, Dana's story simply would not exist. He read the original manuscript and helped me untangle knotty phrases and paragraphs. Beyond that, he listened to certain patches of edits multiple times and gave his opinion, using his expertise as a copywriter and two decades of reporting and writing for his website, freedomisknowledge.com. God answered my prayers and gave me you.

I am grateful to everyone at Ambassador International for giving me a chance to tell Dana's story. Thank you for making it possible. A special thank you goes to Kate Marlett, perceptive reader and extraordinary editor, who went the extra mile.

For reading the entire manuscript, my thanks to Joyce Gould, Patty Kalber, Jerry and Judy Sands, and Terry Weiss. The older I get, the more I recognize time as a gift; and your reading was a gift to me. Special thanks to Patty for suggesting I promote it as Christian fiction. Judy, my forever friend since fourth grade, once showed me how to find the "hider" beans as Seth did for Dana. A gesture like that can end up in a book.

For offering opinions along the way, I am indebted to Maxine House Cunningham and Sharon Van Alstine, whose friendships date back to Oakland, New Jersey, where my sons Chuck and Bill Connolly grew up.

Feedback also came from Ann Stembridge, originator with Lynn Bumgarner of The Red Hot Readers, a book club I belonged to for sixteen years. The women in the book club first met as members of The Red Hats of Weaverville. To all the women of both groups: I miss you and your spontaneity and laughter.

My sons Chuck and Bill were in school when my work was first published in magazines and journals. Over the years, they have been my sounding boards. For this book, Chuck was my go-to guy for sports-related questions and Bill, for fishing and outdoors. And Gary brought with him my second family—John, Hope, Mark, and Matthew. Hope gave me a gift of a delicate gold and silver dragonfly necklace that unexpectedly found its way into the plot. Thank you all for your encouragement and for alerting me to writing and publishing websites. You have changed my life in so many ways.

Many other friends provided inspiration in ways they may not have realized. I can't imagine the story without their input.

Maria England Burnette's memories about her aunt who lived in the mountains of Western North Carolina without running water into the 1970s gave me a model for an off-the-grid cabin and the possibility of a grandmother spending the summer there in 1974 with her grandson.

Donna Lerette, my Canadian nurse friend, described Luke's injuries in the hospital after his accident.

Gail Moore's late husband, Creighton, showed our family how to make a game of trapping frogs with badminton rackets, offering great fun without harming the frogs.

Ben and Judy Spangler's property and burn pile in North Carolina became a significant setting in the fictional town of Laurelsville. Neighbors there are thankful to Ben for his many years of tending the burn pile, where they could dispose of fallen trees, branches, and other yard debris. Thank you for being wonderful neighbors.

Luke's accident is drawn from an experience of Christopher Wright, son of long-ago dear friends, Karen Wright and her late husband, Chuck. Christopher and high school friends took a boat ride on a lake, where a surge in wave action bumped one of the boys off the side into the propeller's path, causing his death. Chuck told us about the priest's message from the funeral, and I've never forgotten it.

If I could thank a place, it would be the Wyoming State Capitol building in Cheyenne that I envisioned as the Fenton Library when I wrote the book. My older brother and I walked that ledge when we were in first and second grade and are still alive. Thank you, Cheyenne.

For all these relationships of family and friends, and for His constant guidance and care, I give thanks and praise to my Lord and Savior, Jesus Christ.

DISCUSSION QUESTIONS

1. Grief is one of the themes in *Chasing the Blue Boat*. How does each member of the Foster family react to losing Luke? Why do they react in different ways?
2. Forgiveness, another theme, is difficult for Dana and her father. What does Dana learn about forgiveness? Who does she need to forgive and is she able to do it? Who should her father forgive? Is there anyone you need to forgive?
3. Discuss how the blue boat becomes a metaphor for the book. What does it symbolize? What other symbols play a role in the novel?
4. What motivates Dana to set the boat free? Is she successful? Have you had a goal that became disastrous in some way?
5. Although many of the character's names are biblical, Seth's is important as it relates to the story. Why is it significant?
6. Luke seems to talk to Dana after he's gone. When does he do that? Where is he at the time of his final words? Does he talk to her at the cabin?
7. Do you recall passages or incidents that foreshadow Luke's death? Do you recall other comments or warning signs that function as foreshadowing?

8. Meeting Gram and Seth is not only life-saving but life-changing. Discuss the ways Gram and Seth change Dana's life. Have you unexpectedly met someone who changed yours?
9. Discuss the subplots of Rachael meeting Taylor and Kaye fearing a reconciliation of Rachael and Jesse. How do they add to the plot?
10. How old were you or your family members during the early 1970s? Did the book trigger memories for you or topics you heard about from others? Think about events, clothing, music, and more.

ABOUT THE AUTHOR

Connie Kallback grew up on the plains of Cheyenne, attended the University of Wyoming, and graduated from the University of Washington in Seattle with a BA in English. She transitioned from being an English teacher to publishing in New Jersey with CCMI/McGraw-Hill, Prentice Hall, and CPP, Inc., in positions from writer to acquisitions and managing editor. Her early writing, penned while teaching, appeared in magazines, newspapers, and literary journals. No longer wearing the hats of Mary Poppins or Sherlock Holmes, necessities of raising six children in two separate families, she writes in South Carolina, where she lives with her husband.

To contact Connie or learn more about her, go to chasingtheblueboat.com.

Ambassador International's mission is to magnify the Lord Jesus Christ and promote His Gospel through the written word.

We believe through the publication of Christian literature, Jesus Christ and His Word will be exalted, believers will be strengthened in their walk with Him, and the lost will be directed to Jesus Christ as the only way of salvation.

For more information about
AMBASSADOR INTERNATIONAL
please visit:

www.ambassador-international.com

Thank you for reading this book. Please consider leaving us a review on your social media, favorite retailer's website, Goodreads or Bookbub, or our website.

MORE FROM AMBASSADOR INTERNATIONAL

If it's true that "all comic novels must be about matters of life and death," *The Honest Atheist* obliges. This entertaining and thought-provoking tragicomedy provides clues to where our loss of public decency originates while telling a moving story of an unlikely friendship between an atheist and an evangelical Christian.

Charlotte Hallaway needs to come to terms with her father's death. He had been her only family, and she wasn't handling her grief well. It was just supposed to be a few weeks of peace and quiet to process it all, but then she saw them—a drug deal and a murder within seconds of each other. And they saw her. Now running for her life, Charlotte boards a bus to escape her pursuers and wakes up the next morning in the woods without a memory of how she got there or of who she is.

Betty is sure that Ida Lou does not belong in their church when the woman shows up to the Good Friday service with her small dog in tow. But before she knows what's happening, Betty—along with the other women of the WUFHs (Women United For Him)—is pushed into helping the woman. God works in mysterious ways—and through ordinary people. The town of Prosper is about to experience some drama—and it all starts with a dog who comes to church.

Made in United States
Orlando, FL
25 October 2025